BLOOD GAMES

A VAMPIRE ANTHOLOGY

Jonathan Maberry
Linda D. Addison
Jeff Strand
Gabrielle Faust
Sèphera Girón
David C. Hayes
JG Faherty
Roh Morgon
Rain Graves
Michael H. Hanson
Sumiko Saulson
John Palisano
Gustavo Bondoni
Jonathan Fortin
Andrew Robertson

"Introduction" by Dacre Stoker
"A Word From the Editor" by Gabrielle Faust

Thank you to Lucy Lu Designs and 52 Ravens for allowing the usage of their playing cards in the photo for the cover design.

NIGHTSHADE PUBLICATIONS
Austin, Texas

Print ISBN: 9798321261064

Edited by Gabrielle Faust. Cover design by Gabrielle Faust. Interior formatting, design and copy editing by Gabrielle Faust.

First Edition: March 2024
Printed in the United States of America.

TABLE OF CONTENTS

Image by Enrique Megeuer

INTRODUCTION

By Dacre C. Stoker

I did not first read *Dracula* until I was a university student in 1979. I re-analyzed the novel in a much different manner after I met screenwriter Ian Holt in 2003. He convinced me that I should co-author with him a sequel to my great granduncle Bram Stoker's legendary tale. It was through the process of researching and writing *Dracula the Un-Dead* that I gained a much better understanding of Bram, his own thoughts, and the tremendous research he put into writing his iconic novel. I did not take the process lightly and still find there remains much to learn about the man, his life, and his work.

Bram Stoker was born in 1847 just outside of Dublin, Ireland. He endured a very difficult childhood—he was sickly, mostly bedridden, and near death on a few occasions over his first seven years. He recovered and went on to attend Trinity College where he worked as a civil servant in Dublin Castle before pursuing his passion and moving to London in 1879. In London he worked for twenty-seven years as the Manager of the Lyceum Theater and personal secretary for Sir Henry Irving the most famous Shakespearean actor of the time. Stoker, in his spare time, was also a writer of both fiction and non-fiction: theatrical reviews, speeches, short stories, poetry, and novels, mostly in the mystery and horror genres. The most famous today, of course, is his novel *Dracula*.

Since its publication in 1897, *Dracula* has never been out of print and has been translated into fifty languages worldwide. The sexy and violent modern interpretations of the original vampires in literature have roots predating *Dracula*—in John Polidori's *The Vampire* (1819), James Ryder's *Varney the Vampire* (1847), and Le Fanu's *Carmilla* (1872). In part, because they were integral to folklore and mythology prior to their appearance in Gothic literature, these vampires were very believable, playing on the familiar fears lodged deep in the readers' inner psyche. These authors brought the vampires to life in horror novels that are still haunting us today.

Vampires in the last twenty years have become more multi-dimensional, an evolutionary advancement, if you will, from the character created by Bram Stoker. In the film *Bram Stoker's Dracula* screenwriter Jim Hart and director Francis Ford Coppola gave the Dracula mythos the romantic element of "everlasting love." Count Dracula is on a quest to find a replacement for his wife who committed suicide because she mistakenly believed him dead. Cursed with immortality, he seeks a suitable replacement for his wife so that he may achieve everlasting love. "Taking" Mina as a bride is Dracula's effort to consummate an eternal union and, thus, we see a transformation from a killing machine to a creature with a conscience, feelings, and need for love. In Anne Rice's *Interview with a Vampire* her vampires possess very humanistic morals. Louis and Lestat debate whether to kill humans of elevated stature or simply consume blood from what they consider lower life forms such as vagrants, prostitutes, and rats. The question is raised: is killing justified simply for nourishment or is it justified to convert a human to become an immortal mate?

Now, the *Blood Games* anthology explores a further development in the vampire genre—the manner in which the vampire "connects" with its prey. Just as man has evolved from hunting and killing for survival, these fantasies involve creatures enjoying the hunt, deriving pleasure from both prolonging the chase and the kill. The bar has been raised and so the present day "reinvented" vampire is often associated with the historical figure Prince Vlad Dracula III of Transylvania, and his reputation for torturing his victims by impalement, skinning them alive, or boiling them, to name a few of his more "celebrated" methods. In keeping with his legendary wickedness, present-day authors incorporate similar evil dispositions to keep the vampire fans on the edge of their seats. Of course, there is no record of Vlad actually drinking his victims' blood, but why let the truth get in the way of a good story!

Naturally, vampires who exercise a decision making process instead of just instinctual killing for blood have made for new and interesting twists in vampire literature. Perhaps, as a reaction to high morals being brought into play, vampires have developed other humanistic traits. It is not unusual for vampires to enjoy tormenting their subjects like a cat playing with a mouse, all to extend the pleasure with torture. But, the vampires still possess the ability to shape-shift and control the minds of their victims, as well as great physical power. Murder is horrifying enough, but pre-meditated murder, especially by torture, is particularly gruesome. Instead of the imperial-seeming formal demeanor of the vampires of the last two centuries the vampires of modern literature are, in ways, similar to today's serial killers.

A number of authors, including myself, have intertwined the sadistic tendencies of Jack the Ripper with recent vampire lore. After all, Bram Stoker was living in London during the terrifying years that the Ripper eluded Scotland Yard and terrorized the population of London. In fact many believe that the Jack the Ripper murders were a direct influence on Bram's *Dracula*. The Ripper seemed to take great pleasure in disemboweling some of his victims, possibly while they were still alive.

On a personal note, as a young boy watching vampire movies, I imagined, once the victim was under a vampire's "spell", the resulting bite and blood drinking did not involve much pain, if any. Now, there is no mistake to be made. It is scary and it hurts! Authors have skillfully added believable human traits and themes to their central vampires. Their undead are given emotions and thoughts, becoming characters of sympathy and even envy for their power and immortal life. There is a shift of sympathy from being the damned to being the desired, with these new human-like qualities they are easier for us to identify with them. We have witnessed a literal renaissance of vampire, zombie, serial killer, and werewolf fiction over the last few years, along with an endless list of remakes and sequels to classic horror films to feed the insatiable appetite of the public.

As long as vampires remain original and unpredictable, the fans will come back for more.

A Word From The Editor

By Gabrielle Faust

Games.

The term has been tossed about so much as of late regarding the world of vampires, both fictional and non, that I sometimes wonder if those living within it forget that life itself is but a game. It is one that you never truly know the rules of, and will, most definitely, never win. There is only one victor in life: Death. And Death is a neutral character who claims no victory in any battle, but only an acknowledgement of duty.

The vampire and Death court one another like night-blooming vines wound tight around wrought iron. They are both enemies and allies casting neither shadow, nor reflection upon the veil of night. Death has no interests in games, though. It comes when called by a vibration in the cosmos and leaves when it has dealt the hand the Fates have given to a creature. The concept of playing a "game" with the souls it harvests is meaningless, an abstract manipulation that simply impedes the natural course of existence.

The vampire, however, takes a special pleasure in art of games, be they mental, physical, emotional, strategic, or a simple session of "cat and mouse." After all, if you were the ultimate predator with an unending existence on earth, wouldn't you find yourself devising ways to entertain yourself, whether consciously or unconsciously? By upping the stakes and altering the expected rules of such a sinister courtship, "life" as perceived by the vampire takes on a new dimension, a fascinating new facet that can be savored and explored, pondered, or simply enjoyed. A distraction from the extraordinary that oh so quickly became mundane. A twisted scientific experiment to test the theories one has cultivated about the nature of humanity and immortality. A flourish of good old-fashioned drama to get the adrenaline racing and give one something to cast snide remarks about and flex the wit and venom honed to a razor edge over the centuries.

The end result of such manipulations of the circumstances that surround the vampire's existence may or may not be favorable to the immortal. However, the pursuit of a heightened experience and, perhaps, even a decent dash of paranoia for if they themselves may be merely a pawn in another's more elaborately devised derision, is a driving force that at times can take on a life of its own coming only second to the vampire's thirst. In the end, the question always remains—was it worth it?

The authors of the *Blood Games* anthology understand this innate need and have each explored the concept in unique and fascinating ways. Whether their tales left you cringing or chuckling, it is to be said that the library of the games the undead play is as vast and intricate as the literary voices that portray it. It has been a true honor to have the opportunity to bring this collection together and edit these tales for your reading pleasure. And, I hope, this book will give you pause to contemplate the nature of your own inner predator and the games you may play with those around you, for better or for worse.

THE CONTEST OF INESCAPABLE MISDIRECTION

by Linda D. Addison

Let's play a game
roll the dice
wish for fame
cut a deep slice
    make the board flood
        with blood.

The Beginning:
If you are fully alive, go to Rule #12
Else go to Rule #1.

Rule #1:
Open the second Circle's door
    even as each drop of your tainted blood
howls for sweet innocence. Take 23 steps forward,
    wait gently in the shadows. Rip the vertebral column
from one unlucky living being.
    Award = 115 points & Lust card piece.
Go to Rule #23.

Rule #12:
Breathe in the sweet aroma of sunlight,
    even as each moment brings Them closer,
no Thing can hinder the final heartbeat,
    you are part of the great dis-folding.
Find another living being, become part of their destiny.
    Award = 210 points & Limbo card piece.
Go to Rule #76.

Rule #23:
Avoid drinking blood older than two hours
     even when dizzy with hunger. Hum
the Fear Eater's song, do not brush graveyard
     dirt off your face. Swallow the frontal lobe
of your victim without chewing.
     Award = 48 points & Greed card piece.
Go to Rule #84.

Rule #76:
Play the game like your life depends on it
     even if you don't believe it does.
Pick up the plastic bag in front of you,
     in case Resurrection isn't possible.
Whisper words of self-loathing, swallow all hope.
     Award = 93 points & Gluttony card piece.
Go to Rule #127.

Rule #84:
Take the form of a large taloned bird,
     even while the other undead crawl as wolves.
Deny knowing what they feast on, fly deep into
     the moonless night, to create thunder and lightning.
Land on the game borders' razor edges.
     Award = 48 points & Fraud card piece.
Go to Rule #285.

Rule #127:
Hide while another is turned un-dead
     even though they helped you climb
out of a hole. Are your hands slippery with blood?
     No, it must be the Rain of Ashes.
Take 41 steps forward, walking backward.
     Award = 1 point & Treachery card piece.

Go to Rule #581.

Rule #285:

Renounce your coven by burning their coffins
    even incinerate your own, bathe in the ashes.
Block the entrance to the Fifth Circle
    with the remains of fallen angels.
Let yourself be pulled into the lower circles.
    Award = 2 points & Anger card piece.
Go to Rule #666.

Rule #581:

Wait at the crossroads of the Eighth Circle
    even when dead wings brush your face.
Close your eyes, lift your chin,
    the pain will dissipate as soon as
Despair is finished feeding on you.
    Award = 149 points & Violence card piece.
Go to Rule #666.

Rule #666:

You can not avoid the Game
    even as you try each path,
weep and scream and plead,
    redemption is just out of reach.
Roll the dice, pray to Lady Luck,
    walk the Labyrinth of Unavoidable Suffering.
    Award = 0 points & Eternal Damnation.
Go to the Beginning.

THE CAR

by Jeff Strand

The donors were screaming, which was usually the best part, but Octavian seemed annoyed. It was important to Boriss to be a good host, so he walked over to the closest cage and kicked the metal door.

"Silence!" he shouted. "Cry and whimper if you must, but no more screams! The next one of you who disturbs my guest will be made an example for the rest!"

Actually, the corpse in Cage #2 had been made an example of less than half an hour ago, but in his hundred and forty-one years Boriss had learned to do much worse things than rip somebody's head off. A man in Cage #1 was proof of that, though he hadn't been killed as an example, but rather because they needed an even number of donors.

The donors fell silent. Boriss walked back to the table. "Can I get you anything before we begin?" he asked.

Octavian shook his head, slowly and deliberately, which is how he did everything. Having Octavian in his home was a great honor, and though Boriss had collected the donors from his usual feeding grounds, he'd tried to find the most attractive of the vagrants.

Boriss sat back down. He took a sip of wine, straightened the game board, and smiled at his guest. "Are you ready to begin?"

Octavian nodded. "Indeed."

"Very well, then." Boriss picked up a tiny metal piece and placed it on the board. "I will be the car. And your choice...?"

The nearly three-hundred year-old vampire frowned. "I believe that I will be the car, if you don't mind."

Boriss did mind. He was always the car. He cleared his throat. "Yes, well, with all due respect, I feel that the car does not suitably represent the power you possess. May I humbly suggest that you play as, say, the mighty battleship?"

"I do not like the battleship. I will be the car."

"The car is such a gaudy piece. You are a legend amongst vampires for your great dignity, so perhaps the top hat is more appropriate?"

"I think not. When I play, I am the car."

"Ah." Boriss knew that he should defer to his guest, especially a guest of such great honor...but he wasn't sure he could play if he wasn't the car. He was always always always the car. "But remember, you are hailed by many for your unmatched ferocity. No piece symbolizes your fierce nature more strongly than the dog."

Octavian let out a snort of disdain. "The ferocity of a Schnauzer? Do not insult me."

"Technically, it is a Scottish terrier."

"Even if the piece depicted a pit bull mauling a toddler, it would not be my choice."

"What about the iron?"

"Do you know anybody who has ever wanted to play as the iron?"

"Certainly somebody wants to be the iron, or they would have discontinued it."

"I do not want to be the iron, I do not want to be the thimble, and I do not want to be the man on horseback. I have been one of the undead since long before your great-great-grandfather was born, and I think that entitles me to be the goddamn car!"

Boriss flinched. He had never heard Octavian raise his voice in anger.

"Perhaps I could go fetch a non-traditional playing piece, such as a button...?"

"I think I have made it perfectly clear that I will be playing as the car. If that is unacceptable to you, then I shall look elsewhere for my evening of entertainment."

"No, no, I apologize for my passion," said Boriss. "Naturally I will defer to you." He picked up a different token. "The thimble represents man's efforts to not have a needle draw blood, but of course, even the mightiest thimble cannot defend against our fangs." He smiled, showing lots of fang.

"Your logic eludes me."

"It does not matter. I shall play as the thimble. Let us roll to see who goes first."

Each of them picked up a die and rolled. Boriss's five beat Octavian's four, so he scooped up both dice, shook them thoroughly, and rolled. One of the dice fell off the table and onto the floor.

"Please be more careful," said Octavian.

"I apologize. My enthusiasm got the best of me." He picked up the die and re-rolled. Two ones. "Ah, doubles. Excellent." He moved two spaces and drew a yellow card. "Doctor's Fee. Pay $50."

Boriss and Octavian both looked over at the cages.

"Half a pint, coming right up," said Boriss.

He went over to his cage, #1, and glanced at the four potential donors. He'd start with the smallest one, a young blonde woman who was obviously a crack whore, but seemed reasonably well fed by crack whore standards.

Getting her out of the cage was not easy, but that was part of the fun. One of her companions in the cage did try to be a hero, and now he was a hero with a concussion. Once the woman was out, Boriss bit deep into her throat and then began the process of filling small vials with her blood. Normally on Game Night he would have done this ahead of time, but for a guest with Octavian's level of prestige it was important that the blood be as fresh as possible.

After she was sufficiently drained, Boriss dragged the woman into the corner. He picked up one of the vials, returned to the table, and placed it on the center of the board. Then he picked up the dice again.

"What are you doing?" asked Octavian.

"I rolled doubles," he said, "so I get another turn."

"Not that. Why did you put the blood in the center of the table?"

"That is how it works. Whoever lands on Free Parking gets it."

"No, no, no," said Octavian. "Free Parking is not a real rule. You do not get anything when you land on it."

Boriss frowned. "The way I have always played, you put bail money, income tax, and whatever the cards make you pay into the middle. It is the Free Parking rule. Everybody does that."

"They most certainly do not. That kind of nonsense is exactly why the game has an undeserved reputation for taking so long to finish! You get nothing for Free Parking! It is a ridiculous house rule that creates scenarios in which somebody who should have gone bankrupt is suddenly flooded with money, and because people land on Free Parking all the time, the game never ends."

"Then what is the Free Parking space for?"

"It is not for anything! It is just a free space! That is why it is called Free Parking! Have you ever gone into a free parking garage and been given somebody else's bail money and back taxes?"

"Well, no, but it would not have occurred to me to compare the rules of the game to the way things work in real life."

"Take the blood off the board."

Boriss picked up the vial. "So where does it go?"

"Into the bank."

"The thing is, we don't really use a bank when fresh blood replaces paper currency. I suppose the cage could count as the bank, but it's not as if I can put the blood back into the poor woman, at least not without...no, not even that way. If I put the vials in the cage, I am sure one of the other donors would kick them over, and then we would just have a mess."

Octavian sighed. It was a sigh that conveyed that nearly two centuries' worth of patience was reaching its end. "Tell me, Boriss, have you thought about these rules at all?"

"Yes, of course. I have never had any problems in the past. My friends and I have actually spent many lovely evenings in this manner. I mean absolutely no disrespect, but I feel that perhaps you are being a bit...fussy."

Boriss immediately realized he'd gone too far. Nobody had ever told Octavian that he was fussy and survived.

"I apologize if I have behaved poorly as a guest in your home," said Octavian. "You have clearly put a lot of work into preparing for tonight's festivities, and it was wrong of me to suggest otherwise. You know the rules of your variant better than I do. I'm sure that if we follow your lead the game will play perfectly well, up to and including the auctions."

"Auctions?"

"You don't play with auctions?"

"Am I supposed to?"

Octavian sighed again. This sigh was much longer in duration than the first. "When you land on a property that you do not wish to purchase, it goes up for auction. That is a major component of the game. It ensures that the properties are bought up in a timely manner and it keeps the game from stretching out into eternity, unlike your idiotic Free Parking rule. What other games do you play incorrectly? Do you just move all of your chess pieces one space ahead at a time?"

Boriss bristled. No matter how much respect Octavian had achieved in the vampire community, there was no reason for him to be a dick.

"I don't know how to play chess," he admitted.

"Why am I not surprised? It is only the ultimate game of strategy. But you know how to play Go Fish, I will bet."

Boriss did indeed know how to play Go Fish, but he wasn't sure if he would look worse saying "Yes, I do" or "No, I do not." Instead, he ignored the question, which was almost certainly rhetorical anyway.

Octavian wasn't finished. "Perhaps we should try something more suited to your level of complexity? Do you have Candyland? Chutes and Ladders?"

Candyland actually worked remarkably well when played with vials of blood from screaming victims, but Boriss wasn't going to tell him that.

"How about Trivial Pursuit?" asked Octavian.

"I don't even get how that is an insult," said Boriss. "That is a most difficult game."

"For you, perhaps."

"Well, certainly. We cannot all be three-hundred years old with nothing to do but memorize meaningless trivia! If I had been turned in the 1700's, yes, I would be pretty fucking good at Trivial Pursuit, too!"

"I doubt that."

"I am sorry, I appreciate you coming over, but I am afraid I will have to ask you to leave."

Octavian pushed back his chair. "Very well."

"It is nothing personal. Not everybody is compatible when it comes to Game Night."

"I understand. The game is really designed for three or more players anyway, not that you would know." Octavian stood up, then gestured to the cages. "What are you going to do with them?"

"Hmmm. I am not sure. Save them for next time, I guess."

"Really? You are going to keep seven live prisoners in cages in your home for that long?"

"It is only until next Friday."

"Will not they make too much noise?"

"Well, yes, but the place is soundproofed. A couple of them have been in here for the past three days and it is fine."

"All right." Octavian walked toward the staircase leading up from the basement, then hesitated. "It simply seems like a waste, is all. Seven fresh victims, and I had a light lunch on purpose."

Boriss smiled. "Oh, I get what you are saying. I collected them especially for the game, but if we are not going to play, there is no reason we can't just rip them apart and bathe in their blood, if you are up for that."

Octavian grinned. "That sounds delightful."

"I know that you are a man of complex gaming tastes, but what if we just made it a good old fashioned race? See who can kill them the fastest?"

"It is an uneven number of victims."

"Right. So, uh, we would just let one of them go. I mean, not let him actually go go, but we would let him or her out of the cage so that the numbers were even."

"Is that how you play? You just let them out of the cage? Do you think anything through?"

"Okay, I think you should—"

"Boriss?"

"Yes?"

"I am kidding. Let us shred them."

Though Octavian won the race, as they lay on the gore-covered floor, Boriss had to admit that it was the best orgy of violence of his life.

THE THINGS THAT LIVE IN CAGES
by Jonathan Maberry

-1-

Dillon saw the punch floating toward him and knew that there wasn't a god damn thing he could do about it. The Cuban kid had battered his arms for three rounds and Dillon could not more raise his hands to block that punch than he could have sprouted wings and flown away. His legs were over-cooked macaroni and his heart was beating against the walls of his chest like a hummingbird trying to push through the windows of a burning house.

The punch was going to end him.

He knew it.

Time seemed to have slowed down so he could appreciate that fact. Dillon's corner man was screaming at him to block. The crowd was yelling like they were at the Roman Circus. Mike Dillon couldn't see at all out of his left eye and his right was smeared with sweat, blood, and Vaseline.

Dillon tried to duck his head down, to take the punch on his forehead instead of his nose. That might give him a chance. If the Cuban kid busted a couple of hand bones, then maybe his corner guy might toss a towel into the ring, or the ref might stop the fight.

Yeah, and maybe bright blue pigs'll fly outta my ass, thought Dillon.

Even so, he closed his one good eye and ducked.
He could feel the exact moment when time snapped back to full-speed. The fist seemed to fill the whole world. There was a huge sound inside his head. It was so loud that it muffled the sound of the Cuban kid's knuckles hitting bruised flesh and

cracked bone.

Dillon felt the shock moving at an angle from the point of impact through his sinuses and eye-sockets, past the back of his mouth, the surge of power shifting his head, tilting the opening at the back of his skull toward the brain stem.

There was a cracking sound. Sharp, wet, deep. Dillon knew that it wasn't his skull. It wasn't his jaw. The sound was immediately followed by a feeling of immense emptiness, as if his entire body had been hollowed out—nerves and skin and bone and blood. Everything below the level of his collarbones became a blank.

"I'm dead," said Dillon.

Or maybe he thought it.

He couldn't feel himself fall.

He didn't feel the flat of his back hit the mat.

He didn't feel anything.

All he was aware of was a huge black mouth gaping wide as death leaning forward to swallow him whole.

-2-

"You're awake," said a voice. "Good."

Dillon wasn't sure that the voice was real. Mostly because he was pretty sure that he was asleep. Or, maybe unconscious was the right word. It's not like he drifted off in his La-Z-Boy in front of the big-screen. He hadn't opened his eyes though, so he wondered how anyone could tell he was awake.

His mind was filled with gutter water and debris. His thoughts were broken things that lay scattered around inside his head.

He knew that he'd been in a fight. This wasn't the first time he'd awakened in a hospital bed. A fight. Sure. Okay.

But which fight?

Who beat him this bad?

And how bad was it?

He could feel his head, which hurt so much that Dillon wanted to let the darkness take him back down into the dim nothingness.

He tried to move his arms.

Nothing.

His legs.

Nothing.

Shit, he thought, but beneath that thought there was a second and less articulate thought. It was more of a sense of how bad things might be, but his mind rebelled against putting it into words.

Got to think, he told himself. Got to get my shit together and think this through.

Dillon lay there, letting some internal hand flick on the light switches one by one.

He didn't try to speak. He wasn't sure he could.

There was a soft ping-ping sound behind him. He knew that sound. One of those hospital machines that never seemed to do anything but make soft noises. There was a dull pain in the back of his right hand. He didn't need to look to identify that. I.V.

Fuck.

Unless he was dead and this was some kind of holdover memory.

"Mr. Dillon—?"

The voice again.

Male. He could tell that much. Nobody he knew. If it was St. Peter waiting for him to make his case for entrance through the Pearly Gates, then Dillon wasn't interested. Dillon didn't want to have to explain to St. Pete that he didn't believe in any of that shit. Heaven, wings, halos, paradise. None of that shit.

And if it wasn't St. Pete and it was that other guy, then fuck you to him, too. Dillon did believe in hell, and as far as he was concerned hell was better known as Trenton, New Jersey. Any other place, even if it was all fire and brimstone and shit, would be an improvement.

There was a rustling sound. Like newspapers. Whoever was there didn't speak again and Dillon figured the guy was reading the paper.

Fine. Whatever. Hope he had a comfortable seat because Dillon wasn't in any hurry to wake up and rejoin the world. Any world.

He settled back and let the darkness take him again.

His last thought before he passed out was that nothing hurt. Everything should have hurt, though, so that was a little weird. The Cuban kid had beaten the shit out of him for seven two-minute rounds. Dillon had gotten two good shots in—a roundhouse kick to the ribs and a spinning backfist that emptied the kid's eyes for a few seconds, but that was back in round one. Dillon had come out hard and heavy the way he always did. That was his thing—he wrapped up the fight in the first round or he generally got his ass handed to him. Different when he was young, but Dillon was a lot of miles away from anyone's definition of "young". Cage fighting was not a sport for middle-aged guys, as the Cuban so eloquently proved. After that first round, Dillon hadn't scored a single point that mattered. And the Cuban made him pay for those early hits.

He wondered why it didn't hurt.

Darkness whispered in his ears, but it gave him no answers.

The lights in his mind dimmed and the last thing he saw, or thought he saw, was a figure—a man? A woman? He couldn't tell—move toward the I.V. stand, a small plastic needle in one hand. The figure inserted the dagger-point of the needle into a port on the I.V. Dillon thought he saw some ruby-red liquid, some exotic medicine, flow from the needle into the I.V.

Then the darkness in his mind flared with red shadows and he was gone again.

-3-

When he woke up Dillon knew that he was actually awake. Not dead, not floating in limbo or purgatory or trying to run a shuck on St. Peter outside the gates. *Alive.*

Balls.

He knew from the way he felt that he'd been asleep for a long time. Easiest way to tell was by how much the painkillers had worn off. They don't keep giving you that shit unless you ask for it. Not in crap hospitals in Trenton. Not with his health plan.

And every-damn-thing hurt. His face felt like it had be hand-carved from his skull, diced into little bits, run through a Cuisinart, and put back on, piece by piece, with staples. His teeth felt loose and his hair hurt.

His body hurt, too, but not as intensely. That pain was distant, like an echo.

It took him a while to figure out how to move his hand, but finally his fingers twitched like the thick legs of some obscene spider and slowly crawled across the sheets. He fumbled for the button that would call the nurse, couldn't find it, and then froze as someone pressed the control into his hand.

"It's the top button," said a voice.

It took Dillon a few seconds to make sense of that. Then he remembered the voice that had called his name earlier. Was that today or last month or a year ago?

Dillon decided to open an eye and look at whoever it was.

One eyelid refused to budge. It felt like it weighed twenty pounds and was cemented shut. That was the one the Cuban kid had wailed on every single god damn round. Fucker had a thing for that eye.

The other one wasn't as badly puffed, but opening it was like jacking up a truck.

He said, "Ow."

It took a few seconds for his eye to focus. The hospital

25

room was small and cheerless, with furniture that was purely functional and clearly intended to make people want to leave the hospital as soon as possible. There was a window that gave a wonderful view of a brick wall streaked with pigeon shit. There were no cards or flowers on the dresser. The TV was off.

Dillon turned his head very, very carefully to look at the person sitting in the visitor's chair. He was a total stranger. Young white guy. Twentyish. Rail thin, but thin the way models and art dealers are. Like he enjoyed looking like a rake handle. Dark hair combed back, dark eyes, red lips that Dillon thought were painted with lipstick, but weren't. Expensive suit, expensive watch and rings.

"Who the fuck are you?" croaked Dillon.

The man gave him a bland, friendly smile that curled his lips without showing his teeth. "My name is Viktor Petrov."

"Russian?"

"Russian."

Dillon tried to pry open the file cabinet in his brain. Did he owe anything to one of the Russian bookies? He didn't think so, but it wasn't impossible. The Russians had taken over the kind of mixed martial arts matches Dillon fought in. They'd crowded the Brazilians out a couple of years ago because they were more ruthless but also more organized. And, let's face it, Brazilian street thugs—no matter how tough they were—weren't going to get into any serious pissing contests with guys who were ex-Spetznaz and ex-KGB. The Russians were ass-deep in muscle who were ex-special forces.

Dillon said nothing. His tendency toward smartass remarks did not extend to deliberately pissing off the Russians.

"Are you in very much pain?" asked Petrov.

Dillon licked his lips. "It's…not too bad."

"Can you move your legs?"

The question scared Dillon, but when he tried to move his feet, they moved. Not well, but they moved.

Petrov nodded. "Good."

"Why…did I hurt my back?"

"You had a neck injury," said Petrov. "But it's nothing permanent. Some discomfort for a while."

"Did they have to operate?"

"No."

"I…I thought I saw…I mean, did you inject something into my I.V.?"

Petrov took a while before he answered. "Yes."

"Are you my doctor?"

"I am…part of the treatment team," said Petrov. "A consultant."

"My head's all messed up," said Dillon cautiously, "so sorry if I'm a little slow here. But…do I know you? Have we met somewhere?"

Instead of answering, Petrov said, "I've seen you fight."

"You mean you saw that Cuban kid kick my head in."

"Well, that, too…but I've seen you in better days."

Dillon laughed even though it hurt his chest to do it. "Then you got a long memory, friend, 'cause my better days were so long ago dinosaurs were running the world."

Petrov smiled at that. His face looked like a moray eel when he smiled. "It wasn't that long ago, Mr. Dillon. I can well remember when you were the up-and-coming thing. A real martial artist in a league that has become glutted with brawlers whose only talent is that they haven't evolved enough to feel pain. Mouth breathing Neanderthals."

"That Cuban kid had some moves," said Dillon.

Petrov shrugged. "Five years ago you would have beaten him."

Dillon said nothing. He wanted to give a nonchalant shrug, but that would involve using too many brutalized muscles. "Kid had some moves."

"He had youth and the stamina that comes with it," said

Petrov, dismissing the Cuban with a wave of his hand. "Five years ago he wouldn't have lasted four rounds with you. Ten years ago he would never have made it past round one."

"Yeah, well everyone gets old. One of these days some kid will be handing the Cuban kid his ass. Way of the world."

Petrov crossed his legs and arched an eyebrow. "Way of the world," he echoed, taking his time, tasting each word.

"Fighters aren't built to last," said Dillon. Then he sighed. "But, yeah, once upon a time I had the juice. I was always hard to hurt. Hardly ever bled, which keeps the refs from stopping the fight. And I could take a punch off of anyone."

"And you are trained as a true fighter. A warrior. Daito-ryu aikijutsu, if I'm not mistaken. For how many years?"

"Started when I was six," said Dillon, and for a moment he felt a flush of pride. "So call it thirty-five years and change. Started cage fighting when I was eighteen. Twenty-three long damn years ago."

"I know. Ninety-two fights. Fifty-seven wins, two ties, thirty-three losses. You knocked-out or choked-out forty-three of your opponents, and you were only carried off four times counting last night."

"So?"

"So, you know more about martial arts than most of the fighters in your league put together. Real martial arts. The deep knowledge, the genuine skills. The kind of knowledge that should be preserved, but which is fading in obscurity with each new generation."

Dillon sighed. "Yeah, no shit. I opened a bunch of dojos over the years. Traditional stuff, very old-school, but no one wants to spend the time to learn the old stuff. They want a few flashy moves, a quick belt promotion, and then they want to call themselves 'masters'. Breaks my heart."

"Mine, too. I have very little appreciation for new things, Mr. Dillon. I'm very much an old-fashioned kind of person."

Dillon had to restrain himself from snorting. The Russian looked like he was two or three years out of high school.

"It's a shame," continued Petrov, "that you can't use those old-school skills in your matches."

"Ha! I wish. But the league don't let guys like me bring out my A-game."

"Pity."

"Got to have rules, I guess," said Dillon bitterly. "You can't really unload on a guy, even in a cage match. People'd get killed."

Petrov smiled and he slowly traced the outline of his sensuous mouth with the sharp tip of one manicured fingernail. "That's not what they tell the rubes. The league's advertising goes to great lengths to declare that this is no-holds barred, that everything is legal, that this is—what's the phrase they use all the time? 'Fighting as real as it gets.'"

He gave a derisive snort.

"What do you expect?" asked Dillon, unsure where this guy was going with this. "This is a sport. It ain't Spartacus and shit."

Petrov sighed. "Alas, no. Those were the good old days."

You're a fucking weirdo, thought Dillon, but he kept that to himself.

"I bet you'd give a lot to fight the way you truly know how to fight. With subtlety, with ruthless efficiency, with a deadly grace."

"I wouldn't go that far," said Dillon. "You don't need to kill people to have a good fight. There are a lot of old-school techniques that I could have used…"

"Why didn't you?"

Dillon shrugged. The action was painful, and Dillon winced. "Bad timing. If I knew what I knew now back when I started in this league, it'd be a whole different thing. But even setting aside the lethal stuff, the moves that would neutralize a bull like that Cuban kid doesn't take insane amounts of strength, but it does require speed and control. Thing is, the more damaged your muscles get, the less precise your control is. That's where the problem comes in. The older you get the more you know, but the older your body gets the less able you are to use that knowledge. It's proof that the universe likes playing sick jokes."

"I suppose you would like to have your old speed and control back last night."

"No shit. But…if wishes were horses," murmured Dillon sourly.

Petrov uncrossed his legs and leaned forward. "What if you could get your mojo back?"

"Very funny, ha ha."

"I'm serious."

"Seriously, about what?"

"About getting back in the ring for real. Wouldn't that be great? Wouldn't that be worth anything? To be at the top of your game, to be Killer Dillon once again?"

"Killer Dillon? Christ, nobody's called me that in years. That was from my old boxing days. Corny name—."

"No," said Petrov quickly, "it's not. It's a name filled with great promise. It's a name that used to give your opponents serious pause, and one that could strike genuine fear into anyone who steps into the cage with you."

Dillon laughed even though it hurt his face to do it. He raised the hand with the IV drip and waggled it back and forth. "I'm five years past my expiration date, son. I should've quit after I lost the split decision with that Polish son of a bitch from Detroit. What was his name? Lenny 'the Breaker' Sepulski. That bastard fair beat the white off my ass. Should have realized he was trying to beat some sense into me, but I was too far into my own shit. Back then I still believed all the hype; I was still high off of my win-loss stats from ten years back. And, man, there's nothing sadder than a cage fighter who's losing every fight and still blaming it on a bad streak that's going to end soon. It's not a streak, it's a downward slide, and it doesn't end. But by the time you realize that you've lost your punch and your reflexes are shot from muscle fatigue, nerve damage and too damn many miles on the odometer, you're already into the phase of your life where you're nothing but a punching bag for younger, better fighters and a punch-line to the guys who knew you when."

Petrov was nodding while Dillon spoke. "Yes," he said softly, "but I've seen how you fight. You always make the right choice—kick or punch or takedown. You knew ten times what the Cuban fighter knew. That was true of your fight with Breaker Sepulski. You were the better fighter."

"I lost those fights. And damn near every fight over the last five years."

"You lost because your age and the amount of damage you've sustained over your career have slowed your body and made your reflexes betray you."

"Yeah, well, that's why they call this a young man's game."

"No, that's why this game has become polluted, Mr. Dillon," said Petrov sternly. "When these matches first got started there were some real fighters in there. Men and women who knew the martial arts. Now what do you have? Thugs, barroom bouncers, brawlers—goons who don't understand the martial arts, not in any real sense. Men who don't care about the martial arts. This is just a game to them, and for many of them it's the only work they could get because they lack the raw intelligence even to work in construction, and they take themselves too seriously to go into professional wrestling." He sniffed. "At least the professional wrestlers call it 'sports entertainment'. They make no pretense about it being a genuine sport. These thugs have so crowded MMA competitions that they've become the standard for excellence. People look at them and think that these are the masters of unarmed combat."

"It's as close as you're ever going to get to having real masters climb into the cage," observed Dillon. "Most of them are too smart to risk getting wailed on. Most of them are too old. By the time they really qualify as masters they're too old for full contact sports. Sure, they could kick ten kinds of ass in a street encounter, but self-defense against a junkie with a knife or a couple of gangbangers is one thing. The techniques you'd use in those situations come from a whole different toolbox than the stuff we're allowed to use in cage matches. And just from the point of view of recovering from injuries—I'll bet that Cuban kid won't even show a bruise by Tuesday and my face'll look like a tropical sunset for two weeks. And I'll be walking like an eighty year-old man for at least that long." He shook his head. "No, this is a young man's game. The real masters either aren't interested in showing off in the ring or they can't see how the risk-reward thing tilts in their favor. Too much to lose, not enough worth winning."

He fumbled for the remote and hit the button for the nurse. But she still didn't come. "God damn it…"

"Not necessarily so," said Petrov.

Dillon, distracted by the lack of a nurse showing up, had lost the thread of the conversation. "What?"

"I said that, while I agree with your assessment, there is more to the equation than that."

Dillon squinted at him with his one good eye. "Like what? The only way a master—some guy who's spent forty, fifty years going all the way deep into a martial art—is going to last more than a round with a twenty-something gorilla who can barely feel pain?"

Petrov said nothing; he folded his hands on his lap and gave Dillon a bland smile.

"What?" asked Dillon. "You're saying you know someone willing to take that kind of a risk?"

No answer.

"You're nuts," said Dillon. "Look, it's not even worth it from a purely financial perspective. Guy who's spent his life training to become a master—a real, genuine master of a martial art—he's got a school, or maybe a chain of schools, filled with students who look to him as a the icon of martial arts skill. Now understand, all of this belief is based on what they see in class and a kind of faith that their master could go all Jet Li on the bad guys in a real fight. But these kinds of guys don't get into real fights. Avoidance is a big part of their lifestyles. They're passive, they'll walk away from an insult rather than fighting over it. So their ability to deliver the absolute combat goods is never seen but deeply believed by everyone from the newest white belt to the most senior assistant instructor. Now… if one of these masters does something as dumb as climb into a cage to fight someone like Breaker Sepulski or the Cuban kid, he risks losing. He knows he can't match the younger fighters for stamina, and he probably doesn't have anywhere near the same protective muscle mass, which means he's jousting without armor. He also knows that he can't use his best stuff. He can't dip into his black bag of tricks and do shit like rupture the spleen, smash the hyoid bone, shatter the knee, burst ear drums, pop an eyeball or anything else that he might use in a real street defense. He's facing a fighter who spends all of his time preparing to be hit, and whose arsenal are those strikes and kicks allowed in the cage. It would be like taking a master-level swordsman from Renaissance Italy, giving him a fake sword, and then putting him in the ring with a Viking who has a sharpened war axe. It's an unfair contest on too many levels. The only way it could be fair—and this is pure fucking fantasy here—is if you could take all of the knowledge and experience from the old masters and somehow put it into the heads of the young Turks. Then, even though there would still be some restrictions on certain techniques, you would see what master-level martial arts are like when it goes whole-hog. But…that's a pipe dream."

"Ah," said Petrov, holding up a finger. "That is exactly my point. That's the tragedy right there."

Dillon frowned. "Huh?"

"At no point in this 'sport' that we both love so well are we seeing anything approximating the kind of fair fight you postulate. The game is skewed, the rules are fractured. This is why these matches draw the worst kind of gambler." Petrov laughed. "You are right to feel a measure of disdain for the kind of brawlers who dominate the sport; but I have equal disdain for the breed of gambler attracted to these kinds of blood sports. They are the same lowbrow crowd who bet on cock fights and dog fights. They bet on animals fighting animals."

Now it was Dillon's turn to remain silent. He was smart enough to recognize the insult buried inside that comment, but at the same time he couldn't really take offense. He was a dumb hulk fighting in a league of dumb hulks. No better than chickens or pit bulls except in being smart enough to know that this was no kind of life at all.

Petrov adjusted his cuffs and necktie. He was dressed very well. Expensive clothes, but good taste expensive rather than fuck-up expensive. Attention to quality rather than for display. Russian Mafia guys often dressed nice. You never saw them in those damn track suits the Jersey goombahs wore. None of the open-shirted satin-finish sport coats of the Cuban players. This guy could be selling expensive watches or showing you four million dollar homes with a view.

When it was clear that Petrov wasn't going to say anything either, Dillon cleared his throat and said, "So where's that leave us other than lamenting what I don't have? I ask, because I hurt too much to lay here singing the blues."

Petrov nodded as if that was the right thing to have said.

"I was at your first fight," he said.

"You saw that?" Dillon narrowed his eyes. "Where? On tape?"

"No, I was at the Princeton Stadium when you fought two matches on the same card. Leroy 'The Lion King' Sanders and then Sonny Daye."

"Bet you don't remember much. That was twenty-three years ago. You were—what? An embryo?"

"A lot older than that," said Petrov with a chuckle. "And I remember both fights as if they happened this morning. The so-called Lion King went down in the very first round. He threw two punches and then tried to sweep your leg. You kick-checked his sweep that I bet no one past the first row saw, and then you hit him with a back-wrist strike to the floating ribs that sent a shockwave through his abdomen, which caused his diaphragm to spasm. Very, very subtle. The judges scored it as a backfist because they were too dense to know what they were looking at. And your finishing blows? A two-knuckle tap to the left sinus that had to fill his eyes with tears and cause enough shock to the Eustachian tubes to make him gag. Then you hit him with a tight looping palm that only four martial arts styles teach. It hit the precise point on his jaw that snapped his head around far too fast for his body to follow, which created a corkscrew twist of the brain stem. He was out before he began to fall."

Dillon narrowed his eyes. "Who told you all that? The blow-by-blow in the fight magazines called that last combination a jab-hook-punch combo."

"The trade magazines are staffed by hacks who don't know a hammerblow from a blow-job."

"Fair enough. But that doesn't explain how you know what I did."

"I told you, Mr. Dillon, I was there."

"Not a chance in hell. Even if you're older than you look you couldn't have been more than five or six years old. Only an advanced pro would have recognized what I was doing."

Petrov shrugged. "The second match lasted two rounds," he said.

"Sonny Daye was a better fighter. It was only cause someone

else dropped that I wound up on the card with him. Nobody expected Lion King to go more than a round."

"Sonny Daye was the full contact fighting champion of the Deep South. Forty-four wins, one loss, and that was a split decision."

"Like I said…"

"I remember watching that fight," Petrov reminded him. "Daye only tagged you twice, both with jabs while you were feeling each other out. After that he never scored one single point that mattered. By the end of the second round he was out on his feet. You delivered a series of blows to acupressure points that systematically shut down his ability to defend himself. You could have taken him down halfway through that round and choked him out. He had nothing left."

"He might have been hurt bad if I tried. Get a guy who's that dazed and he might not have enough marbles left to tap out. Better to dance him a little and let the corner man and the ref stop the fight."

"Which they did."

"Sure."

Petrov leaned his elbows on his thin knees. "You were a superior fighter, Mr. Dillon. If you'd have been able to get into the better leagues and better venues while you were still young enough, you could have been a contender. You might have been the champion."

"Lot of good guys up on that level."

"Few of whom are as good as you. Few of whom know as much about real martial arts. Few of whom care about real martial arts. There are people who still bet on you, despite your recent stats, because they know that you have more knowledge, more real skill, than the apes who dominate the league. I've made several such bets. If you were to win one of these fights, the return on the bet would be considerable."

"Then you got money to burn, 'cause even I don't bet on

myself anymore. See these knuckles, the way they're too large. That's arthritis. I got osteo from old damage and now I'm getting rheumatoid. You want to bet on me in a cage match against old age?"

Dillon pushed the button for the nurse, who still didn't come.

"The fuck!" growled Dillon. The pain was getting worse. His whole body felt like it was about to catch fire.

Petrov reached out and closed his hand gently around Dillon's wrist. Dillon immediately flinched back from the man's touch. The Russian's skin was as cold as ice and clammy as a locker room wall.

"Don't worry about the nurse," he said.

Dillon tried to pull his hand away, but the Russian's grip was bizarrely strong. That was weird because even beat up and half-dead in a hospital, Dillon outweighed Petrov by ninety pounds and none of those pounds were fat. At forty-one, Dillon was rock-solid. Maybe past his own prime, but stronger than this pencil-neck.

Except that he wasn't.

Petrov's hand was like an icy cuff locked around Dillon's wrist.

"Please, Mr. Dillon," said the Russian in a soft voice, "please. We're having a nice and very productive talk. Let's continue to have that talk."

"Let go of me you freak."

After a long moment, Petrov opened his fingers. Dillon snatched his arm away and immediately began massaging his skin, which was cold and sore.

"What the fuck, man," he growled.

"I'm sorry for the discomfort," said Petrov.

"Shit, you almost broke my god damn arm."

"I'm sorry, but—."

"What the hell, you're a frigging stick figure. What the fuck are you taking? Steroids? Meth?"

Petrov's smile turned sly. "Ah."

"Ah…what? Is it meth?"

"No."

"Then what? You're on something. A skinny young prick like you shouldn't be that strong. What are you on?"

"What I'm on, to use your word, is part of why I'm here. And before we get to that, I want to correct a small mistake."

"What?" asked Dillon uncertainly. If he wasn't so thoroughly flattened by injury and painkillers he would have bolted for the door. He cut quick looks at the door anyway, wondering if he could make it to the nurse's station.

"How old do you think I am?" asked Petrov, and the question was so weird and unrelated to anything that was happening that it jolted Dillon and made him whip his head around.

"What?"

"You keep saying I'm young, and I admit that I look young, but how old do you actually think I am?"

"Who gives a—."

"I ask, because the reason I'm so strong and the reason I look so young are both side effects of what I'm 'on.'"

Dillon had no idea where this was going so he said nothing.

Petrov fished in his pocket for his wallet and produced his driver's license. "I am fifty-seven years old," said Petrov. "And before you ask, I have never had a facelift or any Botox injections."

Dillon stared at the license and then at Petrov. "Bullshit."

Petrov put the wallet away.

"That's bullshit," insisted Dillon.

Petrov spread his hands. "Listen to me, Mr. Dillon, and give me an honest answer. What if there was a way for you to get back your youth, your strength, your speed? What if that process also repaired any damage, no matter how old, and which also helped you heal at an accelerated rate from any new damage."

"You're definitely on something. Magic mushrooms or something."

Petrov ignored that. "What if you go back into the ring with all of the knowledge you currently possess, but with your body and reflexes at the very peak of conditioning. Stronger, faster, more durable, less vulnerable. Can you lie there and tell me that you wouldn't want to climb into the ring again without age and scar tissue and disease hanging around your neck like a ton of bricks?"

"That's a stupid question," snapped Dillon. "Of course I would. Who wouldn't? But the league dope tests us all the time. I come up positive for steroids or something, I'd be out on my ass, stripped of all my titles, barred from even stepping foot into—."

"This isn't a steroid."

"Or coke or some designer meth. They test for everything."

"They don't test for this," said Petrov. "Or, rather, they can't test for this. I can show you if you're genuinely interested."

Dillon studied him. The things the guy was saying were wacked out, but his tone and body language was calm. There were no crazy lights in his eyes. It was Petrov's calm rather than his words that kept Dillon's own emotions in check.

And…well, Dillon was curious. Really curious.

He was too old not to want to know.

He was too badly hurt, too sore and spent not to want to know.

And the warrior in his soul, the one that time and damage and arthritis was turning into an impotent old joke, wanted to know.

Dillon licked his dry lips.

"Okay," he said, "show me."

Petrov nodded and reached into the inner pocket of his suit.

He produced three hypodermics. One was filled with a dark red liquid; the other two were empty.

"I anticipated your interest," he said softly. "I've already begun the treatment."

"What?" croaked Dillon. "What the fuck!"

"Shhh," soothed Petrov. "Just listen. There are three steps to the process. All very antiseptic, all done with the greatest of care." He held up one of the empty syringes so Dillon could see that there were trace amounts of red liquid in it. "For step one I drew a few cc's of your blood."

"Who gave you permission, you son of a—."

"Please, Mr. Dillon, we both know that we are not talking about an approved medical procedure. It was totally safe, so you have nothing to worry about. And it's already done. So, please, bear with me."

Dillon lapsed into a tense and angry silence. However, fear gnawed at him. What had this maniac done to him?

Petrov said, "I injected your blood into my arm."

Dillon's mouth hung open in shock.

"Then, after a wait of a few hours, I drew off two syringes of my blood. I injected one syringe into you via the port on your I.V. I believe you were semi-conscious at the time. Do you remember?"

Dillon did remember, and his fear began growing into terror.

Petrov showed him the third syringe, the one that was still filled with red liquid.

With blood.

God, though Dillon.

"Why, for Christ's sake?"

Petrov's smile faded. "Because, Mr. Dillon, the injury you sustained in last night's fight was far more serious than you know. The Cuban hit you with a powerful blow at an unfortunate angle. It cracked two cervical vertebrae and the broken bones caused a deep laceration to your spinal cord. The doctors are discussing their options, but so far it is their belief that you will be a quadriplegic. Everything from the neck down died last night, Mr. Dillon. You were destroyed in the ring."

Dillon thrashed backward from Petrov's words, his feet kicking at the sheets, fingers stabbing the device to call the nurse.

"Fuck you!" he roared. "Fuck you. I'm not crippled, you stupid bastard. Look! I'll kick your ass!"

Petrov sat where he was, the syringe held between two slender fingers. He waited for Dillon's tirade to wind down. Dillon flopped back, gasping.

"I'm not crippled," he snarled.

"Of course not," agreed Petrov. "But you were."

Dillon opened his mouth, but nothing came out.

"Before I injected my blood into you, you were dead from the collarbones down. Machines breathed for you, machines pumped your heart."

Dillon raised his hands and looked at them, totally perplexed. "But…but…"

"It's not a drug," said Petrov. "It's blood. There is a very, very old Biblical saying: 'Blood is the life'. That is so very true."

"What are you talking about?"

Petrov waggled the full syringe between his fingers. "The process is simple. I consume your blood, you consume mine. Writers have mythologized the process in all sorts of absurd ways, but in simple terms it's an exchange of certain key biological materials. A virus, a very ancient virus, activates dormant DNA in you, and that begins a process whereby certain biological and genetic changes take place. The initial stages of the process occur very quickly. The complete transformation, however, takes years."

"A…virus…?"

"Oh, don't get hung up on that part, Mr. Dillon, this will

be the very last virus that will ever affect you. After this, no more colds, no more flu, no cancer, no arthritis, not even the heartbreak of psoriasis."

"You're insane."

"Not at all." Petrov got to his feet and came to stand close to Dillon. He plugged the syringe into the port, but did not depress the plunger. "If I do nothing, the effect of the first injection will eventually wear off and you'll be exactly where you were last night. A head attached to a lump of dead meat. The first injection is self-reversing. So, if you want me to walk away, then I'll go."

Dillon said nothing. He could not compose a single sentence, not even a single word, that made sense.

"However, if you give me permission, then I will inject the second dose of my blood and within forty-eight hours you will walk out of this hospital. You'll probably feel so good you'll want to run. Within seventy-two hours you won't be able to find a single trace of any of the injuries you sustained in that fight. Within a week no X-Ray, MRI or CT scan will be able to find a trace of arthritis or scar tissue."

"Who are you?" breathed Dillon. "What are you?"

Petrov smiled, but unlike his earlier smiles, this one was a broad grin that showed lots of white teeth.

Lots of sharp white teeth.

"I think you know what I am," said Petrov.

Dillon wanted to scream. He tried to shrink away, but his body was sluggish, as if the numbness he'd felt last night was creeping back. The sight of those terrible teeth filled his mind with horror-show images of pale creatures rising from graves and tearing the throats out of the innocent. He wanted to shout a word, to put the label on the monster that stood above him, but he could not force himself to say that word. It was an impossible thing. To say it might make it real.

"Why are you doing this to me?" he hissed.

Petrov blinked as if surprised. "Why am I saving your life? Why am I giving you eternal youth and strength and health? I thought we already covered that."

"Be…because of the fights?"

"I already told you that I was very old-school, Mr. Dillon. I, and those like me, appreciate only the finest things. Immortality tends to cultivate more sophisticated tastes, as I hope you'll discover. I've always been a fight fan. Even before I became what I am. I want to stop being a spectator and get involved more deeply in the sport. As a manager, as a promoter. But I don't want to trot out one mouth-breathing thug after another. Just as this process will elevate you to a higher level, I want to elevate the sport of full-contact fighting to a level it has never before been able to reach. A class of masters."

"Are there others…?"

"Like you? Not yet. I want you to be the first. I want you to cut a swath through the brawlers currently in the game and then make room for a new breed of martial arts competitor. Immortal masters. Come now, Mr. Dillon, tell me you wouldn't give everything to see fights where both competitors could use their greatest skills, to showcase the elegant beauty and sophisticated science of the real martial arts? Tell me that doesn't stir your soul."

Dillon stared at him but said nothing.

His arms and legs began to tingle again. His fingers were already going numb.

Petrov caressed the plunger of the hypodermic with one pale thumb.

Tears broke from the corners of Dillon's eyes. "I don't want to be a monster," he said softly.

"We are not monsters," said Petrov with surprising gentleness. "We are elevated beings. Call it the next step in evolution. Call it whatever you want. We don't fear the cross. We don't hunt the innocent. None of that. So, tell me, Mr.

Dillon—Master Dillon—what's your choice? Ordinary or extraordinary? A broken man dying in a forgotten hospital ward…or the champion you were born to be?"

Dillon could not feel his hands and feet.

"Do it," he whispered.

Image by Haider Mahmood

Saving Face

by Gabrielle Faust

"What do you want from me?" Shane screamed into the maw of darkness between frosted gray evergreen trunks. "Leave me be!"

He whirled in a circle, panting plumes of dense white vapor into the winter air, crystals of ice forming on his colorless lips to match his artic eyes. The forest loomed around him closing in with ancient unspoken verdicts of guilt. Black branches bent heavy overhead with fresh snow, which had ceased only an hour before as Thomas's blood had soaked the pristine white bed of death a mile away.

Shane staggered through the knee-high banks, finding tree roots and boulders beneath to propel himself greater distances in hopes of making it out of the forest alive. "He was the one who attacked me!" he screamed into the night, his powerful voice echoing through the dormant maze and circling back upon him like a flock of angry crows.

"Attacked you?" Came a male voice like a rush of wind through fallen autumn leaves followed by the click of a tongue, flint upon granite in rapid succession. "He attacked not at all. He was playing with you. Thomas always played… Now he doesn't…" The voice faded away as if carried out to sea by the wind.

"Played?" Shane shrieked resisting the urge to rip the hair from the sides of his head in frustration and fear. "He tried to rip my face off! You call that playing? I thought he wanted to murder me!"

"Murder, no." The voice purred. "Mangle, bruise, draw, quarter, dissect, compromise, and a variety of other curious acts, perhaps, but you can recover. You always have. Again, it was in jest he pursued. But you didn't play by the rules. You can't help your nature."

"Rules? What rules? And my 'nature'!" Shane scoffed, stumbling on the lip of a badger's burrow as his concentration was consumed by the thoughts of his body rendered in Thomas's long-fingered, pale hands, the feral yellow glee of the intent he was enraptured with obscured by a haze of Shane's own blood. "And what might that be, oh one-who-does-not-dare-show-himself-to-me?"

"A killer." The voice was prompt and unflinching in its verdict. A ripple of giddy laughter scampered around the perimeter of the forest.

"Killer." Shane snorted under his breath in a plume of cold vapor with a mixture of hate and utter terror. "Killer. That's what they think of me. Nothing else, because I am a vampire. After all of these years. Just a killer."

"Not just because you are a vampire, Shane. You've been our friend for many years. But tonight you are just…a…killer."

Shane halted in his tracks, confused and shaking from rage and exhaustion. He could feel dawn's approach in his bones, a deep ache that pulled at the base of his skull and curdled his stomach. "No! I was defending myself you twisted motherfuckers! I was defending myself! He attacked me and…"

"And you enjoyed every last minute of drinking him dry." The voice spiraled through the branches above like sparrows being chased by a hawk up to the patches where the starry midnight blue heavens peeked through the tops of trees. Shane staggered back until he collided with the trunk of a tree. The vacant space of memory he thought erased suddenly emerged. There he stood gasping like a human warrior feeling the cold, undeniable solidity of the bark supporting his wiry frame as he stared up at the hole in the canopy above wishing his ability for flight had evolved sooner. He was still an earthbound creature after all of these long years. He cursed his Maker and himself.

"Yes…" His whisper evaporated before it left his lips as he savored the moment, even in its grisly detail. "It was…exquisite. Horrific and exquisite."

Rustling of branches surrounded him, fifty feet away but closing fast.

"I cannot help how I feel when I kill! You of all of us should know what nature is!" He instantly regretted the confession, especially given that it was a friend that he had slain. The sound of footsteps through the snow halted. Shane dared not draw a breath. "You yourself have told me that we are the more civilized of our species. At least when it comes to such matters."

Silence; some might have believed it a blessing, but Shane knew otherwise. Without hesitation he bolted, running through the glittering white moonlight patches and dark shadows with a speed he did not think he was yet capable of. Pressure like a vice upon his temples tightened until he staggered, dropping to his knees only to scrambling upwards again.

"Perhaps you are. But we are not. You took one of us, giving nothing in return. He only wanted to show you your true face, to teach you a lesson you must learn."

The new female voice echoed through the whorls of his mind, careening from one skull plate to the other like a bat beating itself against a cave wall. The others that had chased him, flitting through the night with sparrow grace and perching just beyond his preternatural sight had been fae, but now it was one of their Court far older than the young ones in pursuit that admonished him now. Incorporeal now in her power, her essence irrevocably interwoven with the strands of time, her capacity for grace the wind, and her ability to hate the molten core of the planet itself. Shane coughed, trying desperately to force the shields around his mind from being obliterated and cast to the corners of the earth like shards of glass.

She'll crush me from the inside out, he gasped silently trying to focus on the snow to keep from colliding with the trunk of a tree.

"I'm sorry!" he screamed into the night, clinging to the base of an old evergreen, his nails deeply scarring the gray bark. The scent of sap rose as the warm coppery scent of blood traced its way down his fingers to his palms, running beneath the cuffs of his long gray coat. He choked on a sob, his fear too consuming even for tears. "What can I do to make this right?"

The silence was deafening. The pressure transferred from his temples to the base of his neck as if a giant had taken hold of him. Before he could protest he was yanked away from the tree, his fingers raking deep long gashes through the trunk.

"Finish the game Thomas started."

Shane wasn't about to ask if he had a choice.

***

"Bet you a bottle of wine I can bed any woman in this bar." Without the faintest of niceties Thomas threw himself with drunken elegance into the bench facing Shane. Settling himself to drape one long thin arm over the back of the booth, he propped his left leg up on the cushion, leaning against the wall, his right hand resting his ceramic stein of ale on the heavily scarred and lacquered tabletop.

Shane looked up from his philosophical meanderings about existence he contained to a small red leather journal. For a moment he considered Thomas with a wry lifting of one eyebrow and a small smile. The man seemed to never change; literally and metaphorically. He laid his pen down across the open spread of pages and folded his hands over the scrawling cursive secrets that were never so secret that he did not torment the willing with them regularly.

"Pray tell why I would enter a bet like that?" Shane asked with a comical smugness that came from an intimate familiarity with this course of conversation with his friend.

Thomas cracked his neck. "Because you like to amuse me." He winked and took a drink from his mug.

"So why not something more challenging than taking the waitress home?" Thomas sighed and leaned back in the booth.

Thomas's lust for the staff, male and female, was legendary. Around them the dimly lit tavern buzzed with the regular patrons, off from work and beginning their Friday nights with hearty laughs and harsh criticism of their coworkers.

"You've already had her, haven't you?" Shane smiled and took a sip of his vodka.

Thomas's grin widened, toothy and mischievous, as always. "A hundred times, my friend. A hundred times!"

"Right, I'm sure." Shane was torn. A particular concept he had been trying to untangle was left dangling like a participle in the middle of the page beneath his pen, yet he could not deny the charisma that was his merry friend across the table. Thomas had accused Shane of being too serious on occasion.

"You're too serious. Lighten up. Have some fun with a mortal or two once in a while," Thomas said with a sigh.

"Serious no, thoughtful yes," Shane had argued.

"The 'Thinking Man,'" Thomas had replied.

"No, just always thinking," Shane said, feeling him fold in upon himself like wings.

"There is your fault," Thomas stated. "You're always thinking. Live a little. Think on it later."

Shane was offended. Thomas had once again belittled his private studies. But he couldn't dismiss the truth and it ate at his core like a cancer he was unsure how to remove without killing its host. It was a symbiotic union, his quiet observation, recollection, and he. It worked. Until questioned.

"That one." Thomas pointed his index finger, stein still gripped in his fist, at the petite raven-haired beauty leaning against a man twice her size at the edge of the bar.

Shane looked the couple up and down—a normal college-aged pair, though probably graduate students, dressed in jeans and T-shirts. Unassuming and innocent, he scanned their auras and, to his amazement, found nothing negative in either. Their sins, if such indiscretions were to be called such, were so minor as to be barely a blemish upon the surface of their beings.

Unicorns, he thought, *they're as rare as unicorns. Fuck. Of course he'd pick those two.*

"They're in love," he stated simply and turned back to Thomas, eager to watch his friend's assessment in body language and facial expressions alone.

"Yes, I know." Thomas grinned as he pulled long and hard at his drink. "That's what makes it all the more a challenge. Look at them. Blissful, sweet, serene, utterly at peace with each other. Everything is perfect. They'll never see it coming."

Shane's stomach turned. Even as black-hearted as he had become over the years toward humanity and the concept of human "civilization", the refusal of manipulation of true love was one torment he stood his ground on. Many had questioned his stance, asking how he could even tell in humans, and other creatures, the difference between lust and love. There was a resonance, a civility of the soul that permeated the combined auras of the two individuals when in the presence of eachother. He may shatter the existence of life itself in the hands of the corrupt and watch the shards glitter in their palms, but to come across a truly innocent soul was a rarity in any age. He had known love once, he was certain of it, though it felt now like a long-abandoned cobweb stretched thin and wavering across his memory. He wanted to believe that he had felt as those two felt now, comfortably ensconced in each other's quiet adoration.

Snorting and clearing his throat he returned to re-read the last sentence he had scrawled in his notebook.

"You're disgusted," Thomas said with a strange smugness that made Shane's skin tighten defensively. Why did his friend always try to provoke him so?

He looked up at Thomas for a long silent moment. "I'm content to write and be one with my inner asylum of muses.

Can we not do this dance this evening? I just don't have the stomach for it."

"Weak stomach. An excuse I haven't heard before." Thomas shifted, his face growing disturbingly serious. In the low ambient light it seemed his eyes shifted from deep brown to a reddish gold.

Shane saw the change and leaned back in the booth, laying his pen down beside his journal and spreading his hands flat upon the tabletop.

"Now, brother, no need for confrontation." Thomas set his stein down and folded his hands properly before him. "I wasn't trying to force your hand in anything untoward. Just trying to have a jest…or two. The night is young."

"What do you want, Thomas?" Shane drew a sharp deep breath through his nose, attempting to not let it exhale as a growl. His body bristled, his defenses on high. "I've seen you play with your conquests. This is different."

Thomas raised an eyebrow, one side of his wide mouth twisting into a sarcastic impersonation of questionability. "What? Them?" He gestured with a pinky finger at the couple by the bar. "Do you really think that they are a challenge? And, yes, I heard the 'unicorns' statement. No, not hardly. Just sheltered. And, no, I do not consider them the lucky ones."

"Why not?" Shane asked.

"Sheltered? Are you serious? You would prefer them to be sheltered? From the pain and anguish and heartbreak that makes the molds that forms the human consciousness? Take a look at them, a really hard look at them. There's nothing there. Just preplanned expectations set forth by their parents, expectations fulfilled with another expectation that other 'dreams' spoon-fed to them by nannies or counselors or media moguls that America is the land of all things good for those of the upper class. They delude themselves with images of an essence of jadedness they could never achieve. They feel untouchable because of their so-called innocence that their religion has beaten into them with visions of an unobtainable heaven and excruciating hell. They fight every day for that balance. They're always perched just on the edge. It wouldn't take much to push either one over the precipice. You know that. We have played with that balance every night for eons. Why do you look so aghast at my evaluation when you've made it a hundred times before?"

Shane swallowed hard, unable to muster a solid argument. He tried, like forcing a lump of granite from his lungs, but before he could formulate words Thomas snatched his journal out from between his down-turned hands—the speed his fae brother displayed still amazed him leaving him feeling slightly inadequate, angering him. He snarled and lurched forward, snatching at the book gripped in Thomas's hand.

"Shhhhhh—My brother, calm yourself! You don't want to draw unwanted attention, do you?" Thomas's infuriating grin never faded.

"Give it back to me!" Shane hissed, low and angry, "I told you once not to touch that which I write in."

Thomas raised an eyebrow. "And I told you I never listen to laws." He thumbed through the pages as the bar swirled around them in a strange uniform complexity of undulating sound and scent—hard-waxed tables embedded with two decades of human emotions, lights dull from age and cheap circumstance, entities of base existence co-mingling for the sake of not being alone.

And it struck him in that instance. Not being alone… If only humanity could appreciate the aspect of "alone" before beckoning to another then perhaps they might not spend so much of it in angst and isolation. He reached for his journal in which to notate the notion but was met with a raised palm. Thomas's attention was on the pages before him, reading carefully.

"The Importance of the Face." Thomas read the title of the page he read and paused. He raised his eyes to meet Shane's for a moment as if begging for an explanation. Shane felt paralyzed.

"The human face has been referred to by psychologists such as Wilhelm Reich as 'character armor' and Wittengenstein as a 'picture of the human soul'. In the case of Levinas, he referred to the human visage as a gateway citing: when we look at a person's face we are gazing beyond empirical reality to something transcendent, to that which cannot be 'thematized' or made a subject for knowledge." Thomas paused and raised his eyes momentarily to meet Shane's. "Well, aren't we the scholar."

He quickly dropped his gaze before Shane could reply and continued his recitation. "It is a mask, this outside presentation, but one that emits the frequencies of the soul that lays beyond. But how does this concept relate when the creature in question is no longer human? Our faces are masks, but are they gateways to our souls?"

"Interesting." Thomas drummed his fingers on the page of the journal as he continued reading Shane's scrawling longhand in silence. "Very interesting." His mouth curled into a feral grin as he concluded the passage on the page. "You make some interesting points. I had no idea you were such the philosopher."

"There are a lot of things you don't know about me." Shane suppressed a snarl. "May I have my journal back now?" Shane held out his hand, offering Thomas the opportunity to return the book willingly.

"I have to beg the question, though," Thomas raised his eyes again to meet Shane's. "How can a creature that never shows his true face ever have the ability to philosophize about the significance of another's features, let alone your own. How many centuries have you hid behind that mask? Do you even know yourself what your true face looks like."

"I do," Shane said quietly. His palms itched as adrenaline

raced through his veins.

"I've never seen it," Thomas challenged.

"You know my rule." Shane snatched the journal out from under Thomas's palms in a flash imperceptible to the human eye.

Thomas's fingers paused in mid-drum after making contact with the tabletop, hovering as he waited for Shane to finish his statement.

"My true face is reserved for those I trust with my life." Shane closed the journal and placed it in his black, leather satchel beside him.

"You don't trust me?" Thomas straightened, leaning back in his seat, his palms flat against the surface of the table.

"There are reasons for that," Shane replied quietly. It was still a sore subject to dredge up a decade later, a decade that felt like a mere few minutes.

"After all of this time? I bet I could pull it out of you." Thomas's voice darkened, though his grin remained etched as if in crystal across his lean face.

"Hardly. And you'd be a fool for trying." Shane glanced over at the couple Thomas had been eyeing as his earlier challenge. The woman was watching Thomas unabashedly even wrapped within her lover's arms. Silently he commended his brother for his ability to seduce without even attempting first contact—his mere mental acknowledgment of interest in the other party was often enough to send an entrancing vibration to snare their attention.

"A fool? Well, I've been called worse."

Shane surveyed the crowd, acutely aware of Thomas's gaze burning into the side of face. He knew the type of mood Thomas was in. "You're going to try, aren't you? Regardless of whatever I say?"

"Of course, brother." Thomas sat back in his seat and raised his mug to his lips.

Shane shouldered his satchel and rose from the booth. Without comment he slithered through the idle patrons like an eel in vintage gray wool to the rear exit. Thomas was quick to follow.

"Must we do this now?" Shane pulled the collar of his coat up against the cold, tucking his scarf inside.

It was a gesture not made for want of warmth, but an old human pantomime irreversibly ingrained on the pattern of his being. He gazed out over the small paved lot with its smattering of snow-cropped cars and up at the sloping dark forest beyond the sleepy little town. The clouds had finally dispersed to reveal a sterling night sky pregnant with a glowing, omniscient moon. Thomas stalked around Shane as if sizing him up for a prize fight before facing him, his legs planted shoulder-width and bent, his hands coming up in unison to gesture the emphasis of his next suggestion, his right still gripping his mug of ale. For a moment he hovered there, his head cocked slightly to one side as a deranged smile torqued his lips in a manner that made Shane desire a few more feet between him and his old friend.

"Truth or dare," Shane said. There was no question here, but a declaration, a statement of the present reality.

"Seriously?" Shane turned away and walked to his rusted 1965 Pontiac Acadian, opened the driver's side door, and tossed his satchel into the back seat. He stared at Thomas, his left hand holding the door open while he leaned against the frame. "You really think a game of Truth or Dare is going to make me drop my guard?"

Thomas arched an eyebrow, his smile fading as a strange darkness crept in around the edges of his features. In the sidelong light cast by the dull tavern exit his eyes shifted colors again, deepening from icy blue to forest green.

"Truth," Thomas said again, slowly, "or dare."

"Fine," Shane exhaled and closed the car door before crossing his arms over his chest. Beneath the irritation that pricked his skin like steel wool an unexplainable, yet stifling anxiety that gripped him cold and hard at the center of his chest. "I'll give you three tries. Then I'm leaving. I have much better things to do with my time than stand out in the snow feeding your madness."

Thomas waited.

"Truth." Shane finally decided.

The cruel smile returned to Thomas's mouth. "You still harbor resentment for my seduction of Diana."

Shane narrowed his eyes, tilting his head slightly to the side, "That's not exactly a secret. Harbor? Hardly. Wear it on my sleeve. Absolutely. Just as you keep your hatred of me for my turning of her in your hip pocket for easy access. It's honestly amazing we even call each other 'brothers' anymore." He paused. The silence between them was accented by the occasional hissing of tires over snow and asphalt.

"Is that what this is about?" Shane felt his defenses gather tight against him, cold and formidable. The unanswered question hung like razor wire between them.

"You don't get to ask the questions." Thomas denied Shane's inquiry. Any and all joviality in his previous demeanor had evaporated like steam, replaced by hostility. "Truth or dare?" Shane uncrossed his arms, his fists curling at his sides. "Truth." Thomas tossed his empty mug aside into the snow and took a step towards Shane. "It eats at you still, the fact that you made her your progeny and yet she still came back to me because she couldn't stomach the idea of being taught her new life by a monster."

"She never left me Thomas. She couldn't of her own volition. I will always be her Maker. I was not her keeper, though. She could sleep with whatever she liked," Shane said the words, but he knew, no matter the iron and ice in his tone his bitterness tainted his conviction. "As for being a 'monster', she would never call me such."

"Really? Are you so certain of that? In all of the atrocities you've committed over the years, the lives you've destroyed, the spirits you've broken, you do not think you have earned that title?" Thomas sneered.

"Who are you to speak? Your body count may not be as high as mine, but trust me, you've done your fair share of destruction over the years." *Including my own…* Shane let the last sentence ring in his mind. His pulse raced until his skin vibrated with adrenaline, his vision tunneling in on his brother.

Why was Thomas provoking Shane so?

Out of the darkness the realization nearly knocked the wind from his lungs—it was the ten-year anniversary of Diana's death. Only a year after her blood transformation she had disappeared. For weeks Shane and Thomas had searched for her, combing the earth for signs of her. In the end it was Shane that finally discovered her remains, tucked into the hollow root system of an old evergreen tree high in the mountains beyond the town. Every night afterward Shane tormented himself as the memories emerged with questions as to how he could not have known she was in distress or why it had taken him so long to locate her body, for their bond could not be severed, even in death. Thomas had been beside himself in his grief—Shane had retreated from the world, sinking into a melancholy that was perhaps far more destructive than even the havoc that Thomas had inflicted on the unsuspecting who dared to cross his path.

"Thomas, careful," Shane cautioned. "I know what night this is. I miss her too. There is no need for—"

"Truth or dare?" Thomas cracked his neck and took another aggressive step toward Shane. "I get one more. Remember?" Shane swallowed hard, his fangs elongating as the scent of Thomas's bloodlust enveloped them both. He didn't want to choose for there was no choice that would not lead to war.

Quietly, cautiously, Shane answered, "Dare."

"I dare you to take me back there. Show me where you

found her."

Shane was speechless. Deadly silence suffocated the space between them. "Why? Why would you want me to take you there? Why revisit that?"

"Revisit? You never would tell me where it was you found her. You never showed me. All of these years I've tried to peel back the layers of your mind, get inside and find just one tiny glimpse, but no. You keep those secrets to yourself, you selfish bastard." Thomas snarled, his lip curling to reveal clenched teeth.

"No," Shane shook his head. Inside he trembled as the memories of Diana's mangled remains awkwardly folded in unnatural angles amidst the gnarled roots and dirt invaded his mind like blue-black beetles scurrying towards his consciousness. "I can't. I won't. Let her rest."

"Why? What are you hiding, brother?" Thomas took yet another step forward, closing the space between them.

"You're never going to let this go until I take you there, are you?"

Thomas's silence was answer enough. Shane felt bile rise in the back of his throat. His keys were still clutched in his right hand, digging into his palm. He turned towards the car and opened the door.

"You can't back out of this. You agreed to my challenge and you chose 'dare.'"

"Shut up and get in the car."

✶✶✶

A few miles outside of town, up a winding dirt road that seemed almost too rough at times to be manmade, they drove with only the sound of the tires hissing through the snow. Shane kept his eyes focused on the treacherous highway illuminated by dull headlights whose only purpose was to keep the local authorities from pulling them over. Thomas leaned against the passenger door, his forehead pressed against the glass as he stared blankly out into the night. The aggression that had seethed just below the surface of his being a half hour before had curled in upon itself, tucking in its tail and laying its head low. From behind their carefully constructed defenses each tested the other from time to time, trying to find the weak point in the wall to slip in undetected and listen. Neither was successful.

Shane pulled off the main road and parked on the shoulder that met the mountain itself. He turned off the engine and dimmed the headlights. The glistening black forest around them came to life in the moonlight, pristine snow lining the ground and dark gray limbs of the trees that towered above them. Shane studied the silhouettes of each trunk certain his eyes were playing tricks on him—the bark seemed to shift from time to time as if a shadow were passing in front distorting the natural patterns.

"Are you certain you want to do this?" Shane asked quietly.

Thomas opened the door and exited the car.

Shane stuffed his keys in his pocket and followed suit. "This way."

Down the side of the mountain they trudged through the ankle-deep snow, winding a serpentine path to where the ground leveled out for about ten yards before plunging down again to a semi-frozen river at its base. Turning east Shane led Thomas through the hibernating forest to the one place he had hoped to never return.

Shane's foot began to crack a twig buried beneath the snow. He halted as he realized his uncharacteristic misstep, but the sound had already escaped, echoing up out of the canyon like a flock of angry ravens.

"I believe this is it." Thomas's voice was dark as the night itself.

Shane whirled around, perplexed and panting as his heart thundered in his chest. Words failed him as he took in his surroundings. Slowly he dropped his gaze to the ground and traced the disjointed line from his staggered footprints to the mouth of nature's tomb that had cradled his love so carefully in death.

"How did you know…?" Shane's blood turned to ice in his veins.

"Look up brother," Thomas whispered. "It's time to answer for your crimes."

The fine hairs along Shane's arms bristled as the sound of wind rushing past in a cyclone about him blotted out the natural sleeping silence of the forest itself. His body perfectly still, he raised his eyes to find Thomas standing directly before him.

"What exactly do I have to answer for?" Shane stood his ground, suppressing a growl that rumbled deep within his chest.

"Your secrets you keep well, but not well enough. Just once was enough for me to slip in and see the horrible truth." Thomas half choked on the words he attempted to snarl. Suddenly, he was behind Shane again, whispering in his ear, "You say you loved her. How can you murder that which you love? Let me show you your true face."

Thomas's arm locked around Shane's throat as a sharp pain arced down Shane's jaw from his ear to his chin, the cold fire of silver splitting his flesh causing him to cry out in agony. Reaching up he grabbed Thomas by the shoulders and hurled him forward over Shane's head sending him flying into the trunk of an ancient evergreen a few feet away with a crack. Snow sifted down from the lowest branches upon impact, dusting Thomas's body in a fine white powder. Hot blood poured down Shane's neck, seeping into the collar of his coat as the silver kept the wound from closing immediately. As the flesh began to knit together again, he drew his forefinger along the incision as he watched Thomas gather himself at the base of the tree, crouching with the bowie knife still gripped in his right hand.

My true face… Shane thought. *The mad motherfucker is trying to skin me!*

"Thomas, please don't make me—"

Thomas launched himself at Shane with a howl, his knife raised over his head. Before Shane could consider his next move his instincts ignited, stifling his reason—the night became a blur of red and black shadows for a heartbeat. As the distortion ebbed he found himself standing over Thomas, his hands covered in gore. Upon his tongue he tasted blood. Reality solidified as he exhaled, the grisly sight of a hole large enough to reveal the blood-soaked snow below gaped through the center of Thomas's chest. Thomas's throat looked as if it had been savaged by a wild animal—Shane's veins hummed with the warmth of new blood, yet he could not remember his fangs ripping into Thomas's veins. The knife was nowhere to be seen.

Shane staggered back a pace, shaking, "Damn you!" he screamed. "Why? Why couldn't you just let it go? You crazy bastard!" He grabbed fistfuls of hair on either side of his head and screamed as the agony of the memories of Diana's broken body, limbs gnawed upon by wild animals and insects, gruesomely resurrected in his mind's eye.

"You shouldn't have done that." A woman's voice hissed through the branches of the trees.

Shane spun around, staring wildly up at the foreboding forest looming over him. "Who's there? Show yourself!" he shouted.

"Thomas only wanted to show you your true face. Now we must do it for him."

Shane looked down. Thomas's body had vanished—only the dark red stain of his life was left as evidence upon the forest floor. Shane began to run.

✴✴✴

Through the sleeping white forest the invisible hands drug Shane, down the steep mountainside to the frozen river below. He tried to speak, to demand answers, to beg for mercy, but could find no force within his lungs to form sound. Upon the bank, between two large outcroppings of boulders the pressure caused him to drop to his knees. There the racing water still rose to the surface where the ice was thinnest, shimmering with an iridescent mystery all its own.

"Look!" came a man's voice, deep as the roots of the evergreens themselves.

Shane stared down into the water and ice at his reflection. Confusion scattered his thoughts like shrapnel against the walls of his skull—the image was not his own, but that of Thomas. He found his voice again, "This is an illusion," he whispered to himself desperately. "This is an illusion!" he repeated, shouting it to the unseen as he struggled to stand.

"This is no illusion, Shane. You've denied your true face for far too long. You've kept too many secrets from yourself, playing games."

The past rushed by in the water between the broken shards of ice and black rock and in it he witnessed the twisted truth— his obsession with Diana and his ultimate destruction of her at the end of an unfounded jealousy. There had been no Thomas to seduce her away, but only a name that had consumed Shane and, in turn, taken on a life of its own.

The pressure on the back of Shane's neck dissipated until only the cold night air crept beneath his collar. He stared down at his hands—they were clean.

"I killed her," he whispered through numb lips.

Dawn hovered at the edge of the world casting a deep purple bruise to the clear night sky and burdening his bones with leaden immortality. He raised his eyes to the water again and this time his own haunted reflection gazed back full of sorrowful disgust. He was only faintly aware of his hand reaching into his coat pocket, his fingers wrapping about the icy steel of his knife. The click of the knife as the blade was released echoed between the mountainsides until it faded into nothingness. He watched himself as if he stood two paces behind his own body as the knife rose to the ear that once before Thomas had cut—he drew the knife in one swift continuous movement around the edge of his entire face. With a howl he threw hurled the blade into the river and before his skin could knit itself back together, he reached into the wound and ripped the flesh from his face.

Blood poured from his exposed skull down his throat, soaking the front of his shirt as he knelt in the snow holding his face in his hands like strange leather mask. Fighting the darkness that crept in around his vision he staggered to his feet and with another strangled cry threw his visage into the freezing current. Shane would not die from his wounds. But, perhaps, he might, in time, grow another face, a mask to hide his future atrocities from himself and the world. Tonight, however, the truth could not be hidden.

HACK

by David C. Hayes

The Yuk Yuk Hut on Clark Street in downtown Chicago was dark as pitch when Jeff "El Jefe" Dolniak entered the front doors. It was long after hours at the upscale comedy club, but Jeff didn't know that anything, anywhere, could be this dark.

This joint is Africa-dark, he thought and, contrary to standard operating procedure, he was too freaked out to laugh at his own joke. He cleared his throat, quietly. There was no response. For a guy that routinely performed in front of hundreds of laughing fans (and whose material is a couple of steps left of just plain wrong), the quiet and the darkness and the, well, creepiness, had really thrown him off. It was worth it, though. At least El Jefe thought it was worth it even if he couldn't exactly explain what it was. Gathering all of his courage, mid-level comedian Jeff Dolniak called out bravely into the darkness.

"Uumm… hello?" he said, "It's, uhh, it's me… Jeff."

Nothing. Wait.

"Mr. Dolniak, it is a pleasure to see you," A voice sluiced through the darkness, the words oily and black. The spotlight blazed from the rear of the club lighting up the stage next to Jeff. El Jefe jumped, his heart in his throat. The round spotlight exposed the small stage, stool, and microphone. This wasn't Jeff's first time in the club and he knew that a house that seated around 200 fell off into the darkness beyond the light. The Yuk Yuk Hut had been a Chicago institution since before World War II. You got to play there and you are up for a major tour. That's just how it worked. Well, Jeff knew how it worked for real, or at least he thought he did. That was why he was there, scared half to death.

A heartbeat behind the light, Kyle Dillon, the club manager, moved into the cast-off glow of the spot. He smiled, like always, and extended his hand. Jeff had never seen Dillon without that smile. It unnerved every comedian that played The Hut and Jeff had always assumed it was a negotiating tactic that effectively made any situation awkward. Jeff tentatively took Dillon's hand in a perfunctory shake and then moved his hand away quickly. The smile never wavered.

"I'm glad you took Mr. Timponi up on his offer. He sees a great deal in you, Mr. Dolniak. A great deal indeed."

"Thank you. Err, I mean thank Mr. Timponi for me." If possible, Jeff thought that Dillon's smile grew wider and whiter.

"Oh, you'll be able to thank him yourself. Follow me to the dressing area. You will have approximately fifteen minutes to prepare and then you will perform."

With that, Dillon turned and disappeared into the murky shadows of the club. Stumbling after him, Jeff tried to keep up. He had played the club before, during business hours, of course, when the lights were on, so he managed not to kill himself as Dillon walked around tables toward the rear of the establishment. They eventually reached the dressing area and Dillon held the door for Jeff.

"Please, Mr. Dolniak, enter." Jeff, managing a weak smile, entered the small dressing room. A bottle of bourbon, his favorite kind, a tumbler and ice were already there. Jeff felt a little more relaxed seeing his best friend on the table like that. Well, one of his best friends. Like most comedians worth his salt, Jeff ran with Jim, Jack, Johnnie and Jose pretty regularly. Too regularly, if you asked his three ex-wives.

"So, it will just be Mr. Timponi?" Jeff asked. He stammered a bit saying the man's name now that he knew the truth.

"And myself. Here are the ground rules: You are to tell three jokes. These are not to be slice of life pastiches where you wax poetic and make humorous observances about the bizarre, uniquely American condition. You will tell three jokes that have a set-up, a body, and a punch line. Do you understand?"

"Yes," Jeff answered, "I guess, but why can't I just do my set that…"

"Mr. Timponi is a purist and he believes that any individual able to tell a joke will be able to enthrall an audience with a story. It is the joke, though, the bare essence of comedy that is so difficult," Dillon's smile, as always, never wavered. Even as he cut off and chastised Jeff.

"I understand."

"In addition, you are not to curse or use profane language. Mr. Timponi believes that is evidence of a weak mind. You do not want Mr. Timponi to believe you have a weak mind, do you?"

"No."

"Good. You will have three attempts to make Mr. Timponi laugh. Three jokes, three attempts. If you succeed in that endeavor, he will see to it that you, Mr. Dolniak, will have an illustrious career as long as you see fit to stay alive. If you do not, well, you're aware of the consequences. I'll leave you to it." Dillon exited, shutting the door behind him.

Jeff exhaled deeply. He hoped it was worth it, at least. He looked into the mirror ringed with small lights, and stared into the eyes of a good, unknown comedian that knew his last shot at something, anything, of value in the industry was right here and right now. If he didn't make it tonight, though… Shit. He didn't even want to think about it. Not many people get this opportunity. At least he didn't think many people did. It's not like you'd hear from the guys that blew it.

Jeff opened the bourbon and filled the glass. He ignored the ice and took a long guzzle letting it burn down his throat. He shivered with the smoothness of the drink and took a deep breath. He was really going to do it—Tony Timponi's challenge.

A couple of years ago he would have laughed off anyone that brought it up, but Jeff knew now. He knew that Tony Timponi was the real fucking deal.

Tony Timponi was the original, and only, owner of The Yuk Yuk Hut, established in 1941. If he had bought the joint at eighteen that would make him 90 years old or so right now and, after glimpsing Mr. Timponi, Jeff could see that the guy was nowhere near 90. He didn't appear often (although legend had it that Mr. Timponi had seen every comedian that had ever played The Hut), but when he did he looked thirty-five to forty years old. People always said that it was a big Timponi Family joke. The sons and the grandsons just kept taking the place and playing Mr. Timponi like some cryptic Andy Kaufman rib, but that wasn't it. Tony Timponi was really the same guy and, with the advent of the internet, it was pretty easy to figure out a timeline.

After Dillon approached Jeff following one of the shows the week before and made the offer, the one that comedians talk about very quietly over drinks or coke or whatever, Jeff did a little research. Any vaudeville historian worth their salt would tell you that it hit its heyday in the 1920's, but the "polite company" variety show really came into vogue in the late 1800's. Gentleman song and dance men, zany comedians, and screwball clownish performances were the hallmark of the vaudeville review. Most of the shows traveled on a circuit, going from town to town, city to city, like modern medieval minstrels. In the early days of vaudeville, running the Midwest territory, there was one name that drew them all in, men and women, kids and adults. That was Top Hat Tony Timponi. He was considered the funniest man in Chicago (and surrounding areas). Most people who read that on a poster may have disregarded it as some kind of clever advertising—Barnum-esque publicity, maybe. Anyone who'd seen a Top Hat show knew better. Chances were their sides still hurt from the last time Tony was in town.

Tony played to sold-out crowds from Elgin to Detroit, Minnetonka to Des Moines and everywhere in between. He had even started to branch out to the East Coast in the mid-1920's and, with that expansion, got a serious look from the Hollywood studios. Top Hat's patented brand of polite, family friendly comedy featured physical work that would put some of the Holly-weird bigwigs like Buster and Charlie to shame. His calling card, though, was the joke. He could set it up, make them wait for it and then knock it out of the park like no one else. The funny man had a rocket strapped to his back and he was headed straight to the top. Until 1929. After that he disappeared. Just like that, poof. The dates were cancelled and a replacement act was quickly booked to fill the empty slot. Top Hat Tony Timponi slowly faded until he was nothing more than a name that fellow comedians would raise a glass to, toasting his genius as they stole the jokes that Tony obviously had no more use for.

The name Anthony Timponi appeared on the requisite documents in the late 1930's to open The Yuk Yuk Hut and it had been there ever since. It was a Chicago institution, along with the blues and Second City. From the onset, The Hut managed to become a proving ground for young comedians. Anyone that was anyone had performed at The Hut at some point and, through the years, it became a destination point for comedians and audiences alike. It wasn't until the 1960's, though, that the whispers started. The little stories told in the dark about Tony Timponi, The Hut, and just how hard it was to make it in this business.

Jeff had heard the talk before. Tony Timponi would make the offer of a game to certain comedians—comedians that he felt had merit. If they agreed, those comedians would be in the same place that Jeff was right now. Each of them was given three chances to make a genuine comedy legend laugh. If you succeeded, the sky was the limit. Although no one ever knew for sure, there had been talk regarding just who benefited from the Timponi Touch. There was Dangerfield, Kinison (imagine him telling a clean joke), Carlin—all of them genius performers and each of them a certifiable success, artistically and financially. They would never indicate whether or not Tony had a hand in their success, no one would, but one can wonder, right?

And those unlucky stiffs that didn't make the big man laugh? No one ever heard from them again. The funny part was that no one heard of them to begin with so it wasn't like there was a big void in the comedy world by their absence. Another slot just became available at an open mic night. It was as simple as that.

Jeff slugged down another drink and refilled the glass. He had to will himself to not suck that one dry right away. It would do no good to go up there sloshed. That's a quick trip to deadsville. Jeff laughed.

It was the other rumor about Top Hat Tony Timponi that really disturbed him, especially after his research. When a comedian is doing poorly and the audience is just crickets the performers call them "dead." Jeff laughed again. He was pretty sure that his audience tonight was already dead. Well, undead, technically. All the whispering about just who Tony Timponi was usually skirted around what everyone actually thought Tony Timponi was. Only very late at night, when the bartender gives you an extra couple hours after last call while the staff cleans up, did anyone dare say what everyone already thought.

Vampire.

There, it was out. Jeff had thought the word and could no longer bring it back. If you didn't get Mr. Timponi to laugh then you became lunch. Dillon did not say that verbatim. He did indicate that, if Jeff lost, he should make sure that all his affairs were in order before coming to The Yuk Yuk Hut. Walking through those doors was acceptance of the terms. Why did Top Hat do this? No one knew. Boredom, maybe? Jeff liked to think that Top Hat was just concerned with the quality of his industry. Tony had been around so long he could see all the bumbling oafs come through over the years. The guys that told dirty nursery rhymes or simply smashed watermelons or celebrated the blueness of their collars…the lowest common denominator of comedy had to anger Tony Timponi. He was a master, a classic. He had a PhD in funny and these hacks only managed to tell toilet jokes. That's what Jeff wanted to believe. He was chosen, he had something that Timponi saw and, by God, he was going to give it his best shot. Comedy was his life, literally now that Colleen had left, and he wanted this more than anything else. There was no 'plan b,' like a college degree or a factory job back home. Failure meant death so, in effect, he had nothing to lose.

It was still scary as shit, though. And he still hadn't thought through his three jokes when there was a knock at the door.

"Mr. Dolniak?" Dillon asked through the door.

"Yup," Jeff answered, surprised he could even squeak that out. The door opened and the club manager had the same smile plastered across his face.

"You're on." Dillon didn't wait for an answer. He turned and walked toward the front of the club.

Taking a deep breath Jeff shot back the last of the bourbon and followed.

Dillon sidestepped to the left as they entered the main show area. Jeff trudged forward, through the murkiness, and aimed right for that spotlight and the stage. He took the steps one by one and felt the weight of the world on each of them. It was all he could do pull himself up the short flight. Once on stage, he moved through molasses getting to the microphone, adjusted it to his height, and cleared his throat. The mic was on and his gurgling phlegm echoed throughout the empty club.

"Oh Jesus!" he said, hearing his bodily fluids all around him. The exclamation was too loud as well. Jeff stood back from the mic quickly and took a deep breath. Dillon's voice slid through the club to the stage.

"Calm down, Mr. Dolniak."

Jeff nodded and took a couple of deep breaths. He made a mental conviction, plastered his "comedy" smile on and stepped up to the mic on more time.

"Good evening everyone. Well, you, Mr. Timponi. My name is Jeff Dolniak, and—."

"He knows that, Mr. Dolniak. Tell your first joke."

Jeff responded by giving in and shutting up. *Jesus Christ,* he thought, *Haven't even said hello and I'm getting heckled. This business is murder!* At the thought, Jeff cracked a smile. At least he could get himself to laugh. His mind working a mile a minute, Jeff started the first joke that came to him.

"Johnny and his wife had fallen on some tough times. This economy, you know what I mean? Johnny can't find a job, his wife can't find a job…but she is quite attractive. So, they concoct this plan where his wife, Evie, would take to the streets. She would become a prostitute and Johnny would play her pimp. They watched a bunch of movies, like *Pretty Woman*, to make sure they were getting it right. So, Johnny sends his wife out on the first night and she comes back smiling from ear to ear. She has had a great night, she tells her husband, and she hands over the loot. It's a hundred-and-two dollars and fifty-seven cents. Johnny can't believe it. Over a hundred bucks! He was curious, though, and asked her, 'Who gave you fifty-seven cents?' His wife smiled and said, 'Everybody.'"

Jeff stepped back, waiting. He waited a moment more. Nothing. No chuckle, no laugh. Not even a derisive snort. Fuck, he thought. Jeff gave Mr. Timponi another moment. Wait for it, wait for it…

"Mr. Dolniak," Dillon shattered the quiet, "You may try

again.'

One down. Jeff's mind raced. He needed something. Maybe Timponi didn't like the hooker thing. Maybe it was too old? Jeff sweated bullets and licked his lips. They were beginning to dry and crack. His mouth felt like it was filled with cotton. *Dead room, that's for sure*, he thought, and laughed out loud this time. *I slay me,* he thought again and laughed one more time. Not even the image of Tony Timponi swooping in from the rafters, fangs bared, eyes blazing, could spoil it.

"Mr. Dolniak?"

"I'm good. I'm fine. I'm ready." Jeff said, between chuckles. He stepped up to the mic again and took a deep breath. *Jokes. He wants jokes? I'll give him jokes.* He went for broke.

"You know," Jeff started, "Ever since I've was a little kid I have been fascinated with prison. No, seriously, I have. What it takes to get there, what you have to do in prison. I must admit, I had been a bit infatuated with the idea that there was free food, free cable TV, and you got to have a roommate. As an only child, I dug the roommate thing. That particular fringe benefit took on a new meaning as I got older, as did the whole prison thing. I realized what you had to do in order to get to prison and I also realized what people did to you when you were in prison…if you know what I mean. So, I developed a plan. I always thought I would end up there, but I saw how these inmates, theses common criminals were approaching the incarcerated thing all wrong. They worked out and got big and buff so they could beat up any gang rapists that came by, right? Well, not me. I'm going to eat. I'm going to eat and eat and eat. As you can already tell, my derriere is a little larger than most. It's plump. Imagine that even bigger. Much bigger. There is a show on TV called the *600 Pound Virgin*. That guy's rear end is smaller than I'm thinking. When all the other tough guys are fighting off the rapists I'm just gonna' let them in. Go right ahead. With an ass that big you'll just be playing in the cheeks anyway. You'd need to be hung like John Holmes to hit my sweetmeat!"

This joke always worked. He had told it across the country. Even Republicans in Kansas were at least ashamed to laugh at this one. It poked fun at all of society's pariahs: fat people, convicts, rapists, comedians…everyone. Jeff waited for that chuckle. Even a hundred-year-old douchebag that had heard every joke on the planet had to laugh at that one. Didn't he? Another moment. Nothing. Jeff threw his hands up in exasperation. He couldn't take it. He was going to die and there was no way out. Screw it.

"One more time, Mr. Dol…"

"Shut up," Jeff cut Dillon off, knowing full well that he was probably signing his own death warrant. "Just shut up. Yeah, I get it. One more joke. Whatever. I don't need some Renfield wannabe with a goofy smile telling me I'm two-thirds dead, ok?" Jeff squinted into the spotlight, trying to make out a shape, anything, in the audience, "And you. Top Hat? Yeah, I know about you. Everyone does. They just won't talk about it. You're some kind of comedy Godfather, right? Lives forever, feeds on comics that don't cut it. I get it. You're probably looking up here like I'm lunch. Well, too bad for me, right?" Jeff stood back. He kicked the stool over in frustration and ripped the mic from the stand.

"Goddamn vampire, they said. Can't trust him, they said. I'm not talking about you, I'm talking about every other goddamn comedy promoter and club owner on the planet. You, Nosfer-fuck-you, you're the only honest one! You admit it! Know what I hope? I hope all the goddamn villagers get their goddamn torches and they come down here. I don't want them to kill you, though. I want them to tie you down to chair and put a fucking TV in front of you. You won't be able to move and I want them to play all of the fucking Twilight movies in a row, over and over again, until you decide to kill yourself. By my estimation, it should be about twenty minutes into the first one."

"Mr. Dolniak!" Dillon shouted from the audience.

"Can it. Go eat a fly or something. I'm almost done anyway. Finally, I just want to thank you for the opportunity and warn you that I'm a borderline alcoholic so what I got in these veins may be a little watered down for your tastes. Any way, have at it."

Jeff laughed then, long and hard. He knew the end was near so he righted the stool, took a deep breath, and sat down. The spotlight shut off, throwing the club into complete darkness. Before he could even blink and start the eye adjustment process, Jeff felt a presence behind him. It was cold and dark. Hands grasped Jeff's shoulders and he went rigid. The hands had long fingers that were almost gentle at the touch, like when humans 'test' a piece of fruit for freshness. Jeff could barely feel their weight, but he knew they were there. He knew their intent as well.

A cold, dry tongue tasted the vein up the side of Jeff's neck. The sound of the tongue scraping against his five o'clock shadow was like Velcro separating and it made Jeff shiver. He pulled the microphone up one last time.

"They told me that comedy was filled with a bunch of bloodsuckers and that I'd never make it. Guess they were right after all." Jeff let the mic drop to the floor. It landed with a thunk that reverberated through the speaker system. Jeff closed his eyes, preparing for the end.

Wait for it. Waaait for it…

The hands left his shoulders and the room warmed up a bit just then. And, from the shadows, Jeff heard the most awful sound on the planet, like nails on a chalkboard underwater. It was music to his ears.

Image by Jerry H.

THE BLOOD COUNTESS

by Sèphera Girón

On that desolate evening in the chilly grip of autumn, I walked with trepidation down the stone tunnel, my fingers clutching the heavy tray of bowls sloshing with foul gruel, my heart beating as quickly as a hummingbird's wings. It was always cold and dank in that castle and worse so since the immurement. It was often a puzzlement to me how life can go from brutally dull, to magnificently glorious, to stunningly fearful.

She had shown me ways that I would never have known. Certainly not as the child I had been when I first laid eyes on her. Her glamour, her generosity, and her beauty were hypnotically legendary with pale porcelain flesh framing eyes as black as buttons and a plump full mouth that had a perpetual sneer. When she stared at me and spoke I would do anything for her.

Alas, it was time to finish the journey that had started in what seemed like a lifetime ago. The astrological forces were too strong to ignore—the call of the night, the wail of the Watchers, all combined to push me down the path I had been dreading. Her screams of anguish were heard throughout the castle, especially when the winds were high. It was a wonder any sound penetrated through all those thick stone walls. But it did. Yowling threats, wailing sadness, high-pitched singing of her favorite operas— all sounds echoing distantly through my dreams and waking life until I could ignore them no longer. The torch-lit, narrow, stone hallway seemed excruciatingly long because of my faltering steps. The flames provided little warmth in the dampness. A light chilly wind blustered by and then was gone like an animal rushing past me. I held the heavy wooden tray in front of me, keeping my eyes straight ahead, each step one closer to her.

She wouldn't be expecting me.

She thought I had been caught too.

I had escaped detection although many pointed fingers at me. By some stroke of magic, or perhaps by my own sheer intellect, I'd been spared the fate of the others. They were caught and found guilty, subjected to punishments consisting of their fingers being ripped off followed by their bodies burned at the stake. Those of us spared kept a low profile after that, skulking around and doing our duties, while hiding evidence of the Countess's carnage as we stumbled across it. We seldom spoke to each other except for an occasional nod in our gratefulness to have survived.

And then there was she: The Beautiful One. Locked in that wing of the castle for the rest of her life. I looked down at the bowls of gruel I carried. Surely not food she craved. She needed more than that.

I put down the tray of food on the floor and wiped the sweat from my brow with the cloth I kept shoved down the front of my bodice. Even though it was cold, I was sweating. Chills ran up my spine. My hands were clammy. I hadn't seen her since the trials. Not face to face.

A wave of weakness washed over me and I braced against the wall, barely able to gulp in the dense musky air. I tugged at my corset strings but the bindings wouldn't be loosened. No matter, I knelt down to retrieve the tray and walked the last few steps to the bricked-up wall. The only opening in its face was a narrow gap in the stones, covered with a sliding wooden window, about four feet off the ground through which to pass rations to the prisoner inside.

I put the tray on the floor in front of me and with trembling fingers began to slide open the slat. My heart beat so powerfully that I feared I would collapse. Could she smell me? Was she there, waiting? I half expected a hand to reach out for me like a ghostly claw. I knew that on the other side of the wall was a stone table. Hesitantly, I slid the first bowl through the opening. I pulled my hands away quickly before she could grab me and reached down to pick up the second bowl.

"Margarite," she whispered. "You have returned to me."

"Here is your dinner, Your Highness," I stammered sliding the second bowl through. Again, I snatched my hands away from the opening before she could touch me.

"How are you feeling, Your Highness?" I asked, standing back from the window, my back pressed against the wall to keep me from passing out from fear.

"I'm not so well, Margarite." Her voice was low. The sound of sniffling echoed out to me as if she were crying. I wanted to leave.

"I fear that I may be dying. Can you imagine? All this work to look young forever and now I don't even care."

The plaintive whine in her voice could have been convincing had I not heard that tone used just before something terrible happened. Perhaps, after four years, she was truly remorseful for all that she'd done.

I didn't answer.

"I'm delighted you're here, my beautiful Marguerite. You have no idea how lonely I am, languishing away in this despicable vestibule."

"I can't speak." I looked down the hallway to see if there were guards lurking about. I knew I could have my tongue torn out for speaking to the Countess too much, the court had ordered such. Yet, disobeying the Countess could bring far worse horrors.

I pushed myself away from the wall and started to slide the slat shut. Her fingers reached out, grasping mine. She was still powerfully strong and easily pulled most of my hand through the opening. I muffled my cries as sharp pain pierced my fingertips and her lips greedily sucked my blood. I prayed no one saw as I let her feast. How I'd missed her. My heart ached as I pulled my bloody fingers away. I stared at the blood dripping down and with the other hand, shut the door.

That night I dreamed of no one but my Countess. Day after day I returned to feed her. I ate her gruel to keep my strength up and concocted a tale of a rose bush clipping mishap, which explained the bandages around my hands. At least for a while. When I looked at myself in the mirror, I saw my cheeks had grown sunken, my reflection more of an essence than an image. No matter how much extra food I consumed, my flesh was pale, my corset drawn tighter.

When the Countess had first been taken away, I had been one of the many servants instructed to clear her room. We were allowed to take what we desired. The family was more interested in her belongings being gone than worrying about where they went. My own collection included a paint box of mysterious pallets that she had used to conceal her own pale countenance. I had held up mirrors for her as she painted a face and body substantial enough to cast a reflection. Of course, her eyes had been the most haunting aspect for there was no makeup to create eyes. Luckily no one really saw the Countess in the mirror, only in person, and if you missed those black pools of unending tortures, then you deserved everything you received. Now, the pallets were drying out from neglect. Mixing in crushed berries and water to revive them, I began to apply the paint as I had seen the Countess do. With time and practice my reflection appeared healthy once more.

One day as I placed the bowls of gruel on the floor the Countess whispered to me through the slot in the door. "Go to your left, three bricks," she said.

I looked down the hallway to be certain I was alone.

"Down here," she whispered.

The Countess grabbed my ankle. "You must come in. Please." She had somehow chiseled a hole in the bricks large enough for my emaciated frame to crawl through. I wanted to scream, to cry, to run in fear, yet curiosity also beguiled me.

"They will not catch you if you hurry."

I crawled through the hole without thinking.

Quickly the Countess slid a few bricks back to hide the hole. Her eyes flashed with excitement. "I have a plan to free me. You must bring me these herbs," she said calmly as she handed me a piece of old linen upon which she had written the list in her own blood.

I stood up from where I knelt, staring in awe at my Countess. It was the first time I had laid eyes upon her face, her body, in nearly four years. She was more beautiful than ever. "After the full moon, I will drink the potion made from these herbs. You will tell the guards that I have not eaten in several days and you are concerned. Urge them to break down the wall. When they discover me I will appear as if I am dead. When they leave to find help you must hide me."

She grabbed my arm tightly, her nails digging through my thin cotton shirt and into my flesh.

"Countess, please," I whispered, pulling away from her. She dropped her hand and turned away, the figure eight of her corseted body a scarlet slash in the dim candlelit room.

"Together we will flee and rebuild my empire. In the East."

"It's impossible," I sobbed and clasped my hands over my mouth.

Countess Bathory stood before me, tall and menacing as she clacked together her long nails. "You will do as I say."

I was unable to look away from those dark pools, a pit into which I fell. I obeyed her command.

We lived in a castle, the Countess reborn as young nobility and I, her faithful servant. We wove a splendid tale about shipwrecks and pirates, and how we crawled ashore in their fair country. The handsome prince who found us was quick to marry Elizabeth, ignorant of her true identity. As princes do, he was soon off to war leaving Elizabeth alone to her devious fantasies. This time I was the one who combed the countryside for poor young girls eager to work at the castle. Delivering the innocents to the Countess had never been hard for me. I had grown numb to the idea that these young ladies were just farm animals. This time, however, as I was aging now, the Countess shared with me her spoils. We worked as a team to harvest the blood and selected bits of flesh as we learned the most efficient ways to reap our bounty. We were drunk on blood, just like in the old times, only back then I was but a servant girl. Now, I was the Countess's faithful companion and lover. We drank each other's blood rolling about on finely spun pillows stopping only long enough to attend ceremonies or watch an occasional jousting match. Life was good.

One morning, as I slept in the crisp sheets the maids ironed every day, the Countess was restless beside me. It wasn't like her to so much as flinch when she slept, but this time she tossed and turned, murmuring in her sleep. I felt the weight of her body shift and then emptiness as she left the bed. I feigned sleep as the soft rustling of her arms slipping through her dressing gown tickled my ears. The floor creaked lightly as she crept from the room. On the fourth day, I decided to follow her. The Countess ran along the front of the lawn, bare feet barely touching the dew-kissed grass as she ran into the woods.

A shadow flitted through the trees, running to greet her. She had a lover.

Would she treat me the way she had her other lovers? Ordering me beheaded or worse? Would she conjure witchcraft blasphemies against me or would she toy with me until she was bored and then hook me up on one of her meat racks, gleefully watching while my blood dripped into bowls for her to bathe in.

Even though I had saved the Countess, I knew she was but a wild animal; her gratitude fleeting, her appetite exponentially expanding. I did not want to become a victim of her sadistic nature. I had to find a way to escape. She wouldn't let me go easily. I had to convince her that I needed to go on a journey. But to where?

The next day I was sitting alone at the long opulent dinner table by myself when the Countess returned. My thoughts raced as scheme after scheme tumbled through my mind. The Countess lowered herself into her chair with a flounce several seats away from me.

"Oh what a lovely morning, you really should go for a walk with me sometime, Marguerite," she said as she raised the dinner bell at her place setting. "The air is wonderful this time of year."

"No doubt," I said, picking at the bread crusts. "I'm sure you saw some magnificent sights."

"Most definitely," she nodded and smiled. One of the servant girls arrived with tea and hunks of bread.

"Are you certain I can't offer you any eggs or meat, your Highness?" The girl asked nervously with a curtsey.

"No. Bread and water is the secret to beauty. And honey. Another pot of honey would please me."

The girl curtsied and the Countess dipped her fingers into one of the pots of butter. She rubbed it across her forehead and cheeks. I watched her perform the morning ritual. Sometimes I performed it myself but that day I wasn't in the mood.

The halls of the castle had grown foreboding, echoing with an emptiness I had never noticed before. As I had packed my trunk, I had reconsidered my plan. I could just play along with her while keeping my wits about me. Her new fancy would pass—it always did. Yet, this time, I'd had enough. Was I jealous? No more than the other times. Was I bored? I chuckled to myself. Could it be true that after all these many years, my hypnotic mistress no longer had a hold over me?

Perhaps I was the one with the straying heart? I watched my Countess as she rubbed honey along her smooth white neck. A neck I had worshipped for so very long with an obsessive hunger. Now, in the bright morning light, as my mistress wove her web of lies, the flesh of her neck was loose and drooping.

"I'm going away for a while," I said, nearly choking on the breadcrumbs in my throat as I trembled, bracing for her reaction.

"Oh?" she asked, raising her eyebrow. "Away? How will you manage that?"

"You will be most pleased, my Queen," I said eagerly.

Her predatory gaze both enamored and terrified me.

"I've heard of a new remedy." My heart pounded so loud I thought she could hear it. "An Egyptian secret for lifting the skin on the neck and chest. It tightens the flesh, rendering you young again."

Elizabeth touched her neck instinctively. "It's true. The neck I saw in the mirror that used to be as enticing as the arc of a swan, is now a hideously sagging nightmare of flesh. Oh, Marguerite, tell me about this potion!"

"I heard the maids discussing a letter talking about an incredible secret of youth and beauty. I had to know. I am determined to bring it back."

"Bring back all of it. And people to make more. I need to have this abomination vanish." The Countess rubbed more honey along her neck. Her face and breasts glistened in the morning light as flies began to swarm around her.

"I'll leave today," I said.

I took my entourage of King's servants on a wild goose chase for several months. I feigned secret meetings in taverns, when the reality was I was carousing with the locals, drunk on wine and flesh. In private, I met with witches, sorcerers, and alchemists, wondering if there were new secrets to youth yet to be found. In private I met with witches, sorcerers, and alchemists, wondering if there were new secrets to youth yet to be found. In the end, the wondrous elixir I had promised the Countess, I did discover. But I was careful to conceal my prize from the King's entourage lest it ruin the rest of my plans. My years with the Countess had taught me well in the ways of hedonistic debauchery. Why not enjoy these wonderful gifts? Why not indulge my libido with the most handsome of men and women while eating and drinking in the most glutinous fashion? A beautiful stranger in town with a team of soldiers and servants was welcomed at the most elaborate of celebrations. I enjoyed myself without once fearing for my life, as I always did around my Countess.

All things, however, must come to an end. One night, I scoured the streets for a lady of the night similar to me in height and build. I lured her into my rooms with the promise of wine and food. When she was giddy with drink, I asked her to strip naked. Playfully, I tied her arms and legs to the four bedposts. I whipped her soundly, across the breasts and stomach and legs. When she cried out, I whipped her face. When she cried out again, I cut out her tongue. Still, her moans disturbed me, her wild eyes glaring at me as I brought down the crop again and again.

Bloody welts rose all along her body. Tears ran down her face. I drank more wine, then crawled onto the bed. I pulled her hair back and drew my knife from its sheath around my waist. She flailed as I held her tightly by the neck, popping out first one eyeball and then another.

I resumed the beatings until she was a pulpy mess. Then I cut off her head and tossed it onto the bed. The blood wasn't wasted. I squeezed some into vials as the elixir I would use later on all of the areas of my body touched by age. I emptied my trunk, throwing my clothes and possessions around as if I had been robbed and murdered before slipping past the drunken servants and guards. Upon my person, within the few possessions I needed for my journey, was concealed a silver tube in which those secrets most precious to my Countess were concealed.

I made my way back to the castle long before the entourage did. They were likely terrified to return to the Countess without her favorite playmate and more importantly, the potion. I became as a ghost, creeping through tunnels and curtains, unseen and unheard. I sat for hours at night, in the walls, watching my Countess sleep through a small peephole. She never shed one tear for her missing Marguerite. Even when the entourage returned and told her they had found me murdered and mutilated, she barely paused for a breath as she continued about her day.

Her time was filled with the gardener and then a servant girl or two. A passing soldier. An ardent suitor hoping to seduce her while her husband was away. As she grew bored of each playmate, she took them to her chambers for one last round of sexual deviance before flogging them to death and then bathing in their blood. She harbored more than a dozen new lovers while I skulked around the castle. Each lovemaking session that didn't end in death was a dagger to my heart.

As the time went on, I grew bolder. I sat in a chair by the bed, watching my Countess sleep, for no matter how many lovers she took, the only one who had ever slept in her bed was myself. Her breath was even, her flesh still pale and beautiful. Her beauty mesmerized me. I ached to touch her, to kiss her, to help her take the blood from the virginal servant girls. I ached for the glory days when she was grateful to me for saving her, when I was her only blood source for that short time. As much as I loved my Countess, the painful truth was that she didn't love me.

Never had. Never would.

My anger and jealousy grew, my stomach aching with rage.

One night, as I sat in the chair beside her bed, my thoughts tumbling over and over, vacillating between lust and envy, my fingers toying with the long cylinder I carried with me everywhere, she spoke.

The sound of her deep melodic voice in the darkness scared me. "I know you're there," she said.

My heart thundered. She must be speaking in a dream. I said nothing.

"Marguerite. Come sit with me," her eyes opened, glittering in the darkness as her pale hand brushed along her bedclothes. "I've seen you there, Marguerite. I knew you weren't dead. I've felt your every movement since you've returned. The way you spy on me in the castle,your aching heart spilling into my soul with every step you take." She patted the bed again. "Come to me, Marguerite. I know you miss me as I've missed you. Your blood is in my blood as my blood is in yours."

I sat frozen in my chair.

Elizabeth sat up, her dark hair shadows on the white pillows in the moonlight. She reached her pale long fingers towards me, her teeth glimmering as she begged me to come to her.

"I love you, Marguerite. I'm so happy you're here. Hug me and love me as only you know how."

The strength of her urgency was useless to resist. My flesh went to her even as my mind cried out not to, yet when she wrapped her arms around me, I knew I was home. I had missed my Countess so much. She was rough with me, her kisses turning to biting.

"You are my elixir, Marguerite. You are the last witch to understand my desires and needs. I could never lose you," she sighed. Her teeth bit into my neck and she ripped out a small bit of flesh. She chewed on it, blood flowing freely down my shoulders.

"I wanted you to be ready." I finally said as I pushed her back. My neck burned as she clawed at me, wanting more. "I found the elixir," I said. My words calmed her.

"You did?" She was still grabbing at me, her mouth fixated on my arm. She licked my arm with her long warm tongue.

"Where is it?" she growled, teasing and sucking my flesh. "Why did you fake your death if you had it all along?"

I was in pain, yet she was so sensuous. It was as always, the pain with the pleasure, the little death flirting with the big death.

"I wanted to test you. To see if you really deserved it." I pulled my arm away.

"How dare you test me?" she said indignantly. "You know you are my companion. For life. Forever."

"I've seen what you've done to companions," I said as I cupped my fingers under my bloody neck and held it to her face. "Do I want to be thrown away because you are bored? Do I spend months looking for your magic potions only to meet the same fates as every other servant?"

"You are special, Marguerite. Without you, I would have died in that horrible castle. I owe you everything, you know that."

"Yes, you do owe me everything," I said, edging back on the bed. I slipped my hand into my robe and brought out a large vial.

"This is the magic. This is the secret," I said as I held it up. The vial of elixir glowed a reddish hue in the moonlight.

"Give it to me!" she cried out. "It's mine!"

"You have to be careful. Only use a drop. No more than a drop at a time," I cautioned. "It's ancient and powerful. That vial contains enough for a hundred women for a hundred years."

"And what else? What else do I do with it?" she demanded.

"Why, nothing at all. Simply apply one drop to your skin." I pressed the container into her hand.

"Why did you hide from me? Why didn't you bring it back immediately as you were supposed to?"

"Because I wanted to be certain you loved me, Elizabeth. That's all. That you actually care."

"I care for you very much, Marguerite," she cooed as she pressed her lips against mine. However, her kisses were short lived as the distraction in her fingers won her attention.

"I need to try it," she cried out, leaping from the bed. Her nightgown billowed around her as she made her way to the dressing table. She lit a candle and gazed at herself in the reflection.

"Be careful," I warned. "One drop. No more."

She looked over at me and huffed as she poured the elixir into her cupped palm. She rubbed it across her face and neck. Within seconds, all visible signs of age had vanished.

"It works," she whispered with wonder. "I can't believe it actually works."
She poured some more into her hands and rubbed it along her arms.

"Only one drop, Countess," I pleaded. "One drop."

"Oh posh!" she said watching as her wrinkled hands grew smooth.

"Be careful."

"Marguerite, this is wonderful. This is magic, this is…" Her joy turned to horror as her flesh began to sizzle with a potent acrid odor like meat cooking over an open fire.

"What is going on? Get it off. Get it off!" she screamed jumping up from her dressing table and running for her water jug. She poured water into the bowl and splashed her face with it.

"Draw me a bath," she cried. "Call the servants, I need this gone."

"No, it'll be fine," I said as I watched her. The flesh that had been so smooth was now dissolving. It fell from her face and arms in meaty clumps to the floor.

"What have you done to me?" she wailed, rolling on the

floor until she fell into unconsciousness.

I said nothing as I picked her up and carried her down the long hallway to the stairs that led to the dungeons. Silently, I transported her through the narrow stone tunnels, past the agonizing screams and cries of prisoners until I found an empty cell. Throwing her inside, I slammed the door shut and bolted it.

The Countess was for all intents and purposes "dead" and back where she belonged—imprisoned. I was exhausted, but there was work to be done. Returning to her room, I set about tidying up. No one would know what had happened to her, no one but me.

As days went by, I watched from my hiding places in the walls as the King, having returned from his mission, and his royal staff searched in vain for the Countess. It was as if she had vanished into thin air. The King punished the servants for losing sight of her. He cried for several days over the disappearance of his beloved wife before setting out again on his journeys. I enjoyed my ghost's life, teasing the servants by moving objects and blowing out candles. I even crept into bed with the more handsome and had my way with them as they danced in and out of sleep with the mysterious succubus.

One night, I awoke in my secret spot in the tunnels to find her standing over me. The Countess, her flesh decayed and bloody, her eyes flashing with fury, her body more skeleton than human.

"You wanted me for eternity," she whispered. "You shall have me."

I woke again—a dream within a dream. Surely the Countess was dead by now. Even the most powerful witches, devils, and demons had to die sometime. Yet, I wondered. Now and again, my heart ached with the recognition of a pang of guilt once in a while but not for long. Not when I remembered her shouts of joy with other lovers and her manipulating stare for me to do her bidding. I was free of the spell of her sick passions. I was free of her betrayals.

I finally drew up the nerve to return to the dungeons and found the cell where I had left the Countess. My eyes took time to adjust to the dim light. Her corpse lay in the dirt and straw, more bone than flesh. I felt an air of sadness. My beautiful glorious Countess reduced to a skeleton in a dungeon. Moans of anguish and despair echoed around me from the other prisoners, pleads of innocence and freedom.

I had to touch her one last time. The sensation was urgent as I unlatched the door. Her pull was strong even in death. Slowly, I walked over to her and knelt beside her. The yellow-white glow of her skull, the bones of her hands, the tatters of what had been her beautiful nightgown were now filthy with blood and feces. I touched what was left of her hair as tears dripped from my eyes.

She grabbed my hand.

"Marguerite," she hissed, her skeletal teeth clattering at me. "I've missed you."

"Countess!" I jumped up but she was faster than me.

"Stay with me. Forever..." the Countess said as she flung herself on me.

Her teeth bit into my flesh with a frenzied bloodlust. I screamed and flailed, trying to free myself from her grasp, but as always, she was incredibly strong. With a blind rage she tore at my hair and my clothes—every inch of my body was on fire with agony. She drank my blood from the gaping wounds rendered in my flesh by her teeth and nails until I lapsed into unconsciousness.

When I woke, I was in the horrible dank cell where I had once left the Countess herself alone to die. I felt eyes watching me through the door. Slowly, I sat up and saw the face of someone much younger than she should be. I ached. Half of my flesh was missing—I should not have been alive, but I was. I put my hands to my face and felt teeth and exposed bone, sticky with cooling gore. Beetles crawled along me attracted by the stench of death.

"You are with me forever, Marguerite," the Countess laughed and stood up higher so I could see her full face through the barred window in the door. In the dim light, I made out a faint patchwork of carefully sewn flesh through the expertly applied mask of makeup. "Your flesh is my flesh."
She laughed long and loud. The prisoners in the other cells screamed and cried, begging for release. She slid a bowl of foul gruel through the door slat.

"And you thought I never cared."

Her cruel laughter echoed down the hallway as she walked away. I stared at the bowl of gruel in the filthy, stinking darkness and prayed for death.

TRUTH CONQUERS ALL

by Michael H. Hanson

The unexpected structure was impressive to behold. Located at the end of an abandoned logging road in a patch of private property deep in South Dakota's Black Hills, the hand-carved, one-hundred-foot face of the small, unnamed mountain was reminiscent of the ancient sandstone Treasury in Petra, Jordan with its beautifully wrought Greek arches and columns that had been chiseled to perfection—an exquisite display of masonry. Dozens of torches rested in rocky cradles, illuminating the odd setting with warm, flickering light. It was a cold autumn evening nearing midnight, but the weather was the last thing on Ganymedes's mind. He was here in search of a challenge, and the promise of secret knowledge.

Three tall, young women in long, hooded black robes stepped from the shadows and gently took his arms to guide him toward the main entrance. The robes were thin enough to reveal swelling breasts, curvy hips, and long delicate limbs. Their feet were bare. Ganymedes almost laughed out loud at the theatricality of it all. He wondered what nearby city's local modeling agency had been hired for just this bit of the fiction. Two of the women moaned periodically in what he surmised must have been an attempt at instilling distracting erotic imagery in his mind before the games were to begin. The irony was palpable.

In moments they passed through a carved stone archway and into a long, dark tunnel. More torches gave scant, but appropriately mysterious illumination along the curving walls. Prying invisible fingers probed Ganymedes's form, no doubt trying to find out what, if any, weapons or recording devices he carried on his person. He could also sense a number of hidden sensors measuring his mass and body temperature, among other things. No matter. He had, of course, prepared for these and other contingencies. A subtle lead and carbon fiber weave stitched into the inner lining of his clothes was playing havoc with somebody's snooping.

After a full mile, Ganymedes and his three escorts exited into a large circular rotunda. Another doorway on the far side of the one-hundred-foot diameter stone floor appeared to be the only other entrance. The three women quickly exited out of it.

Ganymedes stood in the center and looked around. Twelve torches lit the interior—he could clearly see a dizzying array of wall carvings representing the myths of at least a dozen ancient civilizations and religions. Egyptian, Sumerian, Greek, Olmec, Anasazi—a random hodge-podge of clashing stylizations that any professional archeologist or historian would find in extremely bad taste.

Though no doubt it is an impressive stage dressing to the average naïve mortal, Ganymedes thought, even the more well educated ones.

In neat, ordered rows, several open balconies marked ten floors meeting at a domed ceiling far above, the center of which was carved with a large crucifix, the star of David, the Yin/Yang, and the Islamic crescent and star.

Eight robed and hooded figures stepped from the shadows out onto their balconies on several different levels, on all sides of the chamber. Though their faces were hidden, their scents betrayed them as an equal number of men and women with ages ranging from twenty-five to ninety. None appeared to be the three actresses who had led him here. Ganymedes imagined that the trio of beauties were no doubt hopping in their car at that very moment for the long drive back to civilization, comparing notes on the weird, but well-paid gig.

Ganymedes, five-foot-nine, compact, broad shouldered, and wearing an expensive three-piece suit including a cyan shirt, ebony tie, and black snakeskin shoes, smiled. He knew he struck a handsome figure of indeterminate age with his shaved Mediterranean face, pale green eyes, and thick, lustrous, blue-black hair combed back and touching his collar.

"Word of mouth," Ganymedes said in perfect idiomatic English, "is that a wealth of ancient knowledge is the prize for winning this…game of yours."

Muffled whispers suddenly shot forth across the empty space above Ganymedes's head. It instantly became apparent that each of the individuals had microphones and earphones hidden in their cowls through which they could communicate both with each other and Ganymedes. Their mics were off and, though they attempted to keep their voices hushed, Ganymedes heard them all quite clearly.

"What the heck is going on, Frank?"

"This guy is way too smug."

"Not so loud, what if he hears us?"

"We're too high and we've tested the acoustics here. We're on 'mute.' Only a dog could hear what we're saying."

"Shit, he looks confident enough but other than that, not very impressive."

"And what's with the x-ray footage from the tunnel? We get an outline but no interior details!"

"Probably a computer glitch."

"Bull! I ran the diagnostics myself this morning."

"Doesn't matter. The girls shook him down and said he isn't packing anything. Not even a wallet, watch, or any jewelry."

"No car keys? How the hell did he get here? We're forty miles from any paved road."

"Body heat signature, bio-electrical signature, and weight are nominal. I say we give him a shot."

"And if he passes?"

"Then we know he's special. Isn't that what each of these sessions is ultimately all about?"

No whispered replies followed.

Ganymdes continued smiling, knowing it would make them uncomfortable. One by one, the individuals turned their mics back on.

"Very well." A deep male voice boomed. "You supplied us with ten thousand dollars in gold coins. You come here of your own accord, pilgrim."

"Yes, yes," Ganymedes said impatiently. "Free will and all that. Let the game begin already."

The robed man on the lowest level, just two stories above him, coughed nervously after having his obviously memorized script interrupted. A moment later he began speaking again. "We give you five challenges Mr. Gann," the man said, "and if you should succeed in accomplishing, passing, or playing all five of them to their conclusion, we have it within our means to answer any question you have on any subject. We are of a very ancient order and possess knowledge that stretches back across the ages!"

These schmucks were laying it on thick. Ganymedes thought for a moment about leaving. But, he considered, you never know. These bozos just might have stumbled onto some timeless cache of wisdom that could hold what I need.

"I accept," Ganymedes said.

"Then walk through the doorway our three acolytes exited earlier," the man said. "Good luck, pilgrim. Veritas Omnia Vincit!"

Ganymedes shook his head cynically, spun on his heel, and rapidly walked into the darkness. "Caveat consules!" he shouted over his shoulder.

***

A large, carved circle of granite, weighing what must have been a full ton, rolled into place behind Ganymedes, sealing him into a circular antechamber not much smaller than the one he had just left. The first challenge had begun. In the middle of the room was an odd object that rose out of the floor, a full six feet in height.

"You have got to be shitting me," Ganymedes said as he walked forward.

On closer inspection his first impression proved correct. A thick wood post jutted out from the ground with a mass of coiled rope tied tightly around the top foot and a half. It was an impressive recreation of the Gordian knot.

"Mr. Gann," the aged voice of an elderly man came out of an overhead speaker, "using nothing other than your intuition and strength of finger, untie this knot. You can take as much time as you need. If you give up, the stone behind you will roll back and you will be shown the way out. If, however, you manage to solve this puzzle, the doorway on the opposite side of the room will open for you."

Ganymedes gritted his teeth and visually examined the finely wrought prop under flickering torch light. He ran his fingers over the huge knot, taking in every imperfection and textual differentiation. He then gave it three quick squeezes to get an idea of the object's overall density.

Two minutes later he had it figured out. The inner mass of rope was a ridiculously lazy clump of Granny, Manrope, and Turks Head knots. The double-layered outer portion consisted of some intricately layered Overhand and Shroud knots neatly twined with hidden half-hitches. This was a real work of art.

They must have had a seamstress and a mathematician working on this baby for a full month, Ganymedes thought.

Digging away at the ornery clump, he slowly and steadily untied, unraveled, and unspun the clever and insidious macramé until nothing but a pile of peeled twine lay at the base of the post. Grinding stone alerted Ganymedes. He stood up and quickly walked through the doorway opening to the next challenge.

***

The second chamber was almost identical to the first, except for what was set into the floor—a chessboard.

Ganymedes found himself on the black side. The massive board of roughly forty feet by forty feet was fabricated from cut and polished granite. The pieces themselves were two feet tall, one set carved from African blackwood in the style of ancient Chinese warriors, and the other from pure elephant ivory in the style of Aztec royalty.

"Mr. Gann," the daring voice of a middle-aged woman blasted from a speaker, "welcome to speed chess. You have no more than one minute to conceptualize and shout out your moves. The pieces will reposition themselves. If you lose you can exit the way you came. If you win, a new exit will make itself known. Begin."

Instantly, the white E2 Pawn slid forward to the E4 position.

"E7 Pawn to E5," Ganymedes said, and watched his black pawn slide forward in the directly opposing position. A slight hum coming from the board had him surmising the pieces possessed steel cores and were positioned via powerful moving magnets beneath the board.

The white E7 Knight slid to C6, and so began a devilishly challenging and rapid game of chess. Ganymedes never took more than three or four seconds to strategize his moves, and the unseen opponent, definitely not a computer and possibly the woman whose voice he'd heard earlier, played the first half of the game with the same surety. The second half, however, was quite different. Ganymedes took pride in the fact that closing in on the finish, his opponent was taking nearly a full minute to consider their own moves.

It was down to four pieces on the board and Ganymedes closed in with a ferocious Queen versus Rook endgame that he won in fifteen moves.

Checkmate.

***

The third challenge chamber was of the same dimensions as the previous two. Three men waited within, their demeanor unfriendly. Ganymedes stopped in his tracks and efficiently examined the figures before him. The largest, a bald fellow of African descent, stood seven feet tall, and was lean, but weighing nearly three-hundred pounds in pure muscle. The next was a six-foot tall red-haired Caucasian with a blonde beard that was built like a competitor in a strong-man competition. The third was an Asian gentleman whose build was almost a twin to Ganymedes's own. All three appeared to be in their late twenties and were dressed in matching black sweat suits and boxing shoes.

"Mister Gann," a distinguished male voice boomed from an overhead speaker, not unlike that of a boxing ring announcer, "you are an exceedingly clever man. I think we can dispense with the mundane I.Q. tests and go straight to the real challenges."

Ganymedes read his opponents' body language carefully. The way the Asian stood on the balls of his feet and stretched his arms clearly showed his expertise was in Hopkeido, probably a third degree black belt. The Caucasian man's stance betrayed a confidence in combat Judo. The tall African, though, shifted with an elegance that Ganymedes, recognized as an unexpected mix of Aikido and Capoeira.

"The rules are simple." The excited voice of a middle-aged man spouted. "You must defeat these three gentlemen in hand-to-hand combat. As for how far to take things: they have been forbidden from outright killing or permanently maiming you. We request the same restraint on your part. Other than that, you are free at any time to turn around and leave via the entrance you came through, or, during this competition you can at any time yell 'give', and you will be escorted back outside. And this time, the first move is yours, Mr. Gann."

Ganymedes quickly removed his sports coat. He nodded at the Asian and they both simultaneously moved forward. Knowing that the sunrise was not all that far off, he needed to make quick work of things. It took a full minute to wear his first opponent down with a series of lightning-fast kite-strikes from his palms and elbows, roundhouse punches, and a final front snap-kick to the chest. His opponent flew through the air and impacted with the wall, falling to the floor unconscious. It all should have ended much quicker, though. Ganymedes surmised that the gentleman had rather non-chivalrously enhanced his own natural abilities with a nasty cocktail of adrenaline and amphetamine.

The strongman rushed Ganymedes and they both immediately locked arms like two Greco-Roman wrestlers. Surprise flashed in the larger man's eyes as Ganymedes's own strength proved a match to his opponent's. Weight was on the side of the big man, however, who quickly did his best to apply his mass in whatever way would pin or incapacitate Ganymedes.

Another full minute passed until the wrestler had pushed his smaller opponent up against the granite wall. Ganymedes's patience was gone. In a single lightning move he grabbed both of the man's wrists and roughly yanked them up and outward. The elbow dislocation was audible and Ganymedes shoved the incapacitated and shocked behemoth toward his unconscious compatriot.

The African, crouching forward, moved widdershins and studied Ganymedes with narrowed eyes. Ganymedes moved forward without hesitation. A flurry of windmill footwork thrice knocked Ganymedes off his feet and onto the granite floor. The strikes to his head would have killed a mortal man—so much for the non-lethal aspect of the challenge. Ganymedes discovered a newfound respect for the towering African's agility and speed. Several minutes passed as they circled each other nimbly in a mutual dance of death. Sensing a pattern, Ganymedes rushed forward to intersect an exquisite spin kick, just as a size twenty-three shoe was about to make contact with his forehead. Ganymedes ducked and slid forward on his knees under the kick and slammed a brutal joint lock on the exposed leg. With an exaggerated shrug of his shoulders he gave the taller man's right knee a ferocious and unforgivable torque, instantly dislocating it.

Still in the fight, and screaming his pain and rage, the African angled a deadly elbow-kite at the bridge of Ganymedes's nose, which was barely deflected with a forearm block. Ganymedes instantly countered with a ferocious kick to the tall man's groin. A crushed testicle finally downed the giant who was finished off with three right crosses to the chin. As with the other two, he would survive.

Grinding stone brought Ganymedes's attention to the exposed exit. He put his jacket back on, dusted off his pants as best he could, and walked through the doorway.

***

Again, the fourth antechamber was nearly identical to the first three. As Ganymedes entered the surrounding torches instantly extinguished in unison. Their light was immediately replaced by intense infrared beams radiating from three large projectors on the ceiling, no doubt for the benefit of his audience watching on monitors in a nearby room, to see how he operated when blind.

"Mr. Gann," a new female voice emanated from an overhead speaker, "you are full of surprises tonight. However, I think you will find my challenge more than a match for your admittedly impressive skills. Please cross this room if you can, and exit out the door on the far end."

Ganymedes smiled as he clearly saw a wide variety of

tripwires, nets, moving padded pendulums, and projectile devices silently rise and extend from clever recesses in the floor and walls. He also took note of the speaker's declaration that implied each voice greeting him in each room came from the individual who designed the associated challenge. Deciding not to make this look too easy, he walked forward slowly.

In a succession of seemingly awkward leaps Ganymedes avoided the trip wires. Next, two long opposing pendulums, each ending in refrigerator-sized punching bags, swung inward towards him simultaneously. Moving like a caricature of Charlie Chaplin, Ganymedes leaned forward dramatically and, just as quickly, leaned backwards in seeming disdain of gravity. Skipping forward two steps he left the large hazards behind as the pendulums struck and partially fractured the opposing walls.

He was now in the middle of the room.

Short swooshing sounds immediately came from all of the surrounding walls. Ganymedes dropped flat to the floor barely avoiding the flurry of drugged darts that shot over him and shattered on the opposing walls. He hopped back up and walked quickly to the recessed door he could clearly see in the infrared light. Just when he was a few feet from the exit the floor dropped away immediately in front of him. Without breaking stride Ganymedes executed a sudden standing broad jump, clearing the twenty-five foot gap by a mere inch. A pebble fell over the ledge behind him. The eventual strike let him know the water-filled pit had a one-hundred-foot drop. Nice.

Ganymedes twisted his head and smiled at the hidden digital cameras, turned back around, and walked forward through the exit.

***

The fifth and final challenge room was the expected duplicate of the previous four. The doorway closed behind him as quickly as it had opened.

This was no longer a game. The African's brutal fight tactics might possibly have been an anomaly, the lack of restraint and control in the heat of combat, but the last room was intentionally lethal. The darts could have permanently blinded a human being, the pendulum crushing a lesser man, and the fall into the pit would most likely have resulted in death. The game-masters knew this, and were obviously upping the stakes extensively with each new room.

A feral grin stretched Ganymedes's lips. For a so-called ancient and altruistic coven promising enlightenment as the prize of difficult physical and intellectual challenges, it seemed unfair that the last test would be a rigged affair. When arriving at the remote locale he had assumed the these were con men looking to dupe fools out of their money. The strategy behind these rooms, however, ranged from clever to ingenious, leaving a larger and decidedly shady conspiracy looming in the shadows of Ganymedes's imagination. If a trap it was, it was an intriguing one—he felt he was more a curiosity and an experiment than mere victim here. He was beginning to get the impression that his faceless hosts actually wanted him to succeed in this venture implying they were learning more about him than he would normally allow any mere mortal to do. Still, they had caught his interest and he was determined to see this play all the way to its finale.

"Mr. Gann," a man's voice with a British accent drifted from an overhead speaker, "we applaud you on this unprecedented achievement. You are certainly…more than you appear to be."

"That judgment swings both ways," Ganymedes retorted.

There was no reply, except for the sound of multiple pieces of stone sliding against stone. Under flickering torchlight the room slowly took on a new shape. A series of curved transparent walls dropped from the ceiling to settle on the smooth granite floor forming a three-foot-wide spiraling corridor ending in the exact center of the room. Large granite slabs, each weighing several tons and lowered by steel cables, capped all of the jutting walls. The opening to the narrow labyrinth was a mere stride in front of him.

Why do I feel I'm going to regret this, Ganymedes asked himself. Not hearing any answers, he walked forward.

The moment his shoulders were flanked by the transparent barriers a ten-foot-high slab of granite dropped into place behind him. There was no option of refusal. He slammed his right fist roughly against the clear wall, sending echoes throughout this trap but leaving no more than the slightest of smudges on the multiple layers of bonded aluminum oxynitride and spinel. There was no way he was busting his way out of this trap. The only escape lay in moving forward.

Ganymedes took four steps forward. The air suddenly took on a strange tang. In moments he realized that the normal oxygen-nitrogen mix had been replaced with one hundred percent carbon dioxide. Smiling, he resumed walking, traveling sixty feet and traversing most of the outmost loop.

A sudden change in air temperature made him stop again. White frost rapidly spread across the walls and he estimated it was now close to zero degrees Fahrenheit. Ganymedes rubbed away crystals forming on his eyes and started walking again. Condensed water vapor, of course, never exuded from his nose or mouth.

He was halfway through the spiral toward the center when the flow of air rapidly turned into a treacherous wind that nearly knocked him to his feet. He braced his arms tightly between the walls to ride it out. In moments it ceased. He was standing in a perfect vacuum. Ganymedes opened his mouth wide and clenched his eyes shut as tightly as possible. The pain from the increased internal pressure was nearly overwhelming, but somehow he managed to keep from blacking out or panicking and staggered forward as quickly as possible.

When he was a mere twenty feet from the end of the

torturous maze Ganymedes was knocked off his feet by a flood of water that rapidly filled the interior. The equalizing pressure outside his body put an end to the earlier agonizing pain and he opened his eyes. Snarling, Ganymedes swam through the clear cold water until he reached the very center. There he discovered a circular hole where the water had been pumped into the room. Considering his lack of options for a full minute, he finally shrugged his shoulders and swam into the pitch-black hole.

In moments the current suddenly reversed and Ganymedes felt himself sucked into an adjoining channel, his body battering brutally against granite walls. Five minutes later, feeling like he'd been in a giant blender, he spilled out over a towering waterfall and plunged downwards into a massive square pool of water. Ganymedes swam to the nearest edge and pulled himself up and out.

He certainly looked the worse for wear. He had lost his sport coat, shoes, and socks some time ago. His shirt was in shreds and he roughly stripped it off. His pants and belt seemed to have survived mostly intact. Ganymedes was sure his eyes were blood red from the earlier explosive decompression. He looked at his arms and stomach and was not surprised to see a wealth of bruises and lacerations, no doubt looking more than odd to his hidden audience as no blood leaked from his wounds. The mammoth square chamber he stood in was lit by dozens of burning torches jutting from the walls that reflected off of the pool at its center.

"Well," Ganymedes shouted aloud, "I think I win."

In reply, a vertical line of light appeared on the far wall. Two massive panels of granite slid sideways revealing an even larger chamber where waited a platoon of mercenaries dressed in combat fatigues. They held a variety of weaponry including M16A2 assault rifles equipped with grenade launchers, M249 SAWs, M82A1 SAMRs, and Chinese military Naptha flamethrowers. Behind them, on a raised platform, stood nine robed figures.

Ganymedes walked toward the platoon, stopping within twenty feet of them. Beyond the crowd he could see a large chrome and ivory control room where forty or so technicians in white lab coats sat in front of long white benches covered with the latest laptops. Huge video monitors covered the walls and Ganymedes could see each of his recent challenges being played back in digital loops.

He shook his head. It was like something out of a bad James Bond film. What had he gotten himself into?

"Why do I have the feeling you're not going to honor your promises from earlier," Ganymedes said, "even after you took my money, and I subsequently beat all your challenges. None of which, by the way, you told me ahead of time would be of any real danger to me."

The robed figures all looked at each other and then quickly removed their cowls. They appeared much as he had imagined, men and women of a wide variety of ages, shapes, sizes, and races. From the way they all stood, the expensive haircuts, glasses, and jewelry on display, he was beginning to get an inkling of what was going on. None of the mercenaries were pointing their weapons directly at Ganymedes, but he certainly noticed they held their armament at the ready.

"No one has ever made it past the third room." An Asian-American man in his thirties said in wonder. "You're the first."

"What Carson says is true. I knew you were special, Mr. Gann," an attractive twenty-something woman with blonde hair and blue eyes said. "I knew my money wasn't wasted on this project."

"Your money?" Ganymedes asked.

"We've each paid ten million to get in on this action," she replied, "but to see the fruit of our labors, it's just so…"

"Enough," said a bald, elderly man. "You talk too much

Christina."

Ganymedes took three slow tentative steps forward towards the soldiers. The mercenaries tensed at his approach, though their weapons were still not quite pointing at him. Ganymedes could see the elderly fellow was the true power behind this cabal.

"My name is Terrance Altros, Mr. Gann," the old man said, "and you are now going to answer our questions. First, how did you…"

"Are you an angel?" Christina shouted out, cutting off Altros. "You have to be. I knew angels had to be real ever since I dropped acid while filming my last music video. You're so brave and handsome. I dreamed that—"

"Bah!" A middle-aged woman with red hair spat. "You're a mutant aren't you? Born into a world where you realized you were different and did all you could to hide your superior abilities and powers?"

"Please!" Altros said, trying to take back control of the situation, "We have a protocol we all agreed to—"

"You're an android," Carson spouted. "You have to be— your strength and speed, the fact that you don't need to breathe and are unaffected by vacuum or extreme alterations in temperature. I demand to know who built you. Was it the Japanese?"

"You are all idiots!" an overweight middle-aged Hispanic man shouted. "Gann is an extra-terrestrial alien. Nothing like him could have evolved or been constructed on this planet. His race has probably been studying us for centuries."

Ganymedes was now within ten feet of the nearest mercenary whose M16A2 was now blatantly pointing at his mid section.

"So no wealth of knowledge or answers to any questions I might have?" Ganymedes asked. "You're all just a bunch of liars and would-be puppet-masters who think you can toy with me as you please."

The robed figures were silent for a long moment.

"Very well. I started this venture forty years ago," Altros said. "I knew there was more to humanity than what we saw on the daily news or read in text books. And I knew that one day, if I played it right, prepared this elaborate construct, planted rumors in all manner of locales online and around the world, we would eventually snare an exotic being holding the answers to all of life's hidden secrets. And I believe now that you, Mr. Gann, are the reward of a lifetime of efforts. Now, we ask again, who and what are you? You have no choice but to answer our questions." Altros nodded toward the mercenaries. "I demand all of your secrets."

What the hell, Ganymedes thought. "My real name is not Gann, but Ganymedes," he said. "I was born in ancient Alexandra, the former tutor and protector of Queen Cleopatra's half-sister Arsinoe. In forty-seven B.C. I was incorrectly believed deceased whilst fleeing the conquering forces of the mighty Julius Caesar, whereupon I returned to my secret duties as head Librarian of the surviving royal branch of the main Library of Alexandria, much of which had been torched by bumbling soldiers under Caesar's employ."

"What?" Altros said in confusion. "How…how could you be still alive."

"Now, that last word you used is an interesting one," Ganymedes replied.

"I'm getting a negative reading on body heat and bio-electrical activity, and I've run diagnostics twice," a technician in a far back corner of the room shouted.

"The greatest library of ancient lore that ever existed," Ganymedes went on, "containing all the secrets and mysteries of the ages. And yes, I read every scroll and sheet of papyrus it possessed."

"But your age," Altros pressed.

"The x-rays are working now," the technician yelled out even louder. "All of the organs are there, but there's no heartbeat or blood flow."

"Yes," Ganymedes said, "I first had to find a way to extend my life so I could embrace my ultimate dream, the pure pursuit of knowledge. In a book of ancient lore I learned of the dark breed—their existence, their ways, their weaknesses and strengths, their…breeding grounds."

"Dark breed?" Altros shook his head. "Just what are you saying?"

"That I am probably the only one of my kind who achieved his transcendental state not as a victim," Ganymedes said, "but rather as a matter of planning, choice, and ingenious execution."

Ganymedes raised his eyebrows then tilted his head toward a wide, well-polished chrome panel that stretched up to the ceiling. All those in robes slowly turned and examined it. It took a few moments longer for the realization to ripple through all present—though they could see their own reflections in the mirrored metal, as well as the soldiers and technicians, Ganymedes was not present.

Altros's eyes opened wide in surprise. The soldiers slowly raised their weaponry, but it was all too late.

"Cheaters never prosper," Ganymedes said with quiet but resonating finality.

The slaughter that followed was bloody, horrific, and absolutely necessary. It took Ganymedes two full minutes to subdue and execute the mercenaries, snapping necks and ripping out throat with efficient abandon. Bullets flew in all directions, a few striking his abdomen and thighs. The remaining humans fled in a panicked rush toward three exits on the perimeter of the room. Ganymedes snapped up fallen M16A2's and launched several grenades. Their detonations turned each doorway into dusty piles of boulders. Ignoring his robed hosts who were desperately trying to dig their way through the nearest rubble pile, Ganymedes turned his attention to the small defenseless crowd of technicians. It took little time to dispatch all of them and he did so as humanely as he was able.

The deed done, he turned to the would-be puppet-masters, still pathetically trying to dig their way through a collapsed archway.

Of the nine robed conspirators, two lay dead upon the ground, victims of the crossfire. The middle-aged woman, whose mewling betrayed her as his chess game opponent, lay in shock and pain, a fallen boulder having crushed both of her legs and hips. The remaining six cowered back against the rocks at his slow approach, their eyes wide with terror. Blood and gore covered his form.

Christina dropped to her knees. "Please, you don't have to do this! We're all millionaires. We'll give you whatever you want if you spare us. For the love of god, no!"

Ganymedes grabbed her first, suddenly recognizing her as a former pop star from California, a favorite socialite of the American tabloids who was famous for her reckless adventures.

"You possess a treasure alright," Ganymedes said with great anger, "and I think I've earned it."

His mouth opened far wider than normal. Two long fangs gleamed among the rest of his bright white enamel. In a move faster than the eye could follow, Ganymedes sank his teeth onto her throat, draining her blood in a matter of seconds. He flung her lifeless corpse across the room like a rag doll. Quickly he dispatched of the remaining five in a similar fashion. The rapid influx of fresh blood quickly healed the body trauma he had suffered over the course of the night.

The only person left in the room was Mr. Altros.

Ganymedes had saved the mastermind of this debacle for last.

"I… I thought your kind was a myth," Altros mumbled in

clear resignation, "the product of an imaginative nineteenth-century writer's mind and the tripe of popular culture—." Ganymedes grabbed the old man's throat with one hand and slowly pulled him close. Their eyes locked, their faces inches apart.

"I only wanted to know the truth behind all of life's mysteries," Altros whimpered.

Ganymedes's fangs slowly sought Altros's thin, trembling throat. "And the truth will set you free."

COUNTDOWN

by JG Faherty

Too late, too late! You're going to be too damn late! I thought, as I sped along the New York State Thruway. It was almost eleven-thirty at night. Even pushing my Lincoln Navigator as fast as I could, which on this stretch of highway was about 115 miles per hour, I had at least another thirty minutes to go. I wasn't worried about cops, or traffic, or the slick, icy condition of the road. All I could think about was Gwen.

And the deadly game I was trapped in.

Images of my wife staked or beheaded circled through my brain like vultures over a carcass. I glanced at an exit sign as it flashed by, white and yellow in the truck's headlights. Weston, 1 Mile. I was looking for the Shad Lake exit, fifty-five miles past Weston. I pressed my foot down on the gas pedal a little, trying to coax more speed out of the vehicle without losing control.

Don't fuck this up.

As I continued my race against the clock, the part of my mind not occupied with driving wandered back, replaying how I'd come to be in my present situation.

***

"Hey, Ryan, come look at this," Gwen called to me from upstairs.

I clicked 'Save' to store the five pages or so I'd added to my latest book and dragged my six-foot frame from my comfortable leather chair. I didn't want to stop what I was doing; I was on a roll, the kind of groove where I felt I could put down another dozen really good pages. But there was that tone in my wife's voice that let me know she'd keep calling me until I went to see what she wanted.

"What's up?" I asked, walking up the stairs to the kitchen.

"Look at this," she repeated.

I looked. What I saw was my wife of five years wearing nothing but a white tank top and a pair of pink tennis socks. The tank was barely long enough to cover the curve of her ass. The nipples of her small but firm breasts pushed out against the cotton. Add in the fiery copper hair that brushed the top of her shoulder blades and she looked like she'd just stepped out of a men's magazine. I was beginning to feel very glad that she'd called me when she burst my bubble.

"Look at this, not me, you lech!" she said, laughing and holding out an envelope. "It came in today's mail. No return address, no postmark, not even a stamp, but it was inside our mailbox."

Trying to switch gears from Gwen's body to the envelope, I was a little slow on the uptake.

"What's the big deal?" I was still very distracted by the tank top.

"You need a key to open our mailbox, remember?" Gwen gave me a poke to help jog my memory. "So how did it get in there?"

Now I realized why Gwen was feeling creeped out. Physical distractions forgotten, I thought about the different ways someone could have gotten that envelope in our box. Other than bribing the mailman or having a duplicate key, every other explanation involved some type of supernatural being.

All thoughts of romance disappeared.

"I guess the only way to find out is to open it."

Gwen nodded and slid her finger under the flap. She removed a small note, handwritten rather than typed, and held it up so we could both read the elegant script.

Ryan and Gwen James,

I am writing to you because I need assistance, and you are the only ones who can help me. I am in need of your 'special' talents. You are my last chance. Please meet me at the Overlook Inn at seven p.m. I will be near the upstairs fireplace. I am begging you.

— VH

"VH?" Gwen asked.

I shrugged. "I'm guessing it doesn't stand for Van Halen."

"Ha, ha."

"What do you think we should do?" I asked, as Gwen turned the note over in her hands, looking for any clues as to who 'VH' might be.

"I think we should stay as far away from the Overlook Inn as possible," Gwen said, "but I know you're gonna say we have to go up there."

"We don't have to," I said, not looking at her. "But we should. Whoever wrote this knows about us, which means if we don't go, he or she could let the rest of the world in on the secret."

"No." Gwen rattled the letter in my face. "This sounds like a trap. And a trap is something we shouldn't be putting our necks into. We have enough problems as it is."

I sighed and took the letter from Gwen's hand. She was right. The last thing we needed in our lives was trouble. It did a good enough job of finding us on its own; there was no need to actively seek it out. But I couldn't let this go. I sighed again. Looking up, I saw Gwen staring at me. I didn't say anything. The expression on my face was enough.

"Shit. Shit, shit, shit." Gwen headed for the hall.

"Where are you going?" I called after her. It wasn't like her to walk out in the middle of a discussion.

"To clean the guns and find an outfit. We're obviously going to the Inn, and I intend to look good and be well armed."

114

***

The skies were gray and scattered showers alternated with bouts of sleet as we prepared for our meeting. The temperature hovered around thirty-two degrees. It was wet, chilly, and nasty—the kind of day that makes human bones ache. Patches of icy slush pocketed the streets and sidewalks, making driving or walking both messy and dangerous.

Since we had no idea of what we'd be walking into, we both chose outfits that would allow us to carry weapons unnoticed. Nothing too fancy; the Inn is a casual place. I threw on black jeans, a white t-shirt, and a black leather sports jacket. My favorite gun, a Glock 26— loaded with 9mm silver-infused hollow points—nested at the small of my back. It held 12 rounds, but it was small enough that no bulge showed under a shirt or coat.

As usual, Gwen managed to turn casual into stylishly sexy. Black leather pants, a copper-colored blouse that complemented her hair, and a long black leather trench. Tall, knee-high leather boots perfectly matched her pants. Gold earrings and a bracelet completed the outfit. Her Kahr PM9, one of the world's smallest and finest pistols, fit in her clutch without a problem. She looked good enough for a night at Spago or some Beverly Hills nightclub, rather than an ordinary restaurant in upstate New York.

"All right, let's get going." Gwen flashed me a look of annoyance as she swept past me, a hint of perfume trailing in her wake. "Time to step into the mousetrap."

I didn't say anything. After all our years of marriage, I knew better. We took the Navigator because of the icy roads. Twenty minutes later, I was grabbing my ticket at valet parking and rushing inside before my jacket got too wet.

"Any last minute thoughts?" Gwen asked as we walked up the wide staircase to the second floor. Holding hands, we looked like any other young couple in love, heading to the dining room for a nice, quiet meal.

We reached the top and before I could answer her I found myself face to face with a middle-aged man in a bad suit, his gloved hand pressing a silver cross against my chest. I looked down at the cross and then over at Gwen.

"I think dinner is going to be very interesting."

***

The man with the cross pushed himself against me, forcing me back against a decorative wooden column. He was so close that no one in the crowded room would be able to see the cross, although they might wonder if the somewhat rumpled man was hitting on me. That wouldn't do. I was something of a local celebrity. I pushed him back, hard enough to put some distance between us but not enough to create a scene.

"I take it you're the mysterious VH," I said. "Why don't you put that cross away before somebody sees you?"

"Demon!"

Spittle showered my face and I caught more than a trace of a European accent in his angry whisper. I couldn't place it; it wasn't Italian, Spanish, or German. I haven't heard enough of any others to say one way or another. At least he wasn't shouting. I tried to say something, but he interrupted me.

"The power of the almighty Savior protects me from you!"

"Not anymore." Gwen reached over and grabbed the cross out of his hand. One second he had it, the next he didn't. Judging by the largemouth bass expression on his face, he hadn't expected that.

Gwen handed me the cross. With my other hand, I grabbed the man by the arm and led him to some oversized leather chairs well away from the crowd. Gwen followed, keeping an eye out in case our loony friend wasn't alone.

The moment we sat down, his angry scowl returned and he found his voice.

"Vampires!" He practically growled the word.

I looked at Gwen, and she shrugged. What the hell, I could always hypnotize him later. "Yeah, we're vampires. So what? Why did you ask us to come here, besides to wave useless crosses in our faces?" I handed it back to him and he stuffed it into one of his pockets.

"You would not be so cavalier if you knew who I was," the man said. He seemed calmer now. His accent was fading and his eyes were taking on a hardness that slowly replaced his earlier fury.

"Well, why don't you fill us in?"

The man took a deep breath. "Forgive me. My...prejudices still get the better of me. I will tell you why I have contacted you," he began. "But first, you need to know who I am, so you will understand the seriousness of this situation. My name is Abraham Van Helsing." He paused, probably for effect.

He didn't get the one he expected. Gwen raised one eyebrow. Not nearly as polite as my wife, I started laughing.

"Sure you are," I said, as my laughter died down. "And I'm Count Dracula. This is my evil bride, Mina Harker."

Gwen shot me a shut up look, but the man claiming to be Van Helsing seemed oblivious to my sarcasm.

"You are not Dracula," he said. "Dracula is dead. I killed him myself." He must have seen the expression on my face, because he hurriedly added, "I am telling you the truth. I can prove it to you, if I need to."

"And how are you going to do that?" I asked, still smiling. "Show me a picture of you posing next to his dead body? Oh, I have it, you kept his teeth after the body rotted away."

"Watch."

To my surprise, he slowly faded from view, first becoming transparent and then turning into a cloudy, misty blob. He stayed that way for a moment, and then returned to his previous self. Once again, we were looking at an old man dressed in a rumpled sports coat, plaid oxford shirt, and well-worn gray trousers.

"So, what say you now?" he asked, a smug look on his face.

I didn't let my surprise show. "You're a vampire? You and me and she make three. That doesn't prove you're the real Van Helsing. Hell, I don't even know if there ever was such a person. Plus, he was human. Most people believe that was just Stoker's way of putting himself into the story. You know, same first name, same birthday, blah, blah, blah."

"Hmph." He frowned again. "No matter the day and age, young people are all the same. Very well, I will waste valuable time telling you my story. But then you must promise to listen to why I have come to you for help."

Gwen and I nodded. That seemed enough for Van Helsing, or whoever he was.

"The story of *Dracula* was true. I met Stoker several years later and told it to him. He was an aspiring writer and he struck me as the right person to tell the story of the vampire to the world. I could not do it because of my reputation as a man of science. Stoker changed several of the names and events to embellish the story for his readers. The true story was a simple one; Stoker complicated it with unnecessary details and events. Who can say if this was better or worse? Many people learned the name Dracula, but now today no one believes.

"I was still human then, full of self-pity and remorse, and also hubris. I was the fearless vampire hunter who had killed the legendary Dracula. But my work—my obsession—had, over the years, cost me two wives and a son. Was it worth it? I believe so."

I raised an eyebrow. He really believed killing vampires was worth losing his family? The whole obsession thing worried me. Van Helsing continued his story, unaware of my concerns.

"The years went by. I continued my campaign against the vampires until I was too old to endure the endless hours of travel, the hardships of tracking down the undead in remote lands. Before I realized what had happened, I was an old man of seventy, retired, living out the end of my life in a small set of rooms near the hospital where my first wife lay wasting away in her final years. A bitter old man, filled with hate and despair. After all of my education and training, all of my risks, in the end, what did I have? Nothing. Almost penniless, I survived by teaching the occasional class at one of the city's universities, and by providing medical care to criminals and whores."

By this time, Van Helsing had me hooked. I not only believed him, I was eager to hear the rest of his story.

Apparently Gwen was, too, because she leaned forward and said, "Go on."

Van Helsing nodded.

"It was then I began to have doubts about my life's work. Not the killing of vampires, for all that I had known were an evil blight on this world. No, my doubts concerned the state of vampirism itself. I knew that it returned youth and vitality. But did it always create an evil monster, a spawn of Satan? Or was it possible that vampires, like the humans they were molded from, possessed the capacity for good or evil? I thought back to Dracula, and his eternal love. How could a demon love? That was something I always thought reserved for those with a soul.

"After months of deliberation, a simple fact made up my mind. My wife was dying, her body close to the end. I could not let that happen. So I decided to deliver unto her eternal life, and save worries about souls and damnation for the day of God's reckoning. I would be there when she rose from the grave and put her down myself if there was anything evil about her.

"What came next was easy. I enlisted my former associates for one final hunt. Only this time I told them I needed the vampire alive, for medical research. They took this to mean torture, a falsehood I was only too glad to promote. Together we found and trapped one of the monsters and brought it back to Amsterdam bound in silver chains. There I used a syringe to withdraw some of its blood and then I decapitated the monster. I checked my feeble wife out of the asylum, stating that I was moving her out of the country. Back at my rooms, I placed her in a tub of warm water, gave her a strong sedative, and waited until she passed into a deep sleep. I kissed her goodbye and then made incisions on her wrists. I kept a close watch as her life drained away. When her breathing became erratic, I injected the vial of vampire blood into her vein."

His voice choked up and a red tear ran from one eye.

"I watched as she died."

"But she didn't stay that way," I said.

"No." He wiped away the tear with his handkerchief. "Two nights later she rose, looking just as she did the day we married."

"And then you had her change you, as well."

He nodded.

"I explained to her what I'd done, and why. It shocked her, and she cried, thinking herself a monster. But eventually the lure of eternity in each other's arms was enough to soothe her sorrows. I let her drain me and then I drank from her. Two nights later, she was waiting when I rose. And to our great pleasure, we realized neither of us was a demon. For over one hundred years we have been together. Until three nights ago."

"What happened?" I asked.

"Elisabet was kidnapped in retaliation for my killing several members of a vampire coven. Their leader left me a note stating that if I don't give myself to them before midnight tomorrow, they will kill her. I cannot let that happen."

"Wait, you still kill vampires? Even though you're one of us? Even knowing that we're not all evil?" Gwen looked ready to punch him, and I couldn't blame her.

"Yes." His voice carried no regrets. "However, I am more... careful now. I only kill those who are themselves murderers, the ones who drain and kill humans rather than simply taking what they need to survive."

"So why come to us?" I asked.

"You and your wife have somewhat of a reputation, if I may, for being outcasts among vampirekind, much as I am myself. You have killed vampires. I respect that. I am hoping you will be willing to fight alongside me to save my wife."

"We've killed vamps, sure, but only to save ourselves," Gwen told him. She looked over at me for approval for what she was about to say next. I nodded my agreement. "Okay, we'll help you. But no killing unless we absolutely have to."

"Very well. Let us return to your home. We have much planning to do."

***

After following us back to our house, Van Helsing filled us in on what he knew about the kidnappers. His wife was being held in an abandoned warehouse in the small town of Shad Lake, a little more than a hundred miles upstate. Supposedly they had her drugged and chained, and guarded at all times by two or three vampires. Van Helsing had scouted the place and said he had a fairly good idea of the building's layout.

The plan we came up with was fairly simple. We'd drive to the factory early in the evening, create a distraction, and sneak Elisabet out. Then Gwen would drive her to safety while Van Helsing and I covered their escape. The idea was to avoid physical confrontation unless it was impossible; I didn't intend to kill anyone unless it was to save my own life or Gwen's. What Van Helsing chose to do afterwards was his business. By the time we finished laying out our plan it was getting late, or early, depending on your point of view. I offered Van Helsing the spare bedroom upstairs.

"It's not boarded up like the basement, but there's nice, heavy drapes so the sun won't bother you."

He thanked us, and said he was going to retire as soon as he retrieved some blood from the cooler in his truck. I realized

Gwen and I had skipped our evening drink as well, so when he offered us two of the Red Cross bags he brought in, we gladly accepted. No questions asked. He took his bag to the guest room, while Gwen and I chased ours with a glass of red wine in the living room.

***

I awoke in my bed with no idea how I got there. I looked to my left and saw that Gwen's side of the bed was empty, although the covers were rumpled as if she'd slept there at some point during the night. Glancing down at myself, I realized I was naked. My clothes were on the floor next to the bed where I usually leave them. Gwen, neater than I am, folds her clothes and places them on a chair near her side of the bed. A quick glance showed they were right where they should be. The t-shirt she'd planned on wearing to bed was nowhere in sight.

Even worse, according to my phone almost twenty-four hours had passed.

By now I had realized how stupid I'd been. It had all been an act and we'd fallen for it. Van Helsing had needed to get us alone and we'd obliged by bringing him to our house. I'd either been drugged or placed under a spell of some kind. Sure, it was possible Gwen was upstairs right now, safe and sound, but I didn't believe that. Something felt really wrong, and it had a name: Van Helsing. I pulled on my jeans and t-shirt and rose straight up through the ceiling, not wasting time on the stairs. Materializing in the guestroom, I immediately saw the bed hadn't been slept in and there was no sign of our "guest." I moved down the hall to the living room and looked out the bay window. His car was missing.

I clenched my fists as I stared at the empty street. *Bastard!*

He'd taken off with Gwen. But why? If he wanted to kill us, he could have done it while we were unconscious. Was he going to try and exchange Gwen for his wife? I couldn't see what good that would do, if the original kidnappers had a personal grudge against him.

I had to find Gwen and Van Helsing, but I had no idea where to look. I tried contacting Gwen mentally. I'd never tried speaking to her telepathically from more than a few miles away, and I had my fingers crossed that they hadn't traveled too far. Luck was with me, though, as almost immediately I achieved a dim contact.

"Ryan?" Came Gwen's mental voice. She sounded fuzzy, like she was half-asleep or drunk.

"Yeah, babe, it's me. We've been double-crossed."

"That explains why I feel like shit. I just woke up a minute ago. I'm in the back seat of a car."

I could hear the "I told you so" tone in her voice. It would be a long time before I lived this one down. "Can you take a peek and tell me where you are?" I asked.

I felt Gwen try to focus her thoughts. "Give me a sec," she thought at me. "I can't see much; my head's leaning against the window. Wait, here comes a sign. It says...Exit 135, Taylorville."

Taylorville. That was upstate, north on the Thruway. Could it be that Van Helsing was still going to Shad Lake? Taylorville was just a little south of there. "Gwen, can you materialize out of there?"

"I've been trying ever since I woke up. I can't seem to use any of my powers. Let me just—oh, shit!" I caught a brief mental flash through Gwen's eyes of Van Helsing jabbing a hypodermic into her arm, and then all contact cut off. The son of a bitch was keeping her drugged. I had no idea what game he was playing, but I didn't like it.

I glanced at the time on the cable box under the TV. Ten-thirty. An alarm went off in my head. Van Helsing had mentioned midnight as the deadline the kidnappers had given him. Shad Lake was over a hundred miles from here. That meant there was no time to waste. I raced downstairs, grabbed my gun and some spare magazines. Hollow point ammunition, filled with ionic silver solution. Guaranteed to do serious damage to any vamp, no matter where you hit one.

Had they been closer, I might have tried dematerializing and flying, but a hundred miles in mist-form would tax my strength so badly I'd be near powerless by the time I reached them. Instead, I had to settle for the Navigator and pray the roads weren't too bad.

I had ninety minutes to save my wife.

***

The sleet and ground mist had grown so bad I almost missed the exit for Shad Lake. It seemed like I'd been driving for days. I glanced at the dashboard clock; it was already past eleven-thirty. Time was running out.

I turned hard onto the exit, taking it at seventy miles an hour. The Navigator tilted up on two wheels for a moment before slamming back down onto the road. The SUV slid across the ramp and scraped against a cement guard wall with a teeth-rattling screech before I managed to wrestle control back. At the end of the ramp I turned east, fishtailing through two lanes in the process. I said a silent prayer for no oncoming traffic as I straightened out and went roaring down Route 7. Another mile and I reached the industrial park where the abandoned warehouse was located. I stopped the Navigator just past the entrance and rose up into the frigid night air.

From my vantage point in the sky I quickly located his car— an easy trick since it was the only other vehicle on the property.

I aimed my body directly at the back entrance, flying through the air as fast as I could. Just before I reached the door I solidified, hitting the metal with enough force to tear it off its hinges and send it flying ahead of me into the gloomy expanse of the warehouse. I stopped my forward motion a   few paces in, dimly registering the crash of metal on wood deeper in the room as the door took down a twenty-foot stack of pallets. I caught movement to my right and immediately turned in that direction. What I saw brought a dead, cold feeling to my stomach.

Gwen was laid out on a long metal table, clad in only the panties and t-shirt she'd worn to bed. Silver chains bound her hands and feet and her head lolled to the side, eyes closed. That wasn't the worse part.

Van Helsing stood next to the table, a wicked-looking machete in his hands. From the way his eyes went wide upon seeing me, he hadn't been expecting me to arrive before he delivered the final death to Gwen.

"Don't do it!" I shouted. Even my speed wouldn't be enough to get me across the long room before he could bring the blade down. Maybe if he'd been human I'd have risked it, but as a vampire, his reflexes would be as fast as my own.

He gave me a mocking smile.

"Right on time, Mr. James. Well done."

"Playtime's over," I said, my attention still focused on the knife. "Let her go."

I took a step forward but stopped when Van Helsing lowered the blade to Gwen's neck, pressing just hard enough to draw a thin trickle of blood. With my speed and strength taken out of the equation, I had to find a different way to save Gwen.

"One more move and I end her life."

I knew he could do it, but I wasn't worried anymore. While he was spouting his threat, Gwen had opened her eyes. Van Helsing couldn't see her face from where he stood, so he missed the big wink she gave me before she closed them again, playing possum.

I did my part as well, giving Gwen the time she needed to fully recover.

"Can't we talk about this? Why do you want to kill Gwen?"

Van Helsing stared at me and I saw there'd be no rational discussion. In his eyes was something more frightening than the heavy blade he held.

Fanaticism.

I'd seen it before, on the faces of the zealots you see on television or street corners, the ones who preach about the end of the world, or the second coming of Christ, or how the chosen will leave our planet in an alien spaceship.

"I spent my entire life killing vampires. Why would I stop just because I became one? The only difference is now my powers are equal to those of my enemies. And I am paid for my efforts. "

"Paid?" I thought I'd been confused before, but now I was lost. "Someone paid you to kill my wife?"

"They paid me to kill both of you. I chose to make it a game."

"There has to be some kind of mistake."

He shook his head.

"I have made no mistake. The Lords themselves have charged me to do what I do; I am unique among the undead. I exist solely to exterminate all vampires from this world. Only then will I be able to join my Elisabet in heaven. You and all the rest will burn in hell. Tonight your wife dies, as mine did in that hospital so many years ago, and then it will be your turn."

Before I could do or say anything, he raised his arm and drove the machete down with all his strength. Such was the power of his blow the blade shattered like glass when it struck the metal table, leaving Van Helsing with just the handgrip.

And an empty table.

As he stared at the place where Gwen's body should have been, she reappeared next to him. Before he even realized she was there, she grabbed him by the shoulders and delivered a lightning-fast kick to his chest.

"Play time is over, Grandpa," she said, following her kick with an elbow to his face. It was a blow that would have crushed a normal human's cheekbones into tiny pieces, but it only knocked Van Helsing back a few paces. Then he surprised us both by attacking Gwen in the one way we didn't expect: he lunged forward, gripped her by the neck, and bit deep, as if he intended to drain her.

Gwen screamed in pain and pulled back, losing a huge chunk of flesh in the process. A gout of blood sprayed out, splashing Van Helsing, who stood there, staring at us with a triumphant expression on his face and chunks of skin hanging from his teeth like seal meat in the mouth of a killer whale.

I don't know what he expected from us at that point, but he certainly didn't get the reaction he was counting on. He had to know vampires can heal most wounds. Unless he'd thought she'd just stand there and let him chew her head off. Of course, she didn't. She faded out of site, leaving him standing there like a target dummy at a shooting range.

I was more than happy to oblige.

My first shot took him in the shoulder; my second missed as the force of the first bullet spun him around.

Van Helsing snarled and charged at me. I fired again but missed as he dodged from side to side. I turned to mist just before he ran into me, and then solidified again. He stopped, turned, and came at me once more, brandishing a wooden stake in his hand.

By then I'd had enough of his shit. I fired two rounds into his chest just as Gwen materialized next to me. We stood there while Van Helsing collapsed, the hollow point bullets fragmenting inside his body and delivering a nice dose of ionic silver solution.

Ah, the effects of silver on the vampire virus. Van Helsing lay on the ground, twitching like he was holding a live wire. He appeared to be in agony, but to his credit, he didn't cry out.

"Who hired you to kill us?" I asked, keeping the gun pointed at him just in case he was faking. Not all vampires are created equal. We'd met some over the years who could shrug off a few silver-laced bullets like they were bug bites.

"They're watching right now," he said through clenched teeth. "As they have been for many years."

I was tempted to look around the warehouse, but I did the smart thing and kept my eyes on Van Helsing, despite a creepy feeling between my shoulders.

Van Helsing hauled himself to his knees, red-tinted sweat beading on his forehead.

"This isn't over. I will see you both dead."

"Oh, for God's sake." I looked at Gwen, and she nodded.

I put two bullets into his head.

We watched as his body tumbled over, his flesh already melting and running from his bones. A minute later there was nothing left but a wet, stinking puddle on the floor.

We didn't speak much on the ride home. I was lost in my thoughts and Gwen was content to rest her head on my shoulder and hold my arm.

They're watching right now. As they have been for many years.

I didn't like that. Not at all. It meant the game wasn't over; the stakes were just higher.

Who was out there? Who wanted us dead, and why?

I decided that for one night, I really didn't want to know.

Image by Enrique Meseguer

THE GAMES MONSTERS PLAY

by Roh Morgon

Children.

They shuffled through the warehouse, silent and clinging to one another. Nine bedraggled and terrified kids, ranging from three to twelve years in age, escorted by cold-eyed guards from the receiving dock to the private cells.

Colin couldn't help staring. He'd heard the rumors for years, yet the sight still horrified him. But he didn't dare risk unwanted attention by asking questions.

I have to get them out, Colin thought. Even if it means terminating the Paris operation early. It would be his final move in The Game against the European Chosen. But first he had to survive tonight's meeting with Katarina Habsburg.

***

Clack. Clack. Clack.

Katarina's high-heeled boots rang out against the white marble floor, sounding to Colin like a great clock ticking off the final seconds of his life. He stood between Philippe and Hiroki, and wondered if he stank of fear as much as the other two Chosen. Her powerful Elder energy pulsated as Katarina circled them, its heavy aura smothering their weaker ones. When she reached the front of the windowless room serving as her Paris office, she stopped at the ornate mahogany desk and faced the Chosen.

Soft light from fixtures mounted high along the wood-paneled walls created shadows around her sharp cheekbones and bladelike nose, exposing the innate cruelty in a face that might've once been beautiful. Her statuesque figure, clothed in a forest-green pantsuit and framed in tumbling dark red hair, would've stirred his desire—if she didn't scare the shit out of him. Copper-colored eyes, like those of a cheetah, analyzed the three Chosen underlings. Her gaze slid from Hiroki to Colin and he swallowed.

"So…" Her thin lips curved upward as the word slithered from her mouth.

By the Saints, she's even scarier when she smiles.

Colin waited for her to continue, no longer able to breathe. He'd never been this close to Gilles's consort, and, so far the Queen matched her fierce reputation. Philippe, standing on Colin's left, shifted his weight. The pompous Frenchman lacked his usual swagger, which Colin took as a bad sign. To his right, Hiroki remained statue-still, but tension vibrated the air surrounding the lean Asian.

"I've decided to do something special for my birthday." Her British accent carried a hint of Austrian. "I have a new game— one to assist those in the lower ranks elevate their status. It's called, 'The Queen's Birthday Game,' and you are the first to play."

She paused, her red eyebrows arching with expectation.

"Merci. Merci beaucoup, my Queen." Philippe half-bowed, his hand to his chest.

Hiroki mimicked the gesture and Colin hastily did the same. The Elder resumed her feline stroll around the room. As she moved behind them, Colin's back tingled from the weight of her sharp attention.

Why did she pick me? Thought I was keeping a low profile.

He tried to ignore the drain in the white marble floor, as well as Katarina's extensive sword collection mounted on the wall opposite the wet bar. A traitorous shiver ran through his body.

"I'm giving you each the opportunity to present an offering to me—a birthday gift—which will demonstrate you possess the ingenuity and understanding required to become a member of my court."

Oh, shit.

"The winner will receive a place on my Special Council, and the losers..." Her cold laughter chilled the marrow in Colin's bones.

Katarina stopped in front of them, closer than before.

"Well, there are no losers among The Chosen."

Crimson flared once again in her pupils, and this time it spread into her irises, turning her eyes blood-red. Her upper lip curled into a snarl, revealing long, dagger-like fangs.

"You have three nights. Beginning now."

***

Katarina contemplated their retreating forms. Her fangs retracted and the ruby veil through which she peered faded, her eyes changing back to their normal copper.

Two of the players were common Chosen underlings competing for Elder attention in The Game, their scents and auras bursting with ambition. But the third one, the nondescript blond with an average face and medium build... Something was different about him, a careful blandness not normally seen in younger Chosen.

She'd spotted him the previous month from across the warehouse, puzzled by his respectful handling of the livestock. Katarina had recalled the quiet Chosen as she considered the players for her birthday game and decided he would make an intriguing addition to the roster. Peeling back his layers to see what makes him tick gave her something to look forward to.

The idea for the game occurred to her during her long flight back from Colorado. It had kept her mind busy, and now promised to provide a necessary distraction until she could leave Paris for her London home.

She frowned at the rasping sound behind her and turned as Gilles de Rais entered the room through a secret door hidden within the wood paneling. His eyes, normally the rich brown of his hair and finely-sculpted beard, gleamed a pale gold, indicating he'd just enjoyed a bloodmeal.

Her hunger stirred.

"What little game are you up to today, ma chérie?" Her mate strode to the wet bar and opened the refrigerator-sized wine cooler.

Katarina watched him examine the bottles, his hand pulling first one, then another from their slots. She suppressed the loathing generated every time she beheld his trim figure with its military carriage and precise movements.

"Ah. Here it is. And you thought to keep this all to yourself." He straightened, closed the door, and pivoted, smirking at her with his prize in hand. The bottle, a rare bloodwine infused with the blood of humans kept on a special diet, was the last from the case Antonio had given her for her birthday. She'd intended to enjoy it with better company.

I can't wait to get home to London.

Katarina grimaced as Gilles uncorked the bottle and filled two wineglasses. He raised one to his nose, eyes closing and nostrils swelling as he inhaled the bloodwine's honeyed fragrance. He opened his eyes and shook his head.

"Really, ma chérie. You can be so greedy sometimes." He took a sip, swished it around in his mouth, and slowly swallowed.

Nodding, he beckoned her to the bar. Katarina sauntered across the room and picked up her wine.

"A toast, my dear, to a successful trip." Gilles raised his glass. "It was successful, wasn't it?"

The menace underlying his polite tone triggered a surge of rage, and a growl leapt from her throat.

Goddamned bastard, sending me into that viper pit without the least concern for my survival. His eyes flashed scarlet and he snarled, exposing his fully descended fangs.

"Careful, Katarina. You forget with whom you're dealing. Put away your childish angers and let's focus on the task at hand, shall we?" He tipped his head expectantly.

She nodded, seething.

"Your agent disembarked in New York undetected?"

"Yes, as far as I know. His plane landed a few moments after mine. I believe Éva was too focused on my presence to notice." Katarina took a sip of her bloodwine.

She'd sensed the powerful aura of her longtime enemy sweeping through the airport toward her only moments before stepping on the plane to Denver.

"Éva." Gilles snorted. "She's always despised you, ever since you stole that Magyar bastard out from under her nose and persuaded him to break his mate bond with *her*."

Katarina smiled, but deep inside she winced at the heartbreak she'd suffered from Nicolas's later rejection of her. Though it had happened centuries ago, it spurred another flash of hatred, this time directed at Nicolas—the only one she'd ever truly loved.

"And what of the bitch he's proclaimed as his new Queen? You did meet her, I assume."

It wasn't just the threat beneath his words that enraged her. As her vision reddened, she thought about the dark-haired beauty with the piercing blue eyes who now graced Nicolas's arm.

She's as good as dead. I'll savor every drop of her blood, and then she can join Nicolas on the shelf Gilles has reserved for him. They can stare at one another for all eternity.

Katarina glanced over at Gilles and walked to her desk before answering.

"She's nothing. A commoner. She bore a strange scent, and her aura was unusual as well. I could not detect the signature of any major lineages. She's rather puzzling, and my guess is that she's unbound, an independent, and nothing to fret over."

Katarina lowered her gaze, fearful she'd revealed more than she intended to her mate, who was as much adversary as ally.

He'd enjoy using her jealousy against her.

"Unbound? That's curious. I wonder how Nicolas proposes to utilize her if she has no affiliations. What is this Chosen's name?"

"Sunny Martin. I've not had time to investigate her further. Lars and I only returned last night."

Gilles laughed.

"Yes, I heard about that. Who was the designer you wore, my dear? I'm not aware of anyone branching out into straitjackets. Or ball gags." A slow, condescending smile crept across his face.

Katarina's anger mushroomed as she recalled the indignity of Nicolas forcing her into the straitjacket, and the sting of Éva's slaps before that Hungarian bitch thrust the ball gag into her mouth. Thankfully, Nicolas's Elders on his private jet had refrained from further insults on the flight from Denver to Paris, only requesting she give Gilles their best wishes as they shoved her and Lars onto the tarmac.

She slammed her wineglass against the desktop and the fragile stem shattered. Bloodstained droplets flew into the air and the broken glass tipped from her hand, spilling the precious wine across the polished mahogany surface.

"Go to hell, Gilles. I'm your Queen, not your lackey. I deserve better from you."

Katarina flung the liquid from her fingers and stormed past him toward the door. Air exploded from her chest as his weight smashed her into the wall and pinned her there.

"My Queen, you do forget yourself," he whispered, his icy breath chilling her ear. His body pushed against hers and she shuddered.

The pressure on her back eased and he grabbed her shoulders and spun her to face him.

Gilles brushed a strand of hair from her eyes. "How was Lars? Did you have fun with your birthday present, the present

I gave you?"

Fear shot through Katarina. She'd grown somewhat fond of the Nordic giant, and had hoped to get Lars back to London before Gilles realized how much.

Her mate sneered.

"You've bonded with him, haven't you? That's sweet. I'm glad he brought you a little happiness." Gilles released her and stepped back. He appraised her a moment, then nodded. "You're right. I haven't been treating you as my Queen lately, as you most assuredly deserve. We've been together so long I tend to forget." He stroked his beard. "So, with that in mind, the first thing I shall do is reassert my position as your King. And no self-respecting King would allow a member of his court to bed and bond his mate and live to talk about it."

"Gilles, no! He's mine! You gave him to me—." Katarina clenched her jaw.

He'd even said I was free to do whatever I wanted with Lars.

As Gilles laughed, her throat tightened.

He set me up.

Obviously he'd expected her to bond with the young Chosen, knowing what it would do to her when he killed the Norseman.

The pain from the bond breaking… I can't go through that again. How could I have been so stupid?

She had nothing with which to barter—except herself. But she wasn't sure what Gilles wanted from her this time.

Submission? Resistance? Do I cower, or do I fight?

Katarina studied his eyes, trying to see through his impassive mask. His mouth quirked, an indication his mood was shifting toward amusement. She shook her head, weary of the centuries-old game that formed the core of their relationship.

"What do you want from me, Gilles? Whatever it is, just say it and let's be done with this."

"Aww… Did my Kat have a rough weekend? Too tired to play?" Gilles moved closer to her, slowly pressing her into the corner. He nuzzled her ear, her throat. She stiffened as he dragged his fangs against her skin.

"I tell you what, ma chérie," he murmured. "I'll let you keep Lars a little longer, but I want him out of sight, especially mine."

She nodded.

"As always, my generosity has a price." His cold tongue slid along her jugular.

Katarina froze.

"First, I insist you join me for this week's bloodgames. We've assembled fighters from rival street gangs to demonstrate their skills each evening prior to dinner. Which will be them, of course, followed by several special treats. On our final night, the winning owner will have their choice of dessert from a veritable nursery of tender young morsels."

She nodded again, keeping her face expressionless. "When? Where?"

"Ten, tonight, in the game room. We have a delicious evening ahead of us."

"I'm sure."

She waited, hoping he would release her, but he only pressed his body harder against hers.

"Ma chérie, do you realize how long it's been since we renewed *our* bond?" He licked her throat again, and she nearly retched.

Gilles's twisted version of bonding possessed little resemblance to the Chosen mating ritual. The simultaneous and complete exchange of emotion-charged blood was usually euphoric, radiating waves of rapture through the couple as their blood mingled. Katarina enjoyed bonding with the inexhaustible Lars, basking in his worship of her. They renewed their bond frequently.

But Gilles delighted in causing pain, and he relished

inflicting it upon her. "I've missed your flashes of hatred and disgust, my little Kat, as you've no doubt missed my exotic tastes and my joy at your misery."

His hand gripped her hair and a cry slid from her throat as his fangs tore into it. She tried pushing him away, then beating on his head and back with her fists, but nothing slowed the incessant pull on her veins as he drained her blood in great gasping swallows. Her legs weakened and she started sliding down the wall, only to have Gilles yank her back up by the hair and continue drinking. All thought ended as her emptying veins ignited in flaming agony. The burning hunger deep in her belly roared to life and she shrieked.

"Oh, my little Kat, how I love to hear you sing. It's been so long."

She was vaguely conscious of being lowered to the floor, the wall behind her holding her upright. Gilles sat beside her, then shifted her into his lap with her back against his chest. The fiery torture raged throughout her body, and she envisioned her skin blackening, splitting, curling, the imaginary flames crawling within her like molten snakes.

Katarina bit back another cry.

"There, there, ma chérie, it'll be over soon. God, how I love the hatred you bear me. It's your greatest gift," he moaned into her hair and, fondling her breasts, hugged her tighter to him.

You bastard. Finish it.

The blazing torture pulsed through her again and again.

Weakening, she gave in and the screams erupted from her throat.

"Yes. Yes. Oh, my Kat…"

The blackness was crowding in when his arm pressed against her lips. Katarina opened her mouth, bit down hard, and began taking in the blood her body so desperately craved. His hand stroked her hair as she swallowed, and much too soon, he wrenched it from her teeth. The burning in her veins eased, but not the hunger in her belly. She needed to feed—on human blood. Now.

She shoved herself from his lap and staggered to her feet.

"That's the spirit, my little hellcat!" Gilles stood.

"Go fuck yourself."

He laughed, and she felt his amusement echo in his blood coursing through her, accompanied by gloating and superiority.

"Yes. Hate me. Just keep hating me, Kat, because the day you no longer do is the day I'll have no further use for you. And then you can join the others on a shelf."

The steel clamp of fear gripped her and his blood in her reacted with glee.

"Tonight. Ten. And bring your appetite. I'll savor your hunger as much as your revulsion when you see the specialties I've arranged." The door closed behind him.

Katarina resisted blasting him with one last shot of anger, knowing he'd only enjoy it. She realized he must've felt it anyway as his blood in her veins hummed with satisfaction. It blossomed into joy at the despair washing over her as she thought about the months it would take her body to claim the blood as its own.

Months of complete submission to the iron bloodwill of the one who was her Maker. And months of feeling every emotion from the sick monster who was also her bonded mate and her King.

***

Colin parked the BMW in the Metro parking lot and took the stairs down into the station two at a time. He needed to lose whatever tail might be following him as quickly as possible, and wouldn't feel safe until he'd made several transfers on the RER, the Paris commuter train system.

It was bad enough when I just worried about my cover being blown with the slavers. Now I have to deal with the Queen's agents as well. I'm so fucked.

Nicolas had sent him to Europe eighteen years earlier to infiltrate the human trafficking markets, specifically the organizations operating as fronts for the Chosen bloodslave trade. Colin had worked his way up the hierarchy in each of their major cities, installing agents and gathering the information necessary to shut down the entire blood trade. Paris was the last one.

He thought back to the early days when he first arrived in Moscow. Although Nicolas had tried to prepare him, Colin's shock at the barbarism practiced by the European Chosen had nearly sent him running back to the States. He'd since learned that most lineages scattered around the world viewed humans as nothing more than cattle, maintaining the secret of Chosen existence with highly placed human bloodslaves and Chosen Elders in corporations and governments worldwide.

Sometimes I wish I was back in Colorado, just another Chosen peon hanging out at the club.

Colin hopped aboard another train and worked his way down the aisle. Realizing the only empty seat meant sitting between two attractive young women, he elected to stand. The hunger, already roused by his tension, grew more demanding. The scent of human blood pumping beneath the skin of the surrounding passengers stoked it further, and Colin decided to get off at the next stop, wherever it was.

His gaze drifted to the young women again and their long, soft throats. He swallowed.

That's what I get for waiting an extra night to visit Jeanette.

His young assistant had gradually become more than that, and now was both donor and lover. He didn't take from her very often, though the scent of her blood drove him crazy. Colin had seen the long-term effects on the donors who frequented Nicolas's clubs. He cared for her too much to risk the wasting that resulted from excessive use.

But tonight he would savor her essence, because it might be

their last night together.

The train stopped and Colin hurried up to the street level. Several blocks later, he ducked into a neighborhood bar and cut through the crowd and out the back door. As he made his way along the alley, he spotted the retracted ladder of a fire escape. He leapt up and grabbed it, then climbed to the roof. He traveled across the rooftops, leaping from building to building, until he reached his target. A sharp yank opened the locked roof-level door. Colin slipped inside.

Standing before Jeanette's apartment door, he hesitated.

Damn Katarina. That bitch has ruined everything. I'll be lucky to make it out of this alive. Don't know if I should run or stay. But one thing's for sure—Jeanette's got to get out. Tomorrow.

Guilt over his selfishness sent his fist hammering on the door harder than he intended. When she opened it, he realized he stared at her through a crimson haze.

"Colin!" Jeanette's hand flew to her mouth and she shrunk back, her eyes widening.

He spun away and leaned into the doorframe as he fought to bring himself under control. "Jeanette. I'm… I'm sorry." He opened his eyes to cleared vision, straightened, and faced the one human in the world he trusted.

***

Colin regarded the dark-haired woman sleeping in his arms and pulled the bedcovers up over her bare shoulder. He resisted the urge to stroke her cheek, to run his fingers across those full lips, so innocent, yet so inviting.

He wondered, and not for the first time, if he was falling in love with her. Though he and the other Chosen of Nicolas's lineage treated their donors with care and respect, Chosen bore a natural aversion to emotional involvement with humans. Interspecies affairs were not as common as the myths and stories one was led to believe.

But she's been the only bright spot in this dark hellhole.

Jeanette had started last year as his assistant in the export business Colin managed as part of his cover. She was intelligent and observant, more than he'd realized, and it didn't take her long to figure out that his business wasn't really exporting trade goods.

It also didn't take her long to figure out he wasn't really human, a fact hammered home the night she stopped by the office and found him beaten and shot and in desperate need for blood. Though he'd come close to accidentally killing Jeanette that night, she'd stood by him since, protecting both secrets. Her transition from donor to lover had evolved naturally.

Her gentle breathing was a balm to his soul, and a fresh desire crept through him. But he'd taken enough of her blood, perhaps even more than he should have, and he resisted its siren call to that which ran within his veins.

"Jeanette. Wake up, hon," he said quietly.
She stirred. Her dark brown eyes opened and she yawned. Colin eased out from beneath her body and onto the floor. "Jeanette. We need to talk."

She sat up, her eyes wide. "About what?"

"About you leaving."

"What? What do you mean, leaving?" Jeanette flung back the covers and slipped out of bed. She stood there, naked and frowning, her fists on her hips.

Colin fought another surge of desire for both her body and her blood, and turned away to find his pants. "You need to leave the country."

"*I* need to leave the country? What about you? Aren't you coming with me?"

"No, I'm not. I must stay, at least for a little longer." He avoided looking at her again, despising the hurt and tears he knew he'd see on her face, and focused on getting dressed.

"But why do I need to leave?"

"Because things have changed, and you may be in danger."

"It can't be that bad—"

"It is that bad. In fact, it's worse than bad. It's a fucking nightmare." He normally refrained from cursing around her, but frustration and the need to make Jeanette understand the gravity of the situation overrode his usual courtesy.

Colin glanced over at her. The tears he'd expected hovered in her eyes. He crossed the room and gently gripping her shoulders, kissed her forehead.

"I need you to do this for me. I need you to be safe and out of my enemies' reach." He shifted back so he could see how she handled his next request. "I also need you to carry a message to my contact in the States."

They'd never spoken about his other business, the one hidden behind his export company. Colin had elected to keep Jeanette as far from the intrigues of The Game as possible.

Her brown eyes shone as they searched his. He had no idea how trustworthy the mercurial gaze of a Chosen appeared to a human—it had been over a century since he'd viewed the world through human eyes, and most of that time was long forgotten. Apparently satisfied, Jeanette nodded.

"Whatever you need me to do, Colin. I know you wouldn't ask if it wasn't important."

A sudden rush of affection swept through him, and he pulled her into his arms. After a long moment, he reluctantly let go and stepped back.

"You'll need to travel light. A carry-on and no more. I'm sorry." He surveyed the room, noting her artwork and antique doll collection and other bits of her life here in France.

"It's all right. It's nothing." But he saw her lip quiver as his words sunk in.

"Don't worry. The company will pay your lease for the next year. By then, it might be safe enough to come back." He reached out and touched her hair. "But right now, you need to get dressed and pack. It'll be morning soon, and you should report to the office like you would any other day. I'll meet you there in the afternoon, and by tomorrow evening, you should be on your way to the States."

Jeanette nodded, and he leaned forward and kissed the top of her head. The need to protect his donor underscored his love for her, and he wondered how any Chosen could ever abuse the humans upon whom they depended for so much. Guilt tugged at him for not telling Jeanette everything. For not telling her that the small amount of his blood he'd been slipping into her cognac for months made her healthier than normal, or that it elicited pleasure for her rather than pain when he fed.

And for not telling her it created a symbiotic bond that compelled her to protect him at any cost, even if that cost were her life.

He watched her walk to the closet and, shaking his head at his duplicity, left the apartment.

***

Katarina heard Lars's heavy tread outside in the hallway and the ensuing argument with her guards, followed by the inevitable knock on her office door. She slammed her desk drawer. He knew to wait for her summons—she'd trained him better than this.

Poor dumb brute probably didn't know what to make of last night's events in the Gameroom.

Her blood running in Lars's veins must have seemed like it was at war as she fought to keep Gilles's twisted emotions from dominating her. Though she'd enjoyed her share of the scarlet spoils, Gilles's blood had battered her throughout the evening. She'd resisted giving in to his ecstasies, and had soon grown disgusted with his persistent need to wallow in the gore of his victims.

The knock repeated at her door, shifting her thoughts back to her more immediate problem.

Lars had woken several hours earlier. His confusion and

impatience stirred within her, but his emotions were barely perceptible, and she'd managed to block them while reviewing the monthly warehouse reports.

I'm surprised I can feel him at all. But Gilles, that prick, is an expert—he left me just enough of my own blood, Lars's blood, to keep the bond from breaking completely. I'm sure he's saving that until he has us together, which could be anytime now. I can't put this off any longer.

She sighed, closed her laptop, and leaned back in her chair. Pressing her lips tight, she reached beneath her desk and pushed the button signaling the guards.

The door opened. A Chosen guard came into the office and gave her an apologetic bow. "My Queen."

"Let him in, then wait outside. Oh, and you may need reinforcements."

He nodded, pivoted on his heel, and left the room. Several seconds later, the door opened again and Lars strode in. His uncombed blond hair and disheveled clothing mirrored his emotions inside her.

At six-nine, the big Norwegian was one of the largest Chosen in their lineage. She'd been delighted when Gilles gave him to her, suggesting the ruggedly handsome youth might have more uses than just a simple bodyguard. But bonding was a far cry from the idle bloodplay to which Gilles had alluded, knowing her appetites all too well. She'd given in to the temptation.

A union with the low-status Lars allowed her the physical gratification of bonding without the power struggle usually accompanying a match between more equal Chosen. She knew once she tired of her plaything, he'd be unable to interfere as she slowly severed the bond, which would minimize her pain, though likely not his.

Her mistake was underestimating Gilles's awareness of her activities. It had been decades since her mate had shown any interest in her. Though subject to an occasional pang of loneliness, she'd been quite happy living in London, far from the constant turmoil of the King's Paris court—until he'd sent for her to make the trip to the States.

"Rina! What happened last night? I—"

Katarina glared at Lars and curled her lip. He stopped and opened his mouth as though to say more, then snapped his jaw shut. His massive fists clenched and unclenched at his sides. She said nothing as she rose to her feet.

"Rina?" Lars asked again, his voice now tinged with alarm. His knuckles whitened.

Katarina stared through him, ignoring the pull of his fear deep within her. She pressed the button underneath her desk and a few seconds later two Chosen guards entered her office, followed by two more.

Lars half-turned as they came in. He whipped back around to face her, panic twisting his features. "No!"

She gave a sharp nod to the guards, and two of the Chosen grabbed Lars's upper arms before he could react. Though he dwarfed them, he was younger and weaker, and unable to shrug out of their grasps.

"Rina! What have I done? I love you! Don't—"

"Silence!" she hissed. Katarina strolled around the desk and approached her lover. She caressed his throat, then lowering her hand, stepped back and gestured with her chin. The guards dragged the struggling Lars toward the rear of the room.

"No! You can't mean this!"

Ignoring his outcries, Katarina walked past them to the back wall and pressed a button mounted near the corner. The wood paneling slid apart to reveal an eight-foot wide, floor-to-ceiling recess. The interior lit automatically, and the wall-mounted shackles inside gleamed dully in the harsh light. The guards muscled Lars into the recess and his struggle intensified, his words fading into grunts as he tried to break free. Katarina heard the shackles click into place and dismissed the guards with a disdainful glance. As the door shut, she crossed her arms and stared at the swords.

"Rina, what did I do wrong? Tell me, I beg of you. Let me fix it."

His pathetic attempts to win a reprieve irritated her. She didn't owe him anything, especially an explanation. She was his Queen. But when she allowed her gaze to drift to the big Norwegian, a flicker of regret stabbed her.

It's no use. Gilles has all but signed your death sentence.

Pressing her lips tight, she stepped past Lars into the recess and opened a cabinet door. His musky scent penetrated the emotional barrier she'd built between them in the hours since she'd re-bonded with Gilles. It tugged at the tiny fragments of Lars's blood still buried in her tissues, and she tasted her lover's confusion and despair. Her own blood responded, both the remnants in her cells and that which ran within Lars's own veins.

Katarina steeled herself against the protest ringing through her and reached for the duct tape.

"Rina! No—"

His cry abruptly ended, stifled beneath a strip of grey tape. Bloodtears filled his eyes and flowed down his cheeks, running over the tape to drip from his chin.

"Close your eyes," she whispered, suddenly unable to bear the hurt and dismay at her betrayal shining from them.

Lars whimpered, his expression pleading. She tore off another strip, held it up, and waited. She looked into his blue eyes one last time and shook her head.

This is for your own good. And mine.

All fight left him. His huge form sagged in the restraints, and he slowly lowered his eyelids. Katarina pressed the tape in place over his blood-rimmed eyes. Doing her best to block his anguish prickling throughout her body, she pulled an IV tube from its hook within the cabinet, then double-checked the connections before turning to the young Chosen. Remorse tightened her throat as she plunged the large-gauge needle attached to the tube into the vein of his inner elbow.

Katarina flipped the switch on the vacuum pump and watched Lars's blood race through the tube and into an oversized plasma bag. As the bag swelled with the crimson fluid, Lars writhed in the shackles and his howls burst through the tape.

His essence woven throughout Katarina's tissues erupted into fiery pain. She gripped the wall beside her, panting at the waves of flame passing through her. Though only an echo of what Lars experienced, it nonetheless began to take its toll on her and she fought to remain on her feet.

A taste of the darkness enveloping Lars told her it was nearly over, then the torment abruptly ceased as he lost consciousness. The straining pump shook her from her stupor and, exhaling, she opened her eyes. She ignored the limp body hanging beside her and switched off the pump.

That wasn't nearly as bad as I'd feared. But the worst isn't over yet.

She touched the filled plasma bag. "Well, my love. You will live on, after a fashion. I'll think of you every time I speak with the Prime Minister. He'll enjoy the cognac I'm sending him, as he always does, and our blood in it will ensure his continued cooperation."

Katarina faced Lars's unconscious body dangling from the shackles. She reached up and lovingly caressed his throat, then ripped the duct tape from his mouth.

She left it over his eyes.

"Farewell, my love." Katarina gently gripped his head between her hands, stood on her toes, and gave him a passionate kiss on the lips.

She then braced herself, and with a savage wrench, tore

Lars's head from his body.

Shock and pain lanced through her. Katarina held her breath a moment, staggered into the recess, and placed the head on the floor facing the back wall. Though she looked away, she wasn't quick enough. A shudder rippled her skin at the glimpse of those lips she'd just kissed mouthing unspoken words.

His anguish and horror still murmuring through her, Katarina made her way across the room to her desk. She sank into her chair and pressed the button. The door opened, admitting several guards. Katarina ignored them, focusing instead on the stains splashed across her hand.

"One of you take the blood to the distillery and give it to Hans. Tell him to mark it with the initials 'K. L.' and put it in the Reserved cooler." She motioned toward Lars. "The rest of you take him to the incinerator, and be quick about it. Report back when it's done."

Though I'll know well enough when it is. Hopefully with my blood drained from him it won't be quite so tortuous.

She slowly spun her chair to face the wall, listening as the guards opened the shackles, removed the body, and shuffled out the door with their burden. After several long moments, she finally dared to swivel back around. All that remained of Lars was a smear on the white marble where his head had rested.

Katarina sat back in the chair and steeled herself against his lingering emotions. A fresh agony flared within her and she gasped, her nails sinking into the mahogany desk at the sensation of real flames. As the lifespark of the big blond Chosen winked out, bringing him the Final Death, the remnants of their lover's bond died as well. Aching loneliness punched a hole deep in her core, and an empty despair blacker than any she remembered seized her very soul.

Katarina clamped a hand over her mouth and hugged herself, and her shoulders shook as bloodtears streamed down her face.

Damn you to hell, Gilles.

***

Colin woke from his sun-induced slumber and glanced at the clock. *Three. Don't think I've ever woken this early. Must be getting old.*

He laughed at his private joke, pleased at this latest sign of Chosen maturity. Like all younger Chosen, he sank into a dreamless, coma-like sleep from dawn 'til dusk, unable to be roused. But the last couple decades, as he'd neared and passed the century mark, he'd begun waking earlier and earlier in the day.

Looking forward to that magic two hundred, when the sun no longer puts me down and I won't have to worry about nasty burns anymore.

Colin stretched, and then frowned as he remembered his itinerary.

Jeanette. He grabbed his cell phone from the nightstand.

"O'Neill Exports." Jeanette's voice sounded normal and Colin exhaled.

"Hi, Jeanette, it's me. Any messages?" Colin kept their phone calls strictly business—no telling who might be listening in. Jeanette seemed to understand without ever having been told.

"No, sir. It's been quiet today."

"Good. I have some things to wrap up here, then I'll be in."

"Yes, sir."

Colin pressed the end button and rolled out of bed. He pulled on a pair of shorts, padded across the room, and sat at the desk. Opening his latest report to Nicolas on his laptop, he added a few more paragraphs and saved the file, then ran it through a converter, which coded it into a mixture of several Native American languages. He copied the coded paragraphs into his company's sales catalog listing products in a dozen different languages, printed it, and stapled the pages into a booklet.

Jeanette shouldn't have any problem getting this through.

Returning to his computer, Colin inserted a mini-SD card the size of his fingernail and started transferring files. When he had everything he needed, he withdrew the card and wrapped it in a tiny piece of mesh designed to block both electronic scanners and metal detectors.

He stared down at his bare thigh. Picking up the dagger he used as a letter opener, he took a deep breath.

This is going to hurt.

His jaw clenched, he buried the dagger into the side of his thigh and opened a two-inch gash in the muscle. As he shoved his fingers into the bloody wound to keep it open, his vision turned scarlet and his fangs descended in reaction to the assault on his body.

"Son of a bitch!"

Colin set the bloodstained knife on the desk, picked up the mesh-wrapped card, and stuffed it deep into the incision. He withdrew his fingers, and sucking the blood from them, watched the wound close.

It continued to throb, and the hunger flared in response. He could feel his tissues trying to push the card out of his body. *Fuck me. Hope that thing stays put long enough for me to get out of the country.*

Colin massaged his leg a moment, limped over to the refrigerator, and pulled out his last two emergency plasma packs. He bit into the top of one and sucked out the blood through the fang holes, then grabbed the other.

That'll have to hold me 'til later tonight.

Colin had donors scattered across Paris, all former prostitutes whom he'd helped get off the streets and into legitimate jobs. He still endured occasional pangs of guilt for using them to satisfy his blood needs, especially since his sole purpose here in France was to disrupt the bloodslave trade.

Colin rinsed the plasma bags, then ran them through his shredder. He washed the dried blood from his leg, which now bore no sign of injury, headed into the bedroom, and quickly dressed. After making one more sweep around the apartment, Colin picked up his laptop and broke it open. He popped out the hard drive and placed it in a plastic garbage sack, set it on the floor, and stomped it several times. The laptop remains and the shredder contents went into the sack as well.

His overnight bag held a change of clothes and a few toiletries—nothing more than would be expected of someone staying the night at a girlfriend's. Colin shoved the sales catalog into his overcoat, grabbed his hat and the garbage, and headed to the door.

He scanned the apartment as he stood in the open doorway. Eighteen years. Eighteen years infiltrating European warehouse networks, placing operatives, forming alliances. His role in the ancient, never-ending Game between Nicolas and Gilles, brief though it was, filled Colin with pride.

This was a good operation. Too bad it has to end—I could've used a couple more months.

Colin saluted his home, shut the door, and headed down the stairs. It was nearly five when he reached the office.

Jeanette's flight leaves at 8:10 p.m. Better keep this short.

His plane wasn't scheduled until the next night, after Jeanette had delivered his report and the disposable cell phone he'd purchased. Once he'd spoken with Nicolas, he'd know whether or not to make that flight. He tried to suppress his excitement at the thought of finally going home.

Shouldn't celebrate just yet. A lot could go wrong in the next thirty hours.

Thirty hours was plenty of time to die.

***

Katarina finished washing the blood from her face and picked up the burgundy towel lying on the bar counter next to the sink. Glancing down at her blouse, she felt a surge of rage at the blood spray and tears splashed across the black Dupioni silk, the stains a reminder of being bested by Gilles in their private game. Her eyes reddened and her fangs slammed into place.

Gilles might have won this round, but I will find a way to pay him back.

She opened the wine cooler, pulled out a bottle, and uncorked it. As she poured the bloodwine into a long-stemmed glass, a small laugh escaped her.

Glad I thought to switch the labels. The dimwitted pig didn't even notice.

Her mouth tightened as she heard the hidden door open. She focused on her sword collection on the opposing wall and once again fantasized each one slicing off her mate's head.

"Good evening, ma chérie. What have you been up to? Whatever it is, you've certainly provided me with a rare banquet, and so early in the night. I can't recall when I've tasted such a smorgasbord of delightful emotions from you."

Katarina rolled her eyes. She'd ignored Gilles's voyeuristic interest during her last moments with Lars, and the shock which followed when her lover died and the bond broke. But at the moment, she was grateful for her Maker's blood flowing through her veins. It muted the lingering empty pain of the broken bond, and if she gave in a little to his perverse emotions, it would help her recover more quickly.

She could feel his gaze stripping back her skin to peer inside, but Katarina refused to acknowledge his scrutiny. The curiosity probing her body from within shifted to a slow-burning anger. She suppressed her satisfaction and bit back a smile.

"Pour me some wine, ma chérie."

Katarina retrieved a wineglass from the cabinet and did as he asked. When she handed him the glass, his dark brown eyes bore into hers, seeking answers. She kept her face neutral as he took the first sip.

His eyebrows arched, then flattened. Gilles grabbed the bottle from the bar top and examined the label. He looked up at Katarina, the scowl still creasing his features.

"Well played."

A smile tugged at her lips. She allowed herself to gloat just to annoy him.

Gilles stepped next to her and she stopped breathing. His hand snaked out to clutch a fistful of her red hair. She hissed, remembering her vow to cut it.

"I'm waiting for the answer to my question. I know what you did, but I want to hear the words from your lips."

"You no longer have to worry about being cuckolded by a member of your court, my King. I took care of it."

Her dig at him with the word "cuckolded" had the desired effect. Gilles's hot anger blasted through her veins. His eyes glowed crimson and he roared, his fangs flashing. Still gripping her hair, he coiled his other arm and backhanded her across the face. Her ears rang from the force of the blow.

"You think you won by destroying your lover yourself? Think again!"

Katarina laughed when he buried his fangs into her throat. As he drained her body for the second time in two nights, she focused on her revenge.

I am going to find a way to end you, you son of bitch. Only I won't gift you with the Final Death, though you'll beg me to do so. You'll get the same as you've given me—a place by my side for all eternity.

She laughed again, a laugh that twisted into a scream.

***

Colin perused the computer screen in the warehouse office, massaging the kinks in his neck. Ending the operation early complicated things, and he hoped he could pull this off.

One phone call and I'm fucked.

The awaited purchase order finally came through. He checked it over, then hacked into the authorization function, selected "Approve", and sent it to print. Sticking the printout on a clipboard, he headed downstairs.

He spotted Rousseau talking to one of the guards at the loading dock. The swarthy warehouse manager nodded as he approached and reached out for the clipboard.

Here we go.

Colin tightened his jaw and handed it to him.

✳✳✳

Katarina glanced at the clock on her desk. 2:00 p.m.

Irritation squirmed within her veins. Gilles's "bonding" two nights in a row had left her depleted, spawning a bloodthirst she seemed unable to satisfy, even after spending the remainder of the night in his game room. The level of her atrocities had surpassed his—something that rarely happened—and her killing spree had continued into late morning despite being so bloated on blood she had trouble keeping it down.

And it's not over. To hell with waiting.

She pressed the button on her desk. A guard opened the door and stepped inside.

"My Queen?"

"Bring me that Chosen from the warehouse—Colin, or whatever his name is."

"Yes, my Queen."

The door shut and she settled back in her chair. She opened her laptop. Katarina couldn't make sense of the figures on the screen.

There's … there's no money in this account. What the hell?

She clicked open another page and frowned.

There's none in this one, either.

Her fingers tapped a furious rhythm on the keys, and then froze.

All the money in the warehouse accounts is gone.

Katarina stared at the far wall for a long moment before shifting her attention back to the laptop. She clicked the warehouse shipping manifest.

"What the—? No. No! This is impossible!"

***

The slow click of her heels against the dirty concrete floor resounded throughout the warehouse. Katarina strolled up the aisle between the empty cells, not believing her eyes.

"A copy of the sales authorization, my Queen. With your electronic signature." Rousseau bowed and offered the printout. Katarina snatched it out of his hand and scrutinized it, then glared at the filthy cages that should've had people in them.

"How many are left?" She resisted reaching around and tearing off his head.

"None, my Queen. They even requested the sick ones."

She inspected the order again.

CN Industries.

The knot in her stomach tightened.

"But…but… My Queen, the new shipment should be here by this evening."

"What new shipment?"

Rousseau swallowed.

"The one you authorized—" His words choked off beneath the finely manicured fingers gripping his throat.

The only response she could manage was a deep growl.

You're lucky there's no one to replace you right now.

Katarina released him, pivoted, and headed toward the door, accompanied by the loud clack of her heels beating a much faster rhythm than before.

"Call me when it gets here."

***

The web search for CN Industries proved futile. Katarina

hissed and shoved the laptop aside. She considered the two Chosen who'd been standing in her office with their gifts for the last several hours.

Hiroki had been her operative in Asia until he'd been compromised a few months back. She'd offered him a chance in The Queen's Birthday Game to see if he had any usefulness left. Apparently he still had some connections.

The birthday present he'd brought stood beside him, another Asian. The shirtless man wore shackles and a cold, flat-eyed stare. His tattoos told his story.

Yakuza. Japanese mafia. Very impressive.

The other Chosen, Philippe, had become a headache for his Elder. His constant machinations in The Game had earned him far more enemies than friends among his peers.

Someone seems to have missed the lesson on the importance of alliances.

A young human woman in her early twenties, half-supported by Philippe, kept nodding off, only to be jerked upright each time she did.

Wonder what the story is behind his present.

Katarina's cell phone beeped and she picked it up.

"It's Rousseau."

"And?"

"The shipment arrived." He paused. "And so did Interpol. I barely got out of there."

"What?!"

She smashed the phone against the desk, shattering the screen. As scarlet tinted her vision, a loud knock on the door jolted her. Snarling, she stabbed at the button. The guard commander entered, trailed by a second guard. They bowed, keeping their gazes fixed on the wall behind her.

"Tell me you found him." She stood.

No one in the room breathed.

"No, my Queen. Well, maybe."

Katarina moved and the commander blinked at her sudden appearance just two feet from him.

He coughed. "My Queen, someone matching his description boarded a plane at CDG earlier this evening."

She curled her lip. "Bound for where?"

The commander grimaced. "New York, my Queen."

She moved again, fast, snatching at the wall. A Samurai sword whispered through the air and a bright red seam blossomed across the commander's throat. Shock contorted his features as his body collapsed and his head fell to the floor.

The woman with Philippe shrieked. Its piercing sound died beneath the Frenchman's hand covering her mouth.

Katarina glared at the other guard. "You've been promoted. Have that taken away, but don't leave."

She studied the dripping blade.

New York. Nicolas.

A deep growl slipped out from between her clenched jaws.

CN Industries. CN. Corvinus Nicalao.

She marched across the room and slammed the sword onto the desk, then spun the laptop around to face her. Her fingers flew over the keyboard and stopped. Her breath caught.

Rome.

She punched a few more keys.

Warsaw. And Moscow.

All of the European warehouses. Stripped of their merchandise and likely raided by Interpol.

You son of a bitch! Katarina swept the laptop across the desk and it crashed onto the marble floor. *My Birthday Game. No one's going to take the satisfaction of that from me.*

She picked up the bloody sword and slowly pivoted.

A knock sounded on the door. The guard answered it and a large white envelope marked "Special Delivery" passed through the opening.

"Well? Bring it over here," Katarina said through gritted

teeth, placing the sword back on the desk.

He crossed the room and, bowing, held it out to her. She snatched it and tore open the envelope.

The CN Industries letterhead shook between her fists.

Dear Ms. Habsburg,
I apologize for my absence this evening. I trust my
gift demonstrates the ingenuity and understanding of the
requirements necessary to become a member of your court.
However, I must respectfully decline your offer.
– Colin
P.S. – Nicolas sends his regards.

Her nails dug into her palms, soaking the edges of the paper in red as she read the elegant handwriting over and over. With a low snarl, she crumpled the note into a tight, blood-smeared ball and dropped it on her desk.

You're going to pay for this, you bastard.

Barely able to contain the fury boiling beneath her skin, she picked up the sword again and sauntered across the room to the Asian and his captive.

The sword sliced the air just above their heads. Neither one flinched.

Promising.

"Unbind him."

Hiroki shifted behind the man and unlocked the shackles. They hit the ground with a loud clank and the sobbing woman, standing to his left, buried her face against Philippe.

"Yakuza. Can your master offer you immortality?"

The expressionless eyes flickered and his empty gaze met hers.

Katarina handed him the sword, then glanced at Hiroki.

Quick as a cat, the Yakuza spun. The blade flashed and Hiroki's head tumbled to the floor, followed by his body. The head rolled a few feet and came to a rest, face up—the surprise splashed across his face grew even more grotesque with his moving lips as he struggled to speak. The words fell soundless to the marble beneath.

The woman screeched and clutched Philippe, sobbing and begging him to take her home. Katarina ignored her mewling.

"Hiroki fumbled our Asian operation. I need a new agent. You have your Choice: work for me or join Hiroki on the floor."

The Yakuza dropped to one knee and, bowing his head, offered her the bloody sword from his upraised palms.

"Good." Taking it, she signaled the guard.

"Incinerate that mess, and escort our new prospect to the dungeon. I'll tend to him later."

He bowed, opened the door, and spoke through the doorway. Two more guards entered, and Katarina turned toward Philippe. The woman pressed herself against him, tears streaming down her face. Her dark hair fell to her shoulders in thick waves. Terror-filled blue eyes stared up at Katarina.

"So. You've brought me a present. Tell me. What could be better than a Yakuza?"

Philippe bowed, swallowing several times. Fear contorted his features. "My Queen. I… I've brought you a gift I believe demonstrates my loyalty and ingenuity beyond all others." He bobbed his head again.

"And? Why is this young woman so special?"

"She's my sister. I could think of no better sacrifice for you than one so dear to me."

"What? Philippe? What are you saying?" The horrified expression on the woman's face triggered an unexpected flash of pity in Katarina.

The little rat would sacrifice his own sister? She scowled at Philippe and his eyes bulged. *I'm tired of males always using females as pawns in their stupid games.*

"Well, Philippe. I believe you've won my Birthday Game. I

can think of no reward more fitting than a place on my special council." She raised the bloodstained sword. He cringed and the woman screamed again and sagged to the floor.

Katarina used a corner of his shirt to clean the blade. She hung the sword on the wall, then walked over to the desk and pressed the button. She motioned to the guard who entered.

"Take her to my chambers." Katarina ignored the woman's shrill protests as he dragged her from the room.

"Come, Philippe. I think it's time for you to meet your new companions on the council."

Philippe bowed as she passed, then followed, a nervous grin plastered on his face.

Katarina's thoughts drifted back to the collapse of the livestock business as she made her way down the hall toward Gilles's offices. *Gilles will have* my *head if I don't get the supply line up and running quickly.*

The guard outside Gilles's door bowed and opened it for her. Katarina swept inside and signaled Philippe to follow. She strode past the elegant furniture and fine art scattered about the room and knocked on the door at the far end.

"Come in."

The cavernous inner room was a complete opposite of the outer, furnished with only a simple desk and chair. A long counter with an industrial-sized sink occupied one side. Katarina avoided looking up at the wall-mounted shelves lining the room. But it made no difference. Her skin crawled as it did every time she entered Gilles's inner sanctuary.

The flagstones ringing beneath her heels, she kept her attention on Gilles standing next to the desk. Behind her, Philippe gasped. When she reached her mate, he held out his arms. She obediently moved into his embrace and tipped her head as he kissed her on the cheek.

"Welcome, my darling. It's been a long time since you visited. Are you all right? You seemed upset earlier."

"I'm fine."

He gestured toward the door. "Is this the winner of your little game?"

Katarina glanced at Philippe and smiled. The terror blooming across his face was one of the few things that had gone right during this very long day.

"Well, then, shall we introduce him to the other members of your special council?"

She nodded, opened another door on their right, and beckoned Philippe forward. Philippe trembled as he sidled past her and into the small room.

"No!" His body jerked to a halt as he surveyed the interior. Katarina prodded him forward, then strode past him to a smaller version of the sink and counter. Laying on the countertop were three brass plates with names engraved upon them.

Hiroki. Colin. Philippe.

She picked up the last one and smiled at Philippe. Bloodtears ran down his face, and his head shook back and forth in denial.

"Here. You even have your own nameplate," she said, handing it to him.

His knees gave out and he dropped to the floor. A sickly keening sound poured from his lips.

Katarina gazed up at the shelf above a large brass plate engraved with the words "Special Council."

A row of three-gallon, wide mouthed jars, their glass tops sealed with wax, lined the shelf. Blood filled every jar, and suspended within the viscous red fluid of each, was a head.

The eyes of the heads followed her movement as she motioned between Philippe and the shelf. The lips of several opened and closed, like fish attempting to talk.

"Philippe, meet my special council, and your companions— for eternity."

A sob was his only answer.

"Your sister will enjoy a much better fate than you. Who knows, maybe I'll make her my companion. I'm sure I can devise plenty of games to play with someone who reminds me so much of Nicolas's whore."

Katarina left him on the floor and returned to the large room. She again avoided looking at Gilles's shelves—many of those jars were inhabited by Chosen who'd been her friends and allies, before word spread about the dangers of befriending the King's consort. He'd taken great delight in her despair each time he'd jarred one.

"Well, ma chérie, is he excited? I know I am." Gilles's eyes glowed bright crimson as he unbuttoned his shirt.

Shaking her head, Katarina waved her hand toward the other room.

"He's all yours." Her veins pulsated with his anticipation, and she braced herself for the next several hours of his frenzy. *That should keep you out of my hair for a while.*

She watched Gilles walk past her into the room and shut the door. As she turned to leave, Katarina paused to check the shelf above the doorway. It now contained not one, but two empty jars. Her eyes narrowed as she read the brass plates below the jars.

Nicolas Corvinus. Sunny Martin.

Katarina snarled.

Someday, Nicolas. Someday you will be mine.

***

The limousine pulled up the long circular driveway and a sprawling Tudor mansion came into view. Colin lowered the car window, inhaling the crisp Colorado evening air, and finally allowed relief to wash through him.

I feared I'd never see this house again.

As they passed the huge topiary statues in the central garden, his gaze locked onto a slender figure standing at the top of the stone stairway in front of the house.

Jeanette.

He bolted through the door before the car came to a stop. Two bounds up the steps and she was in his arms.

"Oh, Jeanette …"

He wrapped his arms around her as tightly as he dared and buried his nose in her hair as she snuggled against him.

"I thought I'd never see you again." Her musical French voice aroused him and his mouth ached to taste her soft skin.

A cough behind Jeanette broke Colin's focus. Nicolas stood in the doorway with his hands in his pockets, appearing as though he'd just stepped off the cover of *Forbes* magazine. His emerald eyes shone with satisfaction. Colin grinned at him.

Something's different about him. He looks…happy. Happier than I've ever seen him.

"I have taken the liberty of reserving a suite for you at The Broadmoor Hotel. It is yours for as long as you like." A stray breeze ruffled Nicolas's black hair, worn longer than Colin remembered.

Colin nodded.

"Perhaps Miss Marceau would like to wait at the hotel? I have several items of business to discuss with you, and then your time is your own. Meet me in the library when you have seen her off." Nicolas disappeared inside.

Colin embraced Jeanette again.

"How I've missed you." He traced a finger down her cheek and across those full lips he loved to kiss. He wanted to kiss them now, but decided to wait until he could do so more slowly.

"I was so worried for you, Colin."

"Well, I'm home, safe and sound. No more worries." He gave her a final hug before guiding her down the steps to the car. Colin helped her inside, then reached in and caressed her face.

"I'll see you at the hotel."

"I'll be waiting for you." The words were in her bedroom

voice. Colin stopped breathing and forced himself to close the door. He watched as the limo drove off.

God, I hope I can keep from killing her.

He turned and strode up the stairs. When he knocked at the ornate front door engraved with a raven crest, it was opened by a slender, blonde woman—a human woman.

"Marie!"

"Good evening, Monsieur. It is good to see you." She bowed and moved back to admit him.

"You're lovely as ever, I see. How have you been?" He walked inside.

She hasn't aged a day in eighteen years. The benefits of Chosen blood seem endless.

"I'm well. Your mademoiselle has been delightful. She has been very concerned about you."

Colin chuckled.

I can only imagine them chirping away like two little French birds. I'm glad she's still here. It might make Jeanette's transition to whatever life she Chooses a bit easier.

"Mr. Ambrus is waiting for you in the library."

He smiled at her use of Nicolas's modern surname. To Colin, it would always be Corvinus.

"Thank you, Marie."

She knocked on the library door, opened it, and he stepped inside. The door closed behind him. Nicolas stood by the round table next to the room-length window. A carafe of bloodwine and two filled glasses occupied the table's center. The wine's delicate fragrance, with just a hint of copper beneath the scent of Nicolas's special herbs, stirred Colin's hunger.

He stopped in front of Nicolas and saluted, then dropped to one knee and pushed back his sleeve. With his head bowed, he offered the underside of his wrist.

"Not necessary, Colin." Nicolas rested his hand on Colin's shoulder. "There is plenty of time for that later. I am in no hurry to re-establish the Maker bond. You have more than proved your loyalty and are free to remain unbound as long as you wish."

Colin nodded and rose.

"Thank you, sir."

"It is I who must thank you. Without you and your tireless efforts, we would not be celebrating today."

"Then I, we, were successful?"

Nicolas laughed. He picked up a wineglass and handed it to Colin.

Colin nearly choked. *He never serves anyone. Not anyone. He's the Maker.*

Nicolas picked up the other glass. "All four operations were shut down in their respective cities by Interpol. In addition, several human trafficking rings were exposed, resulting in a large number of arrests. The refugees are in protected camps and every effort is being made to reunite them with their families. Many humans, and sympathetic Chosen, owe you their lives."

Colin, still in shock from his Maker's deference, nodded. "And the children?" he asked, remembering their faces.

"Safe."

The last fragment of Colin's tension drained from him. Recalling the data buried in his thigh, he grinned. "I've brought information on their other activities as well. It's enough to cause havoc in their operations for some time."

Nicolas smiled and raised his glass. "A toast, then. To the Blood."

"To the Blood," Colin echoed and raised his.

"And to The Game."

"To The Game."

BONESONG

by Rain Graves

Fair Isle, Before and After It Happened

The evergreen was so tall, that when the Gods had seen fit to plant the tree, she began growing in their hands before she ever reached Earth. Knowing she had a purpose that was grim, she was reluctant to leave the safety of their blessed fingers. The sapling cried out in a great winnowed rasp, ever reaching for the sun. Though she reached hard to attain those heavenly hands once more, she could not. She drooped over in defeat. The Gods gently whispered the name *Bethel* to her and were silent after that. She was left to grow alone.

As the centuries worried by, Bethel saw the deeds of man all around her. Like so many leaves to seasons, so did the people fall to wars. She had dug her roots in deep, reaching the fiery core of the planet, vibrating with its white-hot light, a heat and a shelter all its own. No element could harm her. No winter too harsh; no summer too dry. She was as wide as fifty men by the time Aodh The Terrible had found her and built his keep around her. It was as much a prison to Bethel as a protection.

In captivity her spirit grew taller. The rooks, ravens and hooded crows with all their potent knowledge would roost in her sheltering branches, keeping her company. Each spring when she bore her fruit, they would each take a large pinecone and carry it far and wide, so that her magic would spread and she would do the land justice with the light of the Gods again, in her children. There was no other way out of the castle walls that hid her from the world, and no other way to tell her story.

There had to be seeds. There had to be dreams. There could not be a hero otherwise.

Those that built the castle walls for the high king also dug a tunnel and then a hole beneath her, like a small, one room house, weakening her root structure. The chamber was sealed by his wizard Lethe, and though Bethel knew she was to become a house to someone, she did not know it would be so burdened a heart.

The beast was bleeding from a large arrow wound when it came into her through the small earthen tunnel, and as it was led inside, they broke its legs and dragged it the rest of the way so it could not kick them. They siphoned off the unicorn's blood to weaken it. The blood went into a wineskin and was thrust into the hand of the king.

The great beast had silvery fur, now mottled reddish-brown with dried blood. Its huge, beautiful wings had been broken in several places to fit through the passage. Bethel knew it was also to ensure they would never heal, and it could never fly away. They were so mangled that they almost looked like branches, she thought. If she could have reached her branches down to cradle the unicorn, she would have.

Just before the men left, Lethe took Aodh's sword and called forth fire to set it ablaze. The beast cringed in fear. Lethe brought the sword down on one broken leg after another, chopping them off at the knee joint. The flames cauterized the wounds, but his pain rang out in anguished howls. It echoed through Bethel, like a terrible, unstoppable song.

Lethe took the bones with him and the men laughed as they went. The beast would never run, nor fly again. He also could not die. It was cruel to keep him alive. The great horsehead bowed in defeat to the floor, blinded by agony. The unicorn crumpled itself down in the hay, all burden and sorrow.

Above them all, Bethel looked down to see the men outside making flutes with its leg bones. When they finished them,

Lethe held one up to the sun in the courtyard, said some words that were strange and foreign, and then put the instrument to his mouth. The sound it made was so beautiful that the men wept. There was another sound deep within Bethel's belly, rising to crescendo with each note. It was harrowing, foreboding, and forlorn. Each note was the unicorn's name, and was bound it to anyone that played its Bonesong.

Bethel saw the king command Lethe to bring the wineskin and pour him a goblet of the beast's blood. She watched the sound of the flutes vibrate through the liquid as the notes were played. Lethe placed the goblet to Aodh's lips, and the king drank it down. A great cry of celebration went up as the finished flutes were given to Aodh and his brother, Anradhan, as coronation gifts.

They were the new house of Ulster; they would rule together, forever. No one noticed that Aodh was the only one to receive his draught from Lethe's wineskin, and Anradhan's from another entirely. No one saw the darkening of Aodh's eyes from brown to black, nor the sinister way his mouth curved, holding the shudder of power in as sweat beaded on his brow. It was done. The blood of the unicorn had made him immortal.

***

The Ruins of Fair Isle, Before The Hero Returned

Ferdaid circled the tree once more, holding his fingers lightly on the bark, letting his childhood memories of the legends surrounding its being fly freely into his mind. They danced and weaved a wonderful tale of an impossible hunt, with a beast so mighty that when it fell, the earth shook. Kayt was laughing, hiding just out of sight of him as he went round and round.

He pretended not to notice and watched the trail of her red hair catch the sun before it disappeared behind the great thing between them. He caught her hand and held it. She did not resist.

"When we are married, I will give you sons that will chase you around this tree."

"When we are married, I will no longer have to run." They embraced and kissed.

"Do you know the story of this place?" He asked her.

"I know the legend. Everyone knows it."

"They say she burned him, right here in his bed. Will you do that to me, when I conquer you?"

"Will you deserve to be burnt, then? I am no concubine, and you are no drunkard." Kayt laughed.

"Then let us go to the Chieftains and get our blessings."

"That shouldn't be hard. Our fathers have bidden it so, and we are lucky the match was foretold by Corr. Her futures are always binding." Ferdaid looked into Kayt's eyes, as she took a lock of his black hair and wound it around her index finger.

"Yes. But they always come with a price. I wonder what ours will be?" She said. He stared at her then, as if it was the last time he would ever see her, one hand on the bark of the great tree, and the other caressed her cheek. He kissed her again, and again.

∗∗∗

"Now you must know the price of her dowry." The old, blind witch spoke quietly, as all those assembled from the four villages nearby held their breath. "With every good fortune, comes great responsibility, and Kayt is your destiny. All your wealth resides within her happiness, as with any good woman. Do you still wish to proceed? The price may be too high…" Corr stared into him, her clouded eyes piercing the depth of his soul with so much ease that he believed she could see everything in him.

"You have seen us together since we were children. My

destiny has never been more clear. Name the price. I will pay it." Ferdaid stared right back.

Corr smiled. "The price of your bride is one of the tribes. It is for better, or worse. It will be of great value to all present on this day, though none will believe or know its worth. The Gods have bidden it so."

"Name the price. I will pay it!" Ferdaid said again. Those gathered began to shout the words for him, "Name the price! Name the price! Name the price!"

"The price, Ferdaid of Argyle, is to kill a king who is already dead." The room went silent. The riddle rested on all their heads, as Corr's black eyes glittered. Ferdaid's gaze narrowed, seeking the answer, and then grew wide as the knowledge found him.

"Then it's true?" He whispered.

"It is," Corr said, "You must pay the price!" As the witch held Kayt's fair hands in her own, raising them above her, triumph and relief filled her wrinkled face. As she lowered them, Kayt's eyes found Ferdaid's. The fear came then, looking into them and knowing his soul.

***

Fair Isle, The Day of the Hunt

"Every nobleman from here to the New World will know of this deed, should you carry it out today, Sire." Lethe slithered through the great hall of the high king, the red hand of his father now emblazoned on his own banner, the one shared by his brother.

"No one will doubt your power when it's done," Lethe continued. "Your brother is weak and prone to mercy. Simultaneously, you must be strong and balance the weakness for your own kingship, if not his. His constituents will never choose war to carry the kingdom far and wide, but no man would doubt a warrior in battle that cries the Bonesong."

Aodh was silent, but slick in his resolve. He knew the neighboring kingdoms he'd taken by force would not be enough to overpower Anradhan in banner men or make him cede his will over his named throne. There would have to be unanimous obedience, a unified power, and a sole provider of protection. With the culling of the beast, he would have all those things and more, if the stories were true. Lethe had assured him they were, and even if they proved false, it would be a fantastic tale for the nobles to tell at the feast.

Where Lethe had conjured the unicorn from, Aodh had no idea. He had seen the beast unfettered, wandering at a crooked, stunted pace on its shortened legs at night, when the maids went for their last bucket of water. The forest edge was silent and still in the moments before the great silver mane was seen as it trotted silently to the lucky ones.

It had been how the king chose his concubines of late; they were proven virgins if the beast appeared to them. It would appear no more after he bedded them, and their shame was born brutally amongst the other women. He marked them all with a small, angry scar across the cheek, under the left eye. He used a metal talon he'd had custom made into a ring by the royal jeweler. Aodh sharpened the end of it every day at dusk, as he watched the river from his high window, looking for the ethereal glow of the unicorn in the dark, waiting for it to mark his prey for him.

***

"I have used my cloak to get close enough, and its wings have been further clipped. The beast cannot fly, though its spirit still walks. We must go while the stars are auspicious. Do you agree, Sire?" There was a long pause.

"Yes. We will go tomorrow and not use the horses. I want nothing obstructing the triumph of this. It must be greatly realized by all. I want no comparison to be made. We'll take the hounds."

"As you command, Sire." Lethe's smile was crooked. He left the great hall to go about his business of potions and portents. The hunt was just a formality, Aodh knew. Politics were politics. He wondered if the unicorn knew of its watchful foe above, as it drank the river water. It raised its head then, shied backwards at its own reflection, and bounded into the darkness of the forest night.

***

The sky was grey and pregnant with the promise of rain the next morning. Aodh the Terrible led his pompous group of nobles through the forest for the hunt. Lethe had told Aodh the plan was to return empty handed, only to find the unicorn at the fountain, drinking deep of a spell to keep him tethered without thought to run. Even as crippled as it was, it was still powerful. It would have to be lured there with sweet apples and clumped sugar, tainted to push its splintered-bone hooves onward and cloud its judgment.

As the day grew long, there were complaints. When they grew too restless for Aodh to bear babysitting the nobles any longer, he turned them all towards home, hounds bounding to the quick beyond them. They knew their empty task for the day was done and food was to come.

"I dare say, Sire, chasing myths is tiring for one such as me. My gout protests, but my sense of amusement doesn't. Shall we make a song of it?" One man mused.

"No," said the king. "I think not. Songs are better sung when the day is won."

"Do you ever win your days, my King?" It was a snide remark, but the king bore it. It was irrelevant.

"Only when the sun sets and I am between a moist set of legs, begging to tame a different kind of beast," He said, giving the man a sideways glance. "You do not win many days, I can see, with that face," His smile had vanished, replaced by thin lips that threatened the nobleman to cull his tongue.

The castle came into the distance, its grisly, iron gates open in anticipation of their return.

"That's odd," remarked a nobleman. "Why are the gates open so soon?"

"We have no reason to be over-guarded in such times of peace," Aodh replied slyly. "Our women will wish to welcome us, ready for the feast. Perhaps there will be a wineskin to suckle, or a shapely breast."

They all grinned hungrily. The last twenty paces to reach the courtyard were anxious ones for Aodh. When they reached it, the uniform gasp of his party was a triumph.

Around the Fountain of Fortune was a crowd of women. Young, old, great lady and peasant alike were gathered around a huge, almost ghostly figure. Its silver fur was shaggy and re-grown trotters lined with great sharp edges, like rounded blades of death peace-tied to the most majestic body of muscle and spirit Aodh had ever seen. From afar it had been magical. Up close, it was like being in the presence of a God.

Its great wings were folded at its sides in a glamour that made them look whole and unbroken. It was docile. A small child held up a ripe red apple to its muzzle, much too far up for her tiny body to reach. When it brought its head down to take it from her, it nuzzled her hands as she giggled. Its great golden eyes shot through the gathered women, and into Aodh, as if he knew the king's purpose. The beast's head shot up, alert, and puffing mist from its flared nostrils. It took a guarded stance, closing a few paces between the hunting party and putting itself between the men and the women.

Aodh muttered under his breath, "You seek to protect them, but they cannot protect you." No one heard him as he called sharply to his squire to bring his bow and quiver. The others were too stunned to do anything but watch and follow their king towards the unicorn.

It was so easy a child could have done it, Aodh thought, thanks to his wizard. Without Lethe's workings, he imagined himself impaled upon that pearl horn and tossed like a ragged doll through the sky, until there was no vital organ left unpierced, his body drained of blood.

The unicorn began to advance towards him, but stumbled and shied as an invisible line was drawn in magic where it could not push through. It moved sideways to the left and the right, always with an eye on the king. The unicorn found it could only go around the fountain and never beyond ten paces of it. It angered the beast, and it reared, uttering a sound that was like thunder as the air became electrified. It reverberated off the chests of the women that were close to it and they fled, suddenly afraid of the thing that had captivated them with all its sublime serenity. They kept to the corners of the rough stone walls and outbuilding structures of wood and straw thatch. The king approached with one arrow drawn, bow fixed on the beast. It was clear what was to be done. The women held their breath and a few cried out, "No!"

They yelled to the Unicorn, "Run! Please! Run!"

Aodh was focused. He held himself at a great enough distance from his prey that it could not be said that magic was what stayed its exit. The unicorn paced around and around the fountain, back and forth in front of it, pawing the earth hard as if it would charge. Sparks began to fly off the stone. The king let his arrow loose and hoped that the poisoned tip would work. It met the skin of the beast and penetrated just deep enough.

The ground shook as the unicorn fell, paralyzed by the venom-soaked arrowhead that worked its poison into its blood. The effects would not last long, Aodh knew, and they had to move quickly to harvest the blood when the poison wore off. Golden eyes full of fury and marked vengeance threatened

Aodh the Terrible, but he paid it no mind.

Silence was all around them, pronouncing the deafening thump of heartbeats in the chests of the living. It threatened to mar the day with both terror and joy, until Aodh The Terrible cried out, "I have done it! The beast is slain! Prosperity is ours!"

No one knew whether to run or to shout his name in victory. Some mouths gaped in horror, quickly righting themselves to awkward, masked smiles. They were hesitant, not knowing how the Gods would react. One by one, they clapped their hands and said the words, "Long live the king! The beast is dead…" But it wasn't dead. Not yet.

It was down on its fabled knees, with what was left of its limbs tucked under its body. It panted and foamed at the mouth, dripping precious copper from its veins from the wound in its flank. The unicorn's magnificent, pearled horn sunk down and dragged a sad line in the dirt. It tried hard to lift its head. All the while, its eyes remained fixed on Aodh, as if a horrible curse was being issued.

If it bothered the king at all, he did not show it. He approached the beast, taking its head by the lowered horn, and jerked it upright. The unicorn's teeth gnashed at air, unable to move beneath the magic in Aodh's grip. "Tonight…we feast!"

"Hurrah!" The men shouted nervously as they clamored for feverish hand-shaking with their sovereign, blood beneath them, pooling in the dirt. They never stopped congratulating him in all the confusion, as their women watched coldly from afar. The group slowly lumbered towards the Great Hall. Four strong men dressed in butchering aprons made their way towards the beast by the fountain, beyond the king. Lethe stood behind them in the shadows, hissing instructions.

When every man was inside, Aodh The Terrible followed his wizard to the great tree, under its precious roots, through the tunnel and into Bethel's belly. The body of the unicorn was never seen again. Only the bones were brought forth, and with the bones came a threat and a knowledge that a dark omen was upon them.

Could something immortal die, they wondered as they were served a stew that was said to have been made from the beast's flesh. Some swallowed with indifference. Others did not eat at all. No one made love that night, or the night after that. Washer women cried quietly to themselves at the riverside. Clouds pregnant with anger darkened over the castle and never went away.

The king ordered a tapestry to be made and hung in the Great Hall depicting the men and women who witnessed the hunt of the unicorn in all its glory. Embroidered in rich gold and silver, with threads of vibrantly dyed colors, was the image of the silver beast stayed forlornly by the fountain by Aodh the Terrible. Behind the splendid scene was a simple red background, symbolizing the blood of the red hand of Ulster and the new reputation he was forging for himself.

The hand had always been a bloody hand after all, many thought, and the blood kept flowing after that. As the years passed, it never seemed to never stop.

***

The Ruins of Fair Isle, After The Hero Returned

Ferdaid stood in front of the great tree once more, a broken man. His hair was caked in dried blood, and it was not his own.

The search for the fabled king that slew a unicorn had only been realized after it was lost. The dark road that ran across the land had to be accessed using ancient maps that no longer ran true to the coastline, nor the landmarks that once were. It took him to an outpost Inn, where rumors of a very old man that often grew young were too good to be true.

By the time he'd found the mound carved inside the foothill where the man had fashioned his dwelling, it had been abandoned. Crude wooden bowls and utensils meant only for liquid consumption were littered about the house. Moldering flowers sat atop a sturdy table where runes had been cast and left. Ferdaid could not read runes, but he crossed himself and spat, just in case the portent was unfavorable.

Terrible paintings on swaths of embroidered cloth and wooden planks lined the walls. Hooded monsters with claws reaching towards a spindly, helpless man crying out in pain were the most prevalent. When Ferdaid looked closer he saw that the man was skinless, and he wore a crown of thistles. His raw muscles were illustrated in great detail. Blood dripped from his mouth. Dark figures behind the man held him in tethers. He was being tortured.

Other paintings were of ravaged women and their burning homes, with the skinless man looming high above them. One woman was painted over and over again. As Ferdaid crept closer, he saw the woman resembled Kayt in unmistakable ways. As horror came over him, so did an unnatural green-white fire begin to lick at his heels. He jumped about, stamping his feet to extinguish the flames, knocking over belongings and cursing to himself for wandering into the wizard's abode unawares.

Those paintings are of the High King, Ferdaid thought. His blood ran cold with the image of what was possibly happening at home in his absence. His quest had been a cruel diversion. Ferdaid had to reach Kayt before they did. He knew the paintings would not lie.

It was already too late. Even by boat, she was twenty leagues from his rescue, and no raven would fly fast enough to warn her. A mortal man could only sail as fast as the wind would allow. Inside, his heart hardened and his blood boiled with rage. His mind held a permanent imprint of the images in the paintings in vivid color. Corr had not told him that Kayt would pay a price too. He felt he had been betrayed.

***

Fair Isle, Before The Hero Returned

Aodh crouched over the girl, his skeletal frame covering her like a terrible spider, hands like claws, clutching her clothing at the shoulders. His skin seemed dead and contrived, sliding over sinew and bone as if it were not even his own. His cruel, sharp, claw glittered with rubies in the moonlight, and he poked it through the sleeve of her dress with ease.

"You won't burn me this time, little bitch," he cooed between clenched teeth that reeked of decay. His face was a borrowed leather mask, the whites of his beady eyes shot through with red veins of anger. They fixed on her face. She winced and whimpered, feeling the claw pierce her flesh. This excited him. He held her in the vice of his legs, one hand like an anvil clamped down on her chest, and he brought his claw up to his nose. First to sniff, and then to taste her.

The rape only lasted moments, but to Kayt, it was an eternity. When it was done, he sliced her left cheek, just under the eye, to mark her shame. He violated her again with his mouth at her throat. Greedy, paper lips sucked her life from her neck. Warm rivulets leaked down her throat as the unmistakable stench of blood reached her nose. She vomited the contents of her supper, catching a whiff of his sweat, but he only clamped down harder on her, tearing the skin like a vicious dog eating a bone.

When it was over, she lay on the hard mattress of her bed, needles of hay poking through the linen beneath her. The wee hours of morning cast a ghostly light in her attic room, as a dark mist left and a lighter grey mist set in to chill her further. She could not even sob. It came out as an exhale like the last breath of death. With her blood, so had her voice been taken.

***

When Ferdaid's great-ship landed and they moved him to shore, he hurried up the fishing village embankment to ask questions, but no one would meet his gaze. His home was not his home anymore, and he was a stranger they did not wish to see. High above, on an emerald cliff with rocky crags, he thought he saw Kayt dressed in rags and looking longingly down at the scene. When he met her gaze she went cold and empty. She turned from the edge and retreated until he could no longer see her. He waited all day outside her cottage door. She did not return home until nightfall.

Her gait was limping, her clothing threadbare, with a ragged wool shawl wrapped around her shoulders. Her eyes were red-rimmed and sunk deep into dark circles. They welled with tears as she chewed a thumbnail and stopped five paces from him in the shadows. Her image was framed by the stars behind her. There were lines on her face that had never been there before. She did not speak, and there was a festering wound left uncovered at her throat.

Ferdaid moved towards her and she shrank from him. He stopped.

"Kayt, it's me, Ferdaid, your love… What has happened here? Why were there so few to carry me to shore? Why would no one look me in the eye?"

Kayt said nothing but whimpered and started to cry. Ferdaid's anger took hold of him and he grabbed her, forcing her to look at him even as she turned away. "Why won't you speak to me?"

As the moonlight hit her once-lovely face, what he saw horrified him. The tiny mark of a scar on her cheek. The knowledge of its meaning brought him to his knees before her. She opened her mouth to show him why she could not speak. Her tongue had been bitten off.

He wept and wrapped her shaking body in his arms. There was no way forward for her in this life now, but through the path of release into death, it seemed. He thought he heard thunder in the distance, but it gave way to echoing laughter. Beyond Kayt, hovering over the sea, he saw a pair of hollow eyes, black as pitch. A single red pinprick sliced through the sky and into Ferdaid's soul. Inside himself, Ferdaid only felt murder and gently moved Kayt aside to reach the door. His pace was swift as he followed the laughter above him. It faded into cracks lightning. As the rain began to fall, he roared into the night, "You will die by my hand, Aodh the Terrible! It has been foretold!"

✳✳✳

When Ferdaid reached the cottage of the witch, Corr was nowhere to be found. There was a message etched into a wood tablet for him. He was to drink the herbs she had prepared that would keep him alert and give him strength in battle. A map was drawn that led up to the Great Tree and then beneath it into a tunnel.

When Ferdaid broke through the decayed locks and seals of the wide, heavy door at the end of that tunnel, magic sparkled forth from the sweat of his skin, granting him safe passage over the threshold of the chamber. Whatever the fabled king's wizard had pressed upon past foes, Ferdaid seemed immune to it. He thought he felt the tree sigh as he entered, but the sound quickly gave way to ragged, feathery breathing. It came from the corner behind him. He spun around and caught his breath; there before him was the unicorn.

It was not magnificent. Its brilliant silvery fur had gone dim and grey with age and dust, which covered a skeleton that had long since lost its muscle. The belly of the beast was on the dirt floor entirely, its four limbs jutted out from all sides awkwardly, cut off at the first joint. He could see the pearl color of the bone sticking out of the hide where its legs had been severed and the flesh cauterized long ago. The jutting bone looked like splintered hooves. What was left of its wings had been eaten away by mites.

Ferdaid was humbled by his own emotions at the sight of the creature. He knelt beside the unicorn's head, inched close to the beast and lifted it onto his lap where he could stroke its cheek. The first kindness it had been given in eons. Blood tears leaked from the unicorn's eyes. It uttered a sound unlike any he had ever heard; a terrible and unending wail of pain and sorrow. Ferdaid cried with it, thinking of Kayt and all she had endured, coupled with the cruelty the unicorn had suffered for centuries. The beast raised its head and fixed its yellow eyes upon Ferdaid's. Words came into his mind, then. *Mercy. Please.*

The last of its kind, thought Ferdaid. And it must die.

***

Bethel shuddered when it happened. There had been no sound. The beautiful beast had been so silent as not to stir a single note on the wind in the flutes of his severed bones, so no one would know it had left this world. She moaned. Her bark creaked loudly as Ferdaid came up and out of her belly, and she laid her blessing upon him for freeing her friend from its burden. She could feel the blood of her immortal brother seeping deep into the dirt, down into her roots. The bones of the unicorn, which had turned to dust and ash, now blanketed her insides warmly. It was thanking her for never having truly been alone. But she was empty now. Hollow, but for its soul, which no one else would ever know. Together, forever.

Ferdaid had been careful to step around the blood as he took the pearled horn. He tucked it deep into a large leather pouch beneath his vest as he marched past all the abandoned and ruined cottages of the keep. He went to the edge of the ruins where the wizard's tower had been, then passed it to where the great hall once housed the terrible feast. There was a small dwelling there, with no smoke in the chimney. He could hear the high king laughing like a man unhinged, but when Ferdaid reached the door, there was no one inside.

The scent of layered death was everywhere. The carcasses of several village dogs, half-eaten and laid to waste, were bloated with maggots and piled in one corner. Towards the other was a wooden table fashioned into an altar notched with runes. A name was written beside each symbol. Kayt's was the last name on the list. Ferdaid recognized the shape of it from their marriage contract.

"She burned me, you know," Aodh's voice came from the darkness, somewhere above him. He pulled his sword from its sheath, looking up towards the rafters. He expected to see the king hanging like a bat, but there was nothing visible except for the cracks of daylight let in from the missing thatch in the roof. "She burned me in my bed when I was drunk on virgin blood. A dozen or more had felt my prick wrestling in them, and my mouth at their throats. She had been the first one I took from my brother's bed, but not the last." His laughter sounded like a raven on the hunt, clicking.

"It's a pity you were so stupid then," he continued. "We could have ruled together, you and me…but then you died. I killed you in your sleep!" Aodh sneered.

"I am not your brother, but I will avenge him just the same. I will avenge Kayt!" Ferdaid lunged forward towards the clicking noise, but the shadow of the king dispersed into a hundred actual ravens. They fled to every corner of the cottage. They came quickly at Ferdaid with feathers black as night, then as hungry, sharpened knives, precise in their accuracy. Like little darts, they pinned and pricked him, slicing past his worn clothing and into the flesh of his arms and legs. The wounds burned like acid. He staggered backwards.

The blades were sucked back up suddenly into the darkness and Aodh emerged. He was no more than muscle and tendon, skinless, wrapped taut and moist over bone. His eyes were wide open with no lids to shut them. They gazed at Ferdaid, round and terrible. Aodh launched himself like a harpy coming down fast on a frightened animal. While Aodh was still in the air, Ferdaid struck a blow with his sword. The blade sliced through Aodh's body without damage. It remained jutting out from his ribcage.

The king laughed menacingly. "You are no match for me, brother! I will feast upon your flesh!"

Aodh gripped and held Ferdaid's shoulders to the ground as he bit down hard on Ferdaid's hand like an angry child. He sunk his fangs deep into the flesh. The pain of the bite caused Ferdaid to release his grip on the sword. Slowly, Aodh withdrew the blade from his chest, letting it clatter to the ground.

Ferdaid's one free hand was not quick enough to get to the unicorn horn. Aodh hissed as he pulled his meaty skull up, tearing Ferdaid's skin off as he went. Ferdaid thought he saw a shadow behind the king. He winced at the thought of his wizard coming to finish the deed, but it was not Lethe that flung the bucket of pitch onto the back of the undead thing above him. The figure that sparked the flint to kindling and threw it upon Aodh The Terrible was Kayt. The king's flesh went up in flames with acrid, foul smoke.

"Mmmmmm!" Was all Ferdaid heard, and he knew Kayt meant for him to move. Ferdaid rolled out of the way as the corpse reared and spun towards Kayt. Flames licked and climbed the small cottage, catching the roof on fire. Aodh had the glow of Hell about him as he roared at her. Above him, a disembodied face hovered, barely noticeable through the fire, but it was unmistakable. It was the king's wizard, Lethe. Tendrils of fire shot upward to meet ghostly hands that moved like an adept puppeteer.

"Get out of this place!" Ferdaid shouted to Kayt.

She backed out of the burning building, her eyes deep set with vengeance, ever fixed on the king. Ferdaid moved quickly, placing himself between her and the gruesome puppet before him.

"She tasted like honey and milk with a hint of jasmine and pine when I drank her in. Her cunt was as soft and hot as butter!" Aodh the Terrible taunted Ferdaid.

Ferdaid's anger launched him forward with an unholy strength. It fueled his thrust to slice at the king with his sword again, but to no avail. The evil, given rise by magic, would not die that way.

A distant sound had floated up the bluff, haunting and beautiful. It sounded like sea sirens and the rush of the water itself whistling through rocks. The demon king and the wizard both swung their heads in unison towards the direction of the sound. In the distance, old, blind Corr was slowly walking towards them. An eerie glow enveloped her as she smiled sharply, her hands hidden in her cloak.

Aodh lunged towards Ferdaid again and Corr screeched, "Do it now! The seed has been planted! The hero has returned!" Ferdaid reached for the unicorn's horn in the pouch-pocket of his vest, just as Corr pulled four flutes out of her cloak that she had tied together. Lethe's eyes fastened on the carved bones as she lifted the instruments to her lips, calmly blowing into one at a time. The sound that came from the flutes chilled the blood inside Ferdaid, as if his soul might freeze. The monster and the wizard were paralyzed by the magic of the Bonesong.

Ferdaid did not hesitate. He drew forth the pearl horn as it gleamed and vibrated in the waves of sound that pierced his ears. Ferdaid drove the horn through the flaming heart of Aodh The Terrible. The puppet tethers of flame broke as the wizard cried out in agony. The sound waves worked further on them; both the king and Lethe became a mist of embers that slowly drifted down to the ground into soot and dust. It burned the grass wherever the soot found rest.

Kayt fell to her knees sobbing, and Ferdaid went to her. The witch was not far behind.

When Corr reached them, she put a hand on Ferdaid's shoulder and said, "You are the high king now. The true heir of Ulster!"

Ferdaid did not feel like a hero or a king. He felt like a man cradling woe in his arms. The Great Tree he once played in as a child swayed in the distance, rustling its leaves, scattering seeds on the wind. The pearl horn in his hand was now just a gnarled, twisted stick. His destiny was fulfilled, leaving him with nothing but a kingdom that never existed, except in legend and myth. Corr was halfway down the bluff, ambling nimbly for an old, blind crone. She called out to him as she passed out of sight. "There will be a child, my king! It is best you prepare!"

Ferdaid buried his head in Kayt's hair, bringing the stick up to her belly, pausing for a moment, as hatred welled in his heart. The hatred soon passed. He picked her up and carried her away from that place.

"It does not have to be the child's destiny," he whispered to Kayt. "Not the child's and not ours."

He turned down a different path, opposite of the way the witch had gone. They were never seen on Faire Isle again.

UNSAFE (THE BETRAYER)

By Sumiko Saulson

We made him our hope-favored candidate
Games afoot behind the wrought iron gate
Of a clergyman's palatial estate

With shock and awe, we contemplate his vices
The demand he makes, blood sacrifices
Poured into the cogs of his war devices

He lied to us, we have discovered
All the bruises of his lies uncovered
Betrayed us like a cheating lover

He promised to keep us safe
All his promises are broken
Once we slept in his arms
But we have now awoken

Let us not attack direct
But make our moves patiently
Cloak our minds unkindly still
And find the strength to break his will

On a pheromone cloud, we stepped into his lair
Now unsafe in the arms of our lovely betrayer
Seduced by his charms all his harm uninspected
In this place where we face all our errors uncorrected

Betrayer, taste this poisoned blood
Gorge upon me wantonly

Never know you've been entrapped
Til your eyes cloud, too late to see

Here is where he comes to feed
I give myself to him in need
I make myself a sacrifice
Undress me in your church of lies

Take me down to my knees
Make me beg at your feet
Feed me your nectar bittersweet

In your arms kiss my neck
Bite my hands circumspect
Make me pay for my sins
While your harm goes unchecked

Bleed me dry
While emotions run high
Take me down to the ground
For your pie-in-the-sky

As I fall down to my knees
Understand much too late
You took the wrong one to the ground
And with this blood you seal your fate

THE COST OF VICTORY

By Gustavo Bondoni

Bernarda Eztli wiped her forehead with the back of her hand. It came away wet with blood. The body of the treasurer disappeared in a blaze of fire as the ancient magic holding the vampire together gave out leaving only his charred skeleton. She hurled herself through the door, clutching her prize tight against her chest and sprinted through the metal-lined corridor, bolted up the steps two at a time, tossed aside the bodies of two dead guards, and dashed into the foyer.

She skidded to a stop on the marble. "Dammit!"

Lord Miquiztli stood before her, hand outstretched. A dozen guards flanked him. Bernarda turned to see that two more of the armored, plume-helmeted Deathspears cut off her escape.

"I believe that belongs to me, young lady," Miquitzli said with a voice like the desert wind over cactus spines.

"It belongs to my family," Bernarda hissed.

The slightest hint of a smile, as bitter as the emaciated vampire was old, hinted at the edge of his lips. "Your family belongs to me." The smile widened. "And now, so do you. Take her."

She didn't even try to resist. No one resisted the Deathspears.

***

As far as Bernarda could tell, the training complex was in Polanco, the noblest of the regions in Mexico City. Her family—the few of them that survived, hidden from their vampire enemies—insisted that the modern city was an abomination, an atrocity built on the bones of the regal city the Thirteen

Families had ruled for millennia. But Bernarda, barely twenty-five, less than an infant in vampire terms, had grown up a creature of neon-spangled nights and open rooftop bars. She'd heard the stories of the old town and wanted absolutely no part of it.

To her vampire senses, the underground complex smelled of sweat and blood. Not the appetite-inducing charnel house smell of human blood, but that of vampire blood lost in training. Old blood that would only attract those of her kind too ancient to be able to nourish themselves on.
Other odors, less intense but permanent, wafted into her tiny cell. Moist earth. The distant scent of a storm drain. All the little cues that reminded her that she was underground, training for…

For what, she wasn't sure.

She heard a new rumor every day, every time someone disappeared and every time someone new spoke to her, but nobody knew any more than she did.

"Up!" a voice boomed.

Gerardo was one of the Deathspears, a grizzled veteran of a million skirmishes and even of the war against the Conquistadors, a war that was lost on the battlefield, but then won through immortality. The armies of the 13 Houses might have been vanquished, but time allowed the vampires to reposition themselves in the new order.

After all, a musket ball through the heart might make an ignorant Spanish soldier think you were dead, but after he left, any vampire so wounded could simply get up and go about his business.

At least that was what the old ones always said.

"What's on the schedule today?" she asked.

Gerardo cocked his head at her. "Do you know you're the only person in this whole complex that hasn't given me a moment of grief since they arrived? What's wrong with you?"

"I'm not stupid. I know you can kick my ass. I've never been in a fight with another vampire," Bernarda replied.

"You are in here because you orchestrated a raid on House Miquitzli's largest treasure store. You killed two guards and a curator." The Deathspear captain let his look linger on her. "And now you're trying to make me think that you want to lull me into complacency. Which means that's not it either. I know you're up to something. And I'll find out what."

Bernarda made a sudden decision. "What if I told you that I'm being a model prisoner because that way I'll have the best chance to survive. Because I can tell all this training is going somewhere, and I want to do as well as I can in whatever you're building us up for. Because I know what happens to vampires who fail in our compulsory tournaments. I've seen the ceremonial bones."

"Those bones are only from the ones who earned the honor." His voice hardened. "And no one from your clan should have been in the Palace of the Depths to see them."

"So I snuck in on a feast day. Are you going to rat me out?"

Gerardo stiffened. "I'm a Deathspear, not a spy. Get moving."

There was almost no light in the corridor, but that wasn't a problem. She could see in almost pitch dark, in places where cats would be utterly helpless.

The arena, on the other hand, was lit by four torches, one in each corner of the pitch. The yellow, flickering light made the place look forbidding.

Though it had evidently been rebuilt in the high tech underground complex, the field itself was original. Magic emanated from the ancient stones. Even vampires with much less affinity for archaic sorcery would have been hard pressed to miss the pulsing power of the place.

It was also difficult to miss the brown stains on the rectangular altar at one side of the stone arena. Blood—and not all of it human—discolored the eroded block. The field wasn't flat. The middle, perhaps five paces wide, was a long straight section of flagstones. Outside of that, the walls of the playing field were set at an angle. In the center of each lateral wall, a vertical ring of stone was set in the rock.

The trainer wasn't a vampire. He was a gnarled and bent old human with a mustache who glared at her and growled, "Let's see if you can finally understand how to score." He held a ball slightly smaller than a soccer ball. She could smell the human leather from where she stood.

From rumors she'd heard, Bernarda knew that ball was one of the modifications that the vampire overlords had introduced in the game of pok-ta-pok when they stole it from the Mayans. Another, whispered even more surreptitiously, was that the game was inevitably linked to sacrifices. And not always human ones.

The man threw a ball in her direction, waist high.

Instinctively, Bernarda jerked her hips and connected with the ball, sending it on a high arc towards one side. To her complete surprise, it flew straight through the stone ring without touching the sides.

"I did it!" Bernarda said.

"It's about time," the trainer responded. "I've seen humans do it faster."

Bernarda had grown used to the trainer's insults, but the man must have been held in high esteem to have been shown the location of this complex. If his discretion and worth weren't considered absolute, he would have been killed long before.

In the glorious Aztec Empire, before the arrival of men bearing crosses and holy water, the power of the Vampires over the people of Mexico had been absolute. They'd had their every whim attended to and bred an entire race of slaves to do their bidding. No human dared stand in the way of one of the masters. But the Spaniards, far from being cowed, had simply fortified their position and called for reinforcements in the form of a band of black-robed priests. Apparently, these were experts in vampire lore because wherever they went, nightwalkers fell in vast numbers.

Mexico had converted, becoming a country of believers shepherded by the men in black and their legions of successors. The Thirteen Families had had no choice but to retreat into shadow and fight amongst themselves for the vast wealth they'd accumulated as lords of America's largest and most advanced empire.

But the influence of the Catholic Church was slipping. Scandals, materialism and the ever-changing tides of history had weakened the hold traditional religions once had, even in bastions like Mexico.

Which meant that many activities that had been confined to the shadows were coming forward again. The survivors of the inter-clan wars were now in the news, owners of industrial conglomerates, shadowy lords of drug cartels and leaders of powerful political parties.

Even with the sudden openness that prevailed, allowing a mere human to know the secret that the leather for the balls for the great game must be made from the flesh of a young human male, skinned alive, was not something she would ever have thought possible.

And yet, here was this man, his scowl somehow even deeper than before. The trainer watched the ball bounce into the distance, then sighed. He turned back to her. "It appears that determination can be stronger than talent. Or, perhaps I'm simply the greatest teacher of the game of pok-ta-pok to ever walk upon the Earth." He nodded sagely. "Yes. That must be the reason."

"What now?" Bernarda asked.

"Get the ball. If you can do it again, we'll talk."

Fifteen minutes later, the ball went through the ring a

second time.

She laughed delightedly. The trainer frowned.

"Do you think this is a game, young lady?"

She glared at him. "You know what I am?"

"Yes."

"And you dare speak to me that way?"

"I dare. And I dare more than that. Because I know what you are. You are a mere pup, hardly worthy of the name you carry, even if that name is now forsaken. You're not even my own age, and yet attempt to cow me with the glory of vampires a thousand years old?" He sneered, "I dare because without me, you will die. Not of violence because of my absence, but because without me, you will die without achieving glory. You will come to the true arena of which this is a mere shadow and you will fail."

No one needed to tell her that failure and death were synonymous. She replied more respectfully, "So, what's next?"

"You become part of a team. I've had someone chosen for you for some days. But I was half-expecting you to fail to grasp the movements needed before the time came to assign partners."

Bernarda didn't ask what that would have meant. She didn't need to. The trainer clapped, a noise that echoed in the enormous hall. A door at the other side of the chamber opened.

"Bernarda?" The voice was thin, tremulous, young. She knew it well.

"Cuitlahuac," she said. "I told you they'd get you eventually."

The man—still looking like a boy at twenty—actually smirked. "They got you first, though."

She approached the other vampire—a young bastard probably born of a human mother, a woman who'd died in agony as the beast within crawled out, fully intelligent and aware, and who would never have been content to feed on mother's milk—and hugged him with more emotion than she expected. A familiar face, even that of someone she'd always seen as a slightly ridiculous inferior, was an unexpected pleasure.

"Enough," the trainer said. "You will be facing the best players of this game to emerge in five hundred years. Perhaps the teams are as nothing compared to the glorious players of old, but some will have innate talent that both of you lack. Every team will be playing to survive and to achieve the highest honor. If you want to live long enough to play for that. You will need to get to work."

The training to that point had been nothing, merely basic preparation, honing her superhuman strength and reflexes to perform the unnatural movements of the game. Now she understood why. Any imbecile—even a human—could strike a ball with their foot, or throw it with their hand, but to put a ball through the little stone ring, one of which was set high above the pitch itself, by hitting it only with your hip while another team was doing their best to give you bad angles, that took a vampire.

It was strange to think that people who saw the fields and the rings displayed in museums had not realized the sport was incompatible with human limitations.

The training proved that beyond any doubt.

Vampires don't sweat. Vampires don't need to sleep.

But they can, after uninterrupted nights of rigorous training, feel a weariness deep within the unholy bones of their bodies, a pain that mere mortals couldn't imagine.

It took her a few days to understand why the trainer had chosen Cuitlahuac as her partner. She expected a virtuoso, a man who could score through the ring from any position, with the ball coming in at any angle. Instead, he had even more trouble attacking the ring than she did. She found herself being the one that brought greater skill to the table.

But not for long. Bernarda's great strength was her

relentlessness. However, where Bernarda would try a hundred times, Cuitlahuac would try a thousand. He was indomitable, refusing to quit, refusing to rest. Stopping wasn't an option. He forced Bernarda to match his intensity.

They improved. And when they felt they could beat all comers, the trainer came back in, accompanied by several workmen with heavy equipment.

"You are doing very well," the trainer said as the men unbolted the rings. "And now, we will use the goals as vampires do."

The rings, which had been set close to the ground, were repositioned ten feet in the air.

The trainer looked at them with satisfaction. "Now you know why the fields had two goals. The lower levels were so that the humans could imitate their gods. But the games that matter have always been, and will always be, played in the upper goals."

Just like that, much of their progress evaporated and they had to start over, adjusting their play and their tactics to the new position. Again, Bernarda managed to learn faster, but soon, Cuitlahuac's sheer force of will had him working at her level.

Gerardo returned. "Go to your cells. You'll be called when it's time to play," the Deathspear informed them. "Expect to wait three days."

"We need more practice," Bernarda protested.

"You need to rest," the aged trainer said. "You won't improve enough in three days to make much difference. But the rest. It will work wonders."

Bernarda wanted to argue, but Gerardo's expression convinced her not to try. "All right."

✳✳✳

Bernarda was in deep sleep, that state in which vampires could heal after a battle or other rigors. The three days passed.

Suddenly, a loud knock at the door of her cell startled her out of her sleep. She jumped into a defensive crouch.

"It's time," Greardo said. "Put this on."

A bundle of clothes, red and green, landed on the stone floor beside her, and the Deathspear turned away. She stripped down to her underwear and then realized that the attire she'd been given consisted only of a sort of loincloth of the kind she'd seen the Royal Guards wear for ceremonial occasions.

It took her a few moments to figure out how to tie it, and another couple of moments to build up the courage to abandon her panties and bra, but she wasn't going to fall at this hurdle. Not after all she'd been through.

"You can turn around now," she said.

Gerardo looked approvingly at her attire. "Now, you look like a real vampire." He pulled a small clay pot, about the size of his fist, from the depths of his robes and handed it to her. "Use it sparingly."

Gingerly, she removed the tightly clamped lid. The smell of earth and blood and spices and paint reminded her of childhood. Her mother had showed her a pot like this one once: sacred unguent.

"This…" she began.

"This is a sign of my favor. I've overseen dozens of dissidents in training, and an equal number of loyalists who volunteered for the honor. None of them deserved to be here as much as you do."

Bernarda dipped her finger into the thick salve and placed three stripes on her face, two below her eyes and one running up from the bridge of her nose to her hairline.

Gerardo nodded in approval. "I knew I made the right choice. A worthy design. Humble but unafraid."

He led her through tunnels which opened into a parking garage and then an elevator where Cuitlahuac joined them, dressed in a loincloth of the same color as hers. He did a double-take when he saw—and more importantly, smelled—the lines on her face.

The elevator finally opened onto a black tunnel that ended in a tiny chamber with windows tinted just enough to keep the fierce daylight at bay. They sat on black leather seats and the door to the tunnel closed behind them. She thought they'd been put into a small, extremely luxurious mini-bus with the passenger compartment completely sealed from the driver.

A roar shook the little room, sound and fury and vibration.

"Helicopter," Gerardo shouted needlessly.

They rode for about twenty-five minutes before the aircraft descended.

"Stay away from that door until I tell you to," Gerardo said. "It's noon out there."

A clanging noise from outside was followed by four raps in succession. Gerardo opened the door.

Another tunnel had been attached to the side of the helicopter.

"Where are we?" Cuitlahuac asked.

"If you can't figure that out for yourself, you might not have been the best choice for this," Gerardo said.

"Choice? I was arrested for protesting the Miquiztli Cartel."

"It's Teotihuacan," Bernarda said. "We're going to the ceremonial fields under the Pyramid of the Moon."

Gerardo nodded. "An enormous honor."

Teotihuacan was one of the largest tourist attractions in Mexico, but tourists were never allowed into the sacred fields beneath. The curators of this section were all vampires. Old ones. Even an outcast from a forsaken clan like Bernarda's knew that.

She felt the energy, the hum of voices long before the stone corridor had finished its descent into the bowels of the earth. There were more vampires in there than she'd ever sensed in one place.

The field was exactly like the one they'd been practicing in, but instead of ending at the walls, there was an arena above, lit only by four torches hanging from chains in the center of the playing field. Air currents moved in the enormous space, causing the flames to sputter and flare.

Cuitlahuac and Bernarda waited. They'd been presented first, which meant they were the less important team. The crowd observed in silence as they awaited to learn whether the training had been a cruel hoax and that they were to be sacrificed without ceremony.

Bernarda breathed a sigh of relief as two figures walked into the arena.

Then she tensed. She didn't know who the young man on the other team was, but she knew Silvana. Silvana was bad news. She was a little princess from the Yaoyotl clan. She hadn't been arrested. She was there because she wanted whatever honor was available. And she would have had the best teachers gold could buy.

Without warning, a ball fell from the sky. Bernarda smelled it before she saw it. It smelled like freshly tanned human leather.

She didn't stop to think. She ran to where it would fall and put her hip out.

A single strike sent it through the ring.

A deep gong sounded, the reverberations echoing throughout the dark space.

Strike and counterstrike, but it soon became evident that, though the opposing team were slightly faster and stronger, they just didn't work well enough together to have a real chance; when things got difficult.

When horns sounded up above, Bernarda and Cuitlahuac were up by five goals.

"Contestants, face your judgement," a voice boomed from the stands. It was a voice of power, a command that no vampire or human could disobey. It was the voice of the highest of the

Blood. Helplessly, Bernarda fell to her knees and pressed her forehead against the flagstones of the arena.

Footsteps, heavy and ominous pounded the stones. She saw feet in the war sandals of the Deathspears. Piercing cries and the iron smell of vampire blood filled the air, followed by a muffled grunts.

"Rise," the voice said.

Bernarda and Cuilahuac stood to see their opponents lying dead in pools of their own blood, expertly staked through the back in a way certain to pierce their hearts. She watched in horror as their bodies turned to bones and ash.

"You have earned a single string," the voice said. One of the Deathpears held out a bracelet of blue beads to her and Cuitlahuac. "Retire to await your next match."

The Deathspears marched them into a chamber with a stone bench. They waited in silence, sharing none of the banter they'd enjoyed during training. What could they say to one another? They had to keep winning to survive.

Hours passed before the sound of marching feet reached them again.

"It's time," a Deathspear told them.

They returned to the arena, and again arrived before their opponents.

They're more scared than we are, Bernarda thought. Though the other team also wore the blue beads of a winner, they walked unsteadily, clearly frightened of what would happen if they lost. *Our advantage is that we thought we were dead meat as soon as they caught us.*

The match's progression reflected the first with Bernarda and Cuitlahuac pulling into the lead. The woman on the opposing team jumped forward to block the ball.

"Please," she said in a whisper that only Bernarda could hear. "You're prisoners too. *Please.*"

Bernarda didn't reply, and the young woman cried and

begged most shamefully when it was time to meet her end.

The following four matches progressed similarly, and though it was obvious that some teams had greater skill than they did, the way Cuitlahuac and Bernarda played together brought them through often by the slimmest of margins. They accumulated beads, but were never introduced first.

After five bouts, they arrived in the arena to find a bright bonfire in the center of the pitch, and their opponents being marched in at the same time.

"This is the call to glory," the voice from above said. "To the winner shall fall eternal rewards. Play well."

The ball was falling even as he spoke. The hush grew even deeper.

Bernarda knew they were in for a desperate fight. The team across from them, composed—as they all were—by a young man and a woman played not only with skill and coordination, but with a desperation that none of the others seemed to be able to bring forth, not even after they learned what befell the losers.

The enemy played so well that the only way to keep them from scoring was to land the ball on their side of the court at difficult angles and with unfavorable spin. That was Cuitlahuac's specialty, so when a ball arrived that they would obviously not be able to shoot towards the ring. When a fa-vorable one bounced their way, she would take the shot.

Unfortunately, if she missed, it gave the opponents an easy strike. This round was limited to only three goals. Bernarda knew how important this final shot was if she and Cuitlahauc were to win. So, when a low ball bounced their way, a ball she would normally never have attempted a shot with, she yelled: "I've got it!"

Cuitlahuac almost almost went for the ball, and she had to shoulder him aside as she slid desperately along the stones and managed to get a hip onto the ball. She thought something had wrenched inside her, but the savage twist she gave was the only way to give enough force to the ball.

The ball was too low to attempt to get a decent arc, so she banked it off the slope, and against the wall, a panic-driven shot if ever there was one. But it bounced just high enough to roll over the vertical inner lip of the ring.

The trumpets sounded before the ball hit the ground, before the gong finished marking the score, and both teams looked up to see what would happen now.

Did I just kill all four of us? Bernarda asked herself.

A man in ceremonial robes walked into the pitch and picked up the ball. He disappeared into the stands.

"Play!" the voice thundered, and Bernarda smelled the ball descending again.

It was about to land almost in the center of the pitch, just to the left of the bonfire. Bernarda attempted to reach it to bank it into a difficult corner, but her opponent reached the ball first and placed a wonderful shot into the back of the court, with spin that made the return shot impossible. Cuitlahuac did his best, giving a quick twist and bouncing the ball against two corners to return it. The move was skilled, but not good enough. The second bank and the spin dropped the ball into the center of the court. The woman on the other team actually smiled as she took the easy shot and put it through the ring.

The gong and the trumpets sounded at the same time. Bernarda's heart fell.

"Kneel to receive your due," the voice said, and all four contestants, winners as well as losers, prostrated themselves.

She was determined not to embarrass herself as she'd seen so many of her opponents do, and also certain that by trying to fight she'd just lose any honor she'd gained from getting this far. Bernarda bit her lip, awaiting the sharp stab of the stake between her shoulder blades.

Strangely, Cuitlahuac's stoic silence beside her made her prouder than his performance on the field. Theirs was the only doomed team to face their fates completely silently, as vampires should.

"Winners rise," the voice said.

Bernarda lifted her head just enough to see that the man and woman who'd doomed them stood to receive a ceremonial headdress. The Deathspears around them knelt in deep respect and Bernarda gasped: she'd never seen Deathspears kneel to anyone, not even to Lord Miquiztli.

Then, suddenly, the same royal guards got up from their crouch and grabbed the winners by the arm. Bernarda heard their protests, growing more alarmed as they were dragged to one side of the playing field.

"The highest honor a Vampire can attain has been earned today. Now it shall be imparted to the victors."

"No, please! We won! It's not fair!" The man screamed.

There was always one of the two who couldn't face their fate. But the screams soon turned to gurgles, and the pitch suddenly became crowded. The spectators had decided to come for their portion of blood as the young vampires—too young to know what the games had meant—gave their lives to the vampire lords who'd organized the pok-ta-pok.

And still, the death from above didn't come. Bernarda barely dared breathe, hoping that they'd simply be forgotten.

"And what should we do about you two?" a voice said.

"You can rise." Lord Miquiztli, red eyes glowing from the massive infusion of young vampire blood, stood before them, surrounded by his guards. "You played very well to make it this far. You displayed more teamwork than anyone else if, perhaps, not as much talent. And then you managed to keep your honor in the face of certain death. It's depressing, really."

"Depressing?" Bernarda asked, managing to find her voice. She supposed it meant their reprieve was over, that Lord Miquiztli was lamenting the talent that would be lost.

"Most depressing. That damnable Gerardo is always right.

He marked you for greatness." The overlord pointed at her forehead. "And he was right. I'm going to have to kill him soon. Either that or make him a general before he comes for my job." Miquiztli shrugged. "But then, everyone is after my job. Have been for three hundred years. How would you to like to go into training?"

"As what?"

"Deathspears." Lord Miquiztli said.

"Deathspears killed most of my family," Bernarda replied.

"I'm aware of that. I sent them, after all. My question is whether you prefer to go into training as Deathspears or die here in forgotten ignominy."

"I'll train," Cuitlahuac said in a quiet voice.

"Very good." Lord Miquiztli's red eyes turned to her. They seemed to pulse and glow.

"I'll train too," Bernarda replied. "But I'll be coming for you."

Lord Miquiztli laughed, an evil sound. "You have no idea how many people you will have to go through to get to the front of that line. But I will be delighted to watch you attempt to progress if you do your duty in the meantime."

The ancient vampire turned and left. Every Deathspear, including the two newly appointed novices watched him leave, greed and envy in their eyes.

MIDNIGHT SUN

By John Palisano

I was an unlikely target for Lindsay Taylor. Everyone knew it. She'd come back to Whistleville a year after soaring the highest of heights with her music. Back to the high school she went to. A triumphant return. A victory lap. Who wouldn't be envious? I know I was. I sure hoped that one day, I, too, would end up doing something equally impressive through my writing. Sure, I was good on guitar, and could get through most of the Korn songs without thinking. I liked the '90s Grunge era, and earlier punk material. But Maddie, our singer, kept insisting we do more Katy Perry stuff. I love Katy Perry. She's cute. It's just that I wanted to do our own stuff, and find our own sound, while Maddie wanted to be Katy. That is, until Lindsay made it big. Once that happened? Maddie and everyone else wanted to be Lindsay. Not me.

I retreated back inside my books, and instead of writing songs, I wrote essays and short stories. No one wanted to change my stories to be more like someone else's. They were mine, and that was beyond fine. Our band, Ghost Soul, kept going, but we played less often. Maddie had picked up acoustic guitar and was doing more singer-songwriter stuff. Just like Lindsay.

"How you doing, brother?" That's what Nick always said. Everyone was his brother, it seemed. That was his way of trying to make you feel extra-special, I guess.

I shrugged and said, "Fine like wine." I could see my breath, which reminded me of smoking. My uncle told me everyone used to smoke everywhere. Sounds crazy to think about.

"Cool. You going to the assembly?" Nick popped some of

his Mountain Dew White Out back. He always got the same thing, and with only fifteen minutes between periods, our time outside was precious. He chose a sugar fix. I chose fresh air and looking at something that wasn't the boring school.

"I don't know," I said. "We can go to the library or the lunchroom instead, they said. I can work on stuff."

He shoved me a little. "Come on, Del," he said. "Life's short. You've got to see Lindsay Taylor, if only to see if her legs are really that long."

I shrugged. "Meh. I know what girls look like. I know what she looks like. She's all over social media. It's annoying."

"Well, I'm going," he said. "I think you'll regret not going. You'll have a story to tell."

"Already got plenty of those," I said. "Just need the time to write them all down."

***

So you're probably wondering how do we go from point A to point B here? How did some introverted, slightly grumpy little artistic teen ever become a blip on Lindsay Taylor's radar? Turns out she was looking for a guy with a brain she could pick because she was looking for something new, something authentic. She saw me as market research. But I'm getting ahead of myself here. Let's talk about what happened when Lindsay first showed up at the school.

She pulled up in a pink limousine. Lindsay even had an entourage of four police cars with her, not to mention a couple other vehicles. Anyone on the south side of the building could see and hear her. Those on the other side soon caught wind and rushed over, much to the useless hollering of the teachers who tried to continue their classes.

Maddie leaned in to me. "I'm going to get some tips from her," she said. She looked down at my Sex Pistols shirt and rolled her eyes. She'd grown increasingly hostile toward the bands I loved. It'd only be a matter of time until she'd be done with Ghost Soul. Change was inevitable.

I'll give Maddie that much: had she not gotten me angry, there was every chance I was going to blow off Lindsay Taylor's homecoming and probably sit in the library or something equally blissfully introverted.

When our class left for the assembly, I made sure to keep next to Maddie. She wasn't thrilled at the prospect, I'm pretty sure. Which was fine. I just wanted to watch her reaction and hope like hell Lindsay didn't call her up or anything like that.

When we got to the auditorium, folks were talking really loudly. It was a lot like the lunchroom. Everyone could speak freely. No raising hands or waiting turns. Our class founds its row, which was surprisingly close. I hated it. I'd rather have been in the back

Mrs. Rogers took the stage. She said a little something about Lindsay having been one of our own and that she wanted to do something special for the school as thanks. Mrs. Rogers was off stage as quickly as she had been on.

Lindsay walked out.

The school went nuts. I clapped, too. So sue me. It was exciting. On top of that? Lindsay looked gorgeous. Much more so than online or television. I wouldn't be honest if I left out how attractive I suddenly found her. This made me run through a hundred emotions. I dug her, then thought she was the type that would never date a guy like me. That stung. I looked over at Maddie. She was beaming. That made me mad. I didn't want to hear her yapping about the show endlessly for the next few weeks.

Lindsay said, "Hi Whistleville High." Someone brought out her signature red acoustic guitar. The one with the kitten eating a rainbow popsicle painted on the side. She strummed a few chords. Everyone around me seemed to recognize the song.

If you were born to run down this lonely road

What do you want in this old hotel?
A bottle of whisky on the short nightstand
I think I might hit the bar, and check out the band

She had a slight country accent to her singing voice. I wondered where it came from. I vaguely recalled a story of her growing up in Tennessee before her mom became a Democrat and moved the family up north, minus the dad. When she first came to Whistleville High, I'd heard, she was an outcast, but had quickly won people's hearts.

I was born in America wrapped in red, white, and blue
Just 'cuz I'm a country girl don't mean I can't sing the blues
You've gotta fight if you wanna win anything
Some people want to play, I just want to sing...
I was born in America

I figured the song must have been some kind of a hit for her. I hadn't heard it, but I thought it was bad that she rhymed 'blue' with 'blues' and had two Springsteen references in the same song. Whatever.

She went on, and by the end, it seemed everyone was singing the chorus.

I was born in America
Born in America

I sang along, too, although I changed the words to, "I was bored in America" and pumped my fists.

She strummed the last chord real fast, as if she had Greta Van Fleet behind her, doing one of their trademark song finales, only it was her all by herself. She whistled, then said, "Hoo, that was amazing, Whistleville. Love you," with all the practiced sincerity of an overseas tech support representative. "Well, now, y'all listen up. It was only a few years ago that I was dreaming of one day being a singer and making it to the big time. I swore to everyone that I'd be back, and I'd help other people if that happened. I'm going to do that today."

Lindsay paced the stage. "Hm," she said. "I'm hoping to have one of y'all come on up here and play a song with me. Who will it be?" She went to the other side of the stage. People went crazy, raising their hands, screaming her name. "Who has the most passion? The most creativity?"

I looked over and I swear Maddy's head was about to explode. I hated her enthusiasm. I'm not sure why, but I found it endlessly irritating. She was so not cool enough to be in our band.

This? This is what she was finally getting pumped for? I thought. *Freakin' traitor.*

To spite her, I raised my hand, jumped up and down, smiling ear to ear, and tried to get in front of Maddie. Lindsay came over to our side. I swear to God our eyes met right then. She checked me out for a second. My heart raced. A second later, though, I was relieved when her gaze fell on others. She was gorgeous and charismatic, no doubt about it, but I wasn't about to sell myself out because of it.

Lindsay went to the back of the stage, and conferred with a man, who didn't look much older than any of us. She made gestures with her hands. She spoke in a highly animated manner. The crowd hooted, hollered, and screamed her name. Then she stood back, turned around, and faced us. The man made his way to the lip of the stage. He went to the far side, his finger pointed to the ceiling.

Folks went insane.

He came our way.

Lowered his finger.

Made his way...

Lowered the finger even more...

Until...

It looked just like he was pointing at me.

I quickly looked around. Had to be someone in back of me going crazy. Someone next to me.

He came out into the crowd, his finger still pointed right at me. The crowd parted, and he came right up to me.

Had to be a prank.

Had to be.

No way.

Then he pointed right at me.

All the fluid in my mouth drained out and my heart raced a trillion beats a second.

No. No. No. Not me.

"Hey, man," he said. "You play guitar?"

"Yeah," I said, my voice higher pitched than I'd hoped. I lowered it. "Yes."

"Then come on up!" He grabbed my elbow. "Lindsay wants to jam with you."

"What?"

I looked over to Maddie. She nodded. "Go," she mouthed. Even though she looked disappointed, she still smiled. I instantly felt bad. It should have been her. Not me.

In a flash, I found myself up on the stage being walked over to Lindsay. She was smiling ear to ear. She shook my hand. "Hi," she said, over the din. "Nice to meet you."

I shook her hand. "My name's Del," I said. Her hands were ice cold.

"Hi, Del," she said. "Do you know 'Arrow in My Heart' off the first album?"

"I think so," I lied. "Do you play it in A minor?" I lied some more.

She nodded. "Sure."

Her Consigliere was right there, handing me her famous guitar. I strapped it on.

I'm never going to be able to live this down.

Lindsay put her arm in mine. "Come on," she said. Her voice was like honey. I felt exactly like I thought being a Prom King with the prettiest girl in school might feel like. She was so tall, too. I couldn't look up at the crowd because I was so nervous. I followed her footsteps.

Her legs are so long, I thought. *Wow. It's not just an illusion on television. Crazy.*

When we got to the front of the stage, I finally looked up at the crowd. The entire school was staring at us. I wanted to go to the bathroom and throw up. I suddenly realized why some bands wore make-up, to hide behind. Being up there in front of so many people was as terrifying as it was exhilarating. Now what was going to happen? Lindsay let me go, and I felt like I was cut loose.

No. Keep holding me. Crap. I'll be alone if you do.

But she had, and I was left standing next to her with her acoustic guitar, and no idea how to play the song she'd mentioned.

"Do you all know Del?" she asked the crowd.

They went crazy.

What? Like five people knew who I was.

"He's going to play a little six string on 'Arrow in My Heart' if y'all don't mind?"

Of course, they went crazy again.

She turned to me, that celebrity smile sucking me in. Off-mic, she said, "You ready?"

"Yeah," I said. "Do your thing. A minor."

She nodded. I nodded.

I looked down at the acoustic guitar. Realized I didn't have a pick. Took out my wallet right there in front of everyone, pulled out a pick, because I always kept some there, and put my wallet back in my pocket.

"Is Del too cool, or what?" she asked. "This man is

prepared."

Another jubilant response.

Without further delay, I strummed the only thing I could think of under all that pressure: the opening chords to "Plush" from Stone Temple Pilots.

Lindsay was taken aback, her smile barely fading, but with all the credit in the world, she went into her own lyrics, singing along with me.

I had no idea what I was doing. I'd only ever learned the beginning of that song, so I strummed chords, trying to hear what she was singing, trying to anticipate her next verse or chorus.

A quote ran through my mind. Johnny Ramone, I think. "With rock n' roll, fake it 'til you make it, man."

So I did, leaning into it, grooving, striking poses like I was in the Ramones or the Blackhearts. I had nothing to lose. We were already into it, so might as well make 'em think I knew what I was doing. Just as I was getting into it, Lindsay stopped singing and raised her chin up, universal singer-language for wrap this up sucker. I did just like she had done, made an open E chord, and strummed it like the ending of an AC/DC song.

Lindsay grabbed one of my hands. "I want to talk to you after," she said.

Oh, no. I was going to get a scolded for messing up her gig. Shoot.

In a blink, her Consigliere lifted her acoustic off me, and I was ushered back into the audience.

"Let's hear it for Del," Lindsay said.

Back at my seat, everyone grabbed me and high-fived me and went crazy. Maddie waved at me. She looked genuinely proud. That threw me for a loop.

We settled down as Lindsay sat in a chair on the stage and took questions. I don't recall much after that. I was still high as heck after playing on stage.

Someone asked her, "How's it feel getting to play with a rockstar like our own Del Howard?"

Everyone went nuts. Lindsay laughed. "He is exquisite," she said. "That was a wonderful interpretation. It was like a remix or something." She looked right at me then. "Don't forget to come talk to me after the show, mister."

That brought lots of catcalls.

Then she was off, the curtains shut, and we got up to go back to our regular old curriculums.

There was a tap on my shoulder.

It was him: the Consigliere. "Del?" he asked. "Would you mind just coming with us for a few minutes. The principal knows. It's fine."

"Okay," I said. "Sure."

Everyone stared at me as I was ushered through the crowd toward the door that led to the back of the theater. That was exciting, but all I kept thinking about was how Lindsay was going to cuss me out for messing up her song and screwing around.

When we got through the door, there were lots of people milling about. I recognized a few teachers. Way in back, behind the curtains, near a folding table with lots of snacks and drinks laid out, stood Lindsay. She looked a little out of it and stared blankly at the food. She must have sensed me coming because she turned and almost immediately that celebrity polished grin spread wide across her face.

"There's my rockstar," she said. "Del."

She came over to me and gave me a big hug.

"Sorry," I said. "I think I froze up there. Couldn't remember what the chords were."

Lindsay laughed. "I thought it was great," she said. "You kept me on my toes, that's for sure. Everyone loved it. You did great."

All I could muster were a half-hearted, "okay" and an "all right", before she changed the subject.

"So tell me: what's the deal with the band on your shirt?"

I looked down. "Oh. The Sex Pistols. One of the best punk bands ever."

"What makes them one of the best?" she asked.

"They're loud. Rude. Angry. Raw. Really raw," I said. "Almost primal."

"Oo," she said. "I need to hear them. Where should I start?"

"My favorite song is 'Holidays in The Sun," I said. "They only have one real album, though."

"What made you play guitar?" Lindsay asked.

"Lots of things," I said. "Just something to do, I guess."

"You're pretty good. Do you have a band?"

"I think so."

She laughed at that. "I get it. It's High School. Do you know that U2 started in high school?"

I shook my head. "I did not know that."

"So you never know," she said. "Well, look, I'm not going to take up any more of your time, but I did have a little something for you as thanks." She gestured to her Consigliere, who stepped over and handed her a CD. She, in turn, handed it to me.

I looked at it. It was already signed.

To Del-
A future rock star!
XX OO Lindsay Taylor

"Take care now, hon," she said, and gave me a big hug. She smelled like sugar.

We broke, and the Consigliere brought me over to a small table. "We just need you to sign a little release form, if that's okay."

"A what?"

"Just something that lets us use the footage of you with Lindsay today if we choose," he said.

"Sure."

Once I was done, he walked me out. I looked around to try and see Lindsay again one last time, but she'd vanished.

It was back to the real world for me.

***

Right about now, you're probably wondering where the scary stuff is, right? What's making this story something more than just a guy who got to jam with a rockstar once upon a time?

So why don't we skip to the good part, then? You can imagine Maddie and my band were thrilled. She freaked out over the signed CD. They asked me a million questions. The band started playing again. Maddie tried to get me to figure out what I'd done with Lindsay on 'Born in America' so we could cover it. Despite us watching the TikTok video a hundred times, it never was quite the same. Maddie was no Lindsay Taylor. It was fun, though, to play with them. And when we played Steve Wilson's basement birthday party, well, it seemed the whole school was crammed down in there. You can guess what our encore was.

Life went along with me feeling like I was parasailing day and night.

Suddenly I received an unexpected text…

Hi, sweet Del. It's Lindsay. You should come visit me! I need some inspiration!

My first thought was that it was Maddie. She'd gotten a new number and was playing trick on me.

Is this Maddie?

A moment later. *Who's Maddie? No. It's me, Lindsay. Come hang out with me!*

I responded, *Is this really Lindsay? Are you in town?*

Yes! I'm in Vegas, baby!

That's the other side of the country! I replied.

I can take care of that. Can you come this weekend?

I couldn't resist. *If this is real, and not some joke, then yes!*

No joke, hon! I'll have William call you in a SEC! She replied.

Moments later my phone rang. It was William, her Consigliere. "I'll have a car at your place Friday at 3:30. Would that work?"

"Sure," I said. "What do I need?"

"Pack a small bag. Everything else will be taken care of," he said.

It was Wednesday, and I couldn't wait. My thoughts were filled with her. I Googled her. I watched her videos and awards show appearances, and studied all of her social media. I was obsessed. I couldn't help but think that maybe...just maybe...she was interested in me beyond just messing up one of her songs. Maybe she thought I was cute? Maybe she wanted me to be her boyfriend? I imagined myself walking red carpets on her arm, going to movie premiers, having dinners with famous people like Austin Butler Felt and Cardi B. Maybe I'd tour in her band as her guitarist? Then I could be famous, too.

The hardest thing in the world was keeping it to myself. Of course, I had to tell my folks, who, surprisingly, seemed pretty indifferent. "If you're going to have sex with that girl, please protect yourself, Delbert," my mom said.

"I hate when you use that name for me," I said. "And I think she wants to write songs."

"In Las Vegas? Just leave us the number," she said, shaking her head.

Weren't they afraid something was going to happen to their son? Didn't they find it the least bit odd? And why weren't they even excited for me? My mom said she'd told my dad, but I barely ever saw him. He was always at work, or sleeping, or watching football on TV.

Fine, I thought. *Whatever. At least they're not making it hard on me.*

***

A limousine pulled up outside of my house that Friday. I couldn't believe it. If it were a joke, it was an expensive one, which pretty much counted out my friends. The driver got out, asked my name, opened the door, and I sat inside. It was just me. There was an iPad with a red ribbon on it on the seat next to me. There was a small note attached.

To Del, love Lindsay! Please fill this with all your creative dreams and share them with me!

The trip was already off to an amazing start.

It seemed like we got to JFK airport in no time. We got to a curb, and I was dropped off at the entrance to the United Airlines terminal. The driver said, "Just show your ID at the counter. You're good to go. Have a good time." He put his fingers to the side of his hat and bowed just a little. Then he was off. I wondered why her Consigliere wasn't returning with me to her. I turned and walked through the sliding doors and up to the counter. Before I knew it I was rushed through security as if I was myself a celebrity and sitting in my first class seat. I'd brought a book about Kurt Cobain to read, but the iPad beckoned.

Lindsay had asked in her note that I fill it with creative ideas. Her and I both being musicians, I typed in some ideas I had right away.

Classic rock meets new country. Grunge covers album, with acoustic country instruments. Imagine 'Smells Like Teen Spirit' done at the Grand Ole Opry. Or 'Alive' by Pearl Jam with a ripcord hootenanny group.

That actually sounded like a fun record and was kind of like what we'd done up on stage. Of course, I thought of myself front and center helping her pick the songs, and conducting with my acoustic guitar, Lindsay smiling at me, beaming, maybe even wearing a ring.

Stop thinking like that, I thought. Come on. Take this for what it is. Just have fun.

The other part of me thought I should eek every ounce of whatever I could out of what was happening, and that I should get ready because opportunities like Lindsay Taylor inviting you out only happened once in a lifetime.

The jet took off. It was so fast I couldn't believe it. Once we hit cruising altitude, I looked out the window at the world below. Large patches of white covered most of the landscape. It was so gorgeous. My mind wandered, wondering what it was going to be like in Las Vegas.

✳✳✳

"Prepare for landing."

I slowly came out of my nap. I rubbed my eyes, yawned, and looked around. No one was remotely interested in me, thank heavens. Outside the window, I saw the desert for the first time. Just ahead, like a mirage, I saw the towering casinos coming into focus. It reminded me very much of something that maybe Tim Burton would have dreamt up. Just didn't seem real. Not one itsy bit.

When we departed the plane, as soon as I got in the tunnel leading out of the plane's cabin, the heat hit me. At first I thought it had to just be exhaust from the jet, but I overheard someone saying it was a hundred and five degrees.

I realized I had no instructions as to what to do when I landed. I assumed Camp Lindsay would have something prepared but wasn't sure. Maybe it was a joke after all? Maybe someone had tricked me and I was on my way to my permanent resting place seven feet below the Mojave Desert. How could I have been so stupid?

My fears were quickly dissipated when I spotted a man holding a sign with my name on it. He recognized me right away. Another driver, only this time we were in a town car instead of a limo.

The airport was only a couple of miles from the main strip. The casinos were off the hook. One of them looked like a miniature New York City, and another looked like a small Paris. A volcano erupted. There were huge TV screens all over the place showing loops of glamorous people doing magic acts and dancing, and then I saw one of them that had Lindsay on it, strumming her famous acoustic guitar, the one I'd played. I'll admit I felt seriously starstruck.

"This is it," the driver said.

We'd pulled up to a massive hotel that looked like a cross between a cruise ship and a gothic nightclub. When I got out, I saw its name: The Fountain. I couldn't figure out why they'd chosen that name. It didn't look like a fountain. It looked like a ship turned on its side with everything shiny and black. It was really weird.

"Go on and check in with the concierge," the driver said.

I made my way inside. The lobby was massive. I could have fit my whole house inside with room to spare. There were men and women standing at attention. They reminded me of anime characters: they all had black, straight razor-cut hair, and they all had on black outfits with buckled pockets and black hardware. None of them looked happy. I was intimidated to go up to any of them.

Finally, worked up the nerve to approach one of them, "Where's the concierge?"

The fellow said, "We are all Concierge. How can I help you?" He didn't look the least bit interested in helping me.

"I need to check in, I guess," I said.

He pulled out a small phone, asked my name, nodded, then walked me to an elevator. He went inside with me. He pressed the topmost button, then tapped a code into the screen. What followed was the fastest elevator ride I'd ever had. Made my stomach flip flop.

The doors opened, and there was another very ornate door in front of me. It looked like something out of a steampunk comic if steampunk had originated in hell. There were metal tubes that looked like veins. There were all kinds of skulls on the door, none of them human, all cast in black anodized metal. There was a handle, and a knocker, both made from what I believed were vertebrae. I turned, but the elevator had closed. I hadn't even heard it. Then I turned round again and reached for the knocker. I was pretty sure it was going to come to life and rip my hand off.

I took a breath.

Clasped my hand around it, knocked twice, then pulled my hand back like it was on fire.

Within a moment, I heard, "Give me a sec, hon." Lindsay.

The door opened.

She was radiant. Her cheeks were flushed. Her eyes sparkled in that way that didn't seem real. Her smile was wide. Her hands were on her hips, her long, sharp red nails nearly touching the center of her tiny waist. "There's my little rockstar," she said. "Come on in, love."

Was this really happening?

She took me by the wrist, and I felt her nails scrape against my skin. I felt a shiver through my body, which I chalked up to the extremely high air conditioning. Lindsay walked me to the couch, which seemed like it was made of freezing cold leather as I sat down on it. She sat next to me.

"So good to see you," she said, and threw her arms around me. "You are so talented. We had such a great connection. I'm so happy you came. It's nice to have a friend from Whistleville out here. It's so cold."

"No worries. You know they said it was over a hundred degrees outside."

"I know. That's the problem. I'm locked in these rooms all

the time. I can't just go outside anymore like I used to. Not without an entourage and security." She put a hand on the side of my head. "So what have you been working on?"

"I had a few ideas."

"Great. Care to share?"

"I think a grunge country album would be great. You're known as a country singer, and grunge was like our classic rock, you know?"

She looked upward. "Hmm," she said. "That's kind of like what we did, right? You played something from one of those songs. Then played more in that style. It definitely worked with the words."

"Right. So imagine a record where you cover ..."

She put up a finger. "I don't do covers, hon," she said. "I write my own songs. That way I get publishing."

"Makes sense," I said.

"I got that Sex Pistols record you mentioned. Holiday In the Sun. I loved it. So I wanted to give you a holiday out in the sun, away from the cold New England weather for a little bit."

"Thank you," I said. "That's so amazing of you. Man it is cold in here, though."

She laughed, and her eyes glistened like they were made of glass. "Well, I could make it warmer, but then my hair would get frizzy, and my nails might crack. We don't want that."

"Of course not," I said.

"We are going to a show in a bit," she said. "You want to go?"

"I hope it's better than the ones at Whistleville high," I said.

Lindsay laughed again. "I'm sure it is, Del."

✳✳✳

Afterward, Lindsay had a tricked-out JEEP waiting, and I was surprised she made her way to the wheel. "It's going to be just you and me, buddy," she said.

I was confused. Where was her entourage, her security?

"Where are we going?" I asked.

I climbed in. Her nails made it so she could barely wrap her hands around the wheel. "Out there."

"Out there" ended up being outside the city in the desert. We got on a highway, the only one I saw, and soon Vegas was in our rearview. There were no lights, other than ours and those of other passing cars.

Lindsay didn't seem to realize driving a hundred miles an hour was dangerous.

"Aren't we going to put on the radio?" I asked, hoping it'd distract her.

"I want to hear the desert music," she said.

"How can you hear it while speeding?"

"Not now, silly. When we get there."

"You're not going to kill me and bury my body out here, are you?" I asked, joking.

"Nope," she said. "That's for later."

I hoped she was joking.

She banked the wheel hard right, and I swear we must've gone up on two wheels. There wasn't a road that I saw, but again, it was so dark, I couldn't see.

Finally, we came to a stop.

"Phew." She put the Jeep in park and opened her door. "Come on."

My feet hit the desert, and it was harder than I thought.

"Are there snakes out here?" I asked, seriously concerned.

"Probably somewhere," she said. "But don't worry. They can't have you. You're all mine."

I followed her blindly, her tugging me by the hand. Eventually she stopped, and it appeared we were nearly on the edge of a large, deep overhang. My eyes semi-adjusted to the moonlight, although even that was unreliable.

"What do you think?" she asked. "Beautiful, isn't it?"

"Yeah. What is it?"

"Fountain of Youth," she said. "I'm actually over a thousand years old."

"Amazing what they're doing with plastic surgery these days," I said, jokingly.

She laughed. "That's why I love you, Del. You're so funny. I could just eat you up."

My smile stayed on, but inside, something felt off. I had the distinct feeling she was about to push me over the edge of the canyon.

"Sit down," she said.

She did and I did, and then, Lindsay curled up in back of me, her legs stretching around my middle. Yeah. My heart was racing. Millions of guys, and gals, I'm sure, dreamt of what was happening to me.

Stay cool, I thought. *Don't blow this.*

Then she put her hands on my shoulders and rubbed them. "You had such a long flight out here. You must be tired."

"A little," I lied. No way did I want her to pull away and stop what she was doing.

Her hands moved up my neck and then to the back of my head. I felt her kneading my skull, then her fingernails inched between my hair. She ran them over my scalp and it felt amazing. Her nails were super strong. I shut my eyes. She clamped around me tighter. Her whole body was right on mine. I felt everything: her hips, her breasts, her breath on the back of my neck.

Holy cow. Was she really into me?

When I opened my eyes, ever so slightly, the depressed area just below the ridge seemed different. The moonlight seemed to fall on it stronger than it had even moments before. There were details that seemed so defined. I saw small silhouettes moving near the brush. Maybe they were dogs? Coyotes? All pitch black. There seemed to be a constant, high-pitch buzz coming from the area.

"Is that the desert music?" I asked.

Lindsay smiled. "Yes." Her voice sounded different than I'd ever heard it: deeper, more soulful, more . . . something I couldn't put my finger on. Like it was coming from a different place is the best way I'd describe it.

Her fingers were rubbing my head furiously and I very much wanted to go to sleep, but I also wanted to turn around and kiss her.

I saw a long, noodle-shaped light in the sky, way off in the distance. It grew larger, then seemed to vibrate.

"You see that?" I asked.

She whispered in my ear, her breath tickling my skin. "This is a very special place."

I was convinced I'd just melt right inside of her any second, the two of us becoming one.

The light in the sky became two, then three, then, last I could count, six. Their colors were not all the same. "What's happening?"

"Open your mind," she said.

Every bit of my body felt electric, like her fingertips were shooting me through with energy.

I fought against the drowsiness. I needed to be awake, to see. I needed to be hers. All hers. Only hers.

Down below us, on the depressed plane, I saw several of the dark shapes cornering a lone silhouette. They all pounced at the same time. The thing made a wretched scream.

"What...?"

"Shhh." Lindsay put a hand over my mouth. "It's natural. All of it. Don't be scared. They're doing it for us."

"Why?"

"So you can open your mind to me."

The shadows below seemed to dissolve into the darkness. I stared, but couldn't see any more movement, other than the light ribbons in the sky. She rubbed my head again.

"That's it, love," she said.

It was.

I couldn't keep my head up. As soon as my chin lowered, I was out. I felt like I was on a bed, strapped to it, and it was rolling round and round like a bowling ball going down a hill. The only thing tethering me to the world was Lindsay's hands. Hadn't she been wrapped around me? I wasn't sure. Everything spun. Everything faded.

***

Do you know how much I love you? That I've dreamt of you every night since we met? Last night I held you while you cried. I made sure that you were okay. I took all that pain away.

Lindsay's voice inside my head.

I'm warm. I can't smell the desert anymore.

There's something pressing against my lap. Pretty sure I'm laying down.

As I come to, there's a lot of pressure in my head. I find myself in the hotel room. I'm on a bed. Lindsay's on top of me, straddling me. Oh. My. God. For a moment, I think that I'm the luckiest guy in the world. It's short-lived. Her hands are on top of my head. Her eyes are shut, and her mouth is open. There's so much pressure inside my skull. I can't bear it. Something pops inside my brain, and I recall Mr. Block's Biology class when he said we couldn't feel things deep inside our brains. I want to cry out and yell at him and tell him he's wrong – so very wrong – that yes, indeed, you can feel in there, because I'm feeling in there. Lindsay's nails are probing inside, looking, searching, taking from me. I know this instinctively. How did she get inside?

Open your mind.

She meant it.

Had she taken my skull off?

No. I realize she's stuck a few of her fingernails in through

225

the scalp and down through my skull in just the right places. Like Acupuncture, from hell.

Of course I tried to move but found I couldn't. Not even a bit. Instead, I had to suffer.

She kept her eyes closed.

I thought, *Please get out of my head. Please.*

Oh. You're here. Back with us. Welcome, Love.

My mind froze. There was little I could do.

Small things crawled inside my head. I couldn't see them, but they felt a lot like little spiders. They were worming their way through my head, crawling up the sides. It was itchy and uncomfortable. How would I get them out of my head?

I sensed that insectoid thing dug deep. So deep. How would it ever get out?

Please. Stop.

You don't like me on top of you? I like being on top of you.

I like that part. But not what you're doing.

What am I doing?

I don't know.

You're just opening up to me.

More of the insectoid things slid off her fingers into my brain. The swarm spread out and made quick work of exploring my innermost sanctum. I felt them. I saw them inside my thoughts, on the edges, like oozing, moving dark vignettes.

What were they looking for?

I saw my fingers on the guitar. A replay of myself playing with Lindsay at the school. She could see what I was doing. The insectoids knew, too. I felt a sucking feeling inside my head, drinking in my every thought.

Was she drinking up my memories?

There was a breeze on top of my head. I pictured my head made of big, razor teeth, which would clamp together and chop of her fingers at the knuckle.

Make it real. As real as you can.

Lindsay yelled and suddenly release me. "Are you angry with me?"

I couldn't speak. I reached up to touch my head and was surprised I couldn't find any holes. Instead, there were raised bumps, as though I'd been stung by bees where her nails had gone inside. My head hurt terribly.

I passed out again.

✶✶✶

Her warmth encompassed me. Lindsay wrapped me from behind with her body. I woke slowly. She pet my head, but not with her nails. Then I remembered everything. Were the bugs inside my head? Would they eat me from the inside out? I was so hungry. Starving. The room smelled of hot food. Burgers. Pizza. French fries. All kinds of fast food. I saw a stack of bags on one of the tables.

"I'm sure you're famished," she said. "That's all for you."

I didn't say anything.

On one hand, I didn't want to move. Having a gorgeous woman like Lindsay spooning you was an amazing feeling, and one that took every bit of resistance inside of me to break from. She had stuck her nails inside my brain and injected bugs? Or had I dreamed that?

"What did you do to me?" I sat up and grabbed my aching head.

She laughed, although it was a more practiced and low-pitched one than before. "I didn't do anything," she said. "I just...got to know you."

"You were inside my head."

Lindsay put a hand on my shoulder. "The desert does strange things to people. I think the flight made you tired. You should eat something. Get replenished."

"From what you took, right?"

Again, her laugh.

"What's going on in that head of yours?"

"Not sure. It's been scrambled," I said. "Messed with. By you."

She let go. "Why does it always end up like this? I thought you'd be different. I know being close to me can be challenging."

I turned. "I like you a lot," I said. "It's just that . . ." and I put my head on my hands. "My brain hurts so much."

"Eat," she said.

I went to the table, sat, and gorged.

When I was done, I felt like laying down again. Lindsay had stayed on the bed the entire time. She'd turned on the TV and seemed to aimlessly click through the channels with the sound off. "Come on watch with me."

Maybe she'd been right? Maybe the long flight and the stress of the trip had gotten to me?

Lindsay looked absolutely radiant. Her face appeared impossibly smooth. Her hair fell perfectly around her head. I couldn't resist and joined her. She lifted the covers, and I slid in. We watched TV, the sound raised just enough. She liked to switch the channels every few minutes. Said she got bored easily.

"I'm tired, Del," she said, and put an arm around my shoulders, nestled her head in my neck, and fell right away to sleep.

***

We stayed like that for a long time. I was so conflicted. Everything felt right. Everything felt wrong. Looking down at her, it was tough believing she'd been inside my head, listening to my thoughts, my memories. I felt violated. There were crunching sounds coming from deep inside my head. I thought it had to be my imagination, but the sensation persisted.

Could I just be imagining the whole thing?

At one point, fatigue got the best of me, and I slept again. I woke to the sound of someone knocking on the door. Lindsay was nowhere to be found.

When I answered the door, there was an official looking woman. "Good morning," she said. "I'll be your transportation to the airport."

"Airport? I'm not supposed to leave for a few days."

"I'm sorry, sir. Miss Taylor was called out on business. She said she left you a note." The woman came in without my asking. I looked around nervously. I was freaked out by the night before, but I was still hoping I'd have more time with Lindsay.

I spotted a folded piece of stationery on the counter. It had my name written on the front.

Del. Sorry to have to run. I didn't want to wake you because you were so cozy. I loved our 'Holiday in The Midnight Sun' together. Maybe we can do it again sometime soon?
Love ya!
– Lindsay

"Shoot," I said. "Okay."

I hadn't unpacked, so I just grabbed my bag and we left. I was at the airport and sitting on the plane in no time. Several yellow, crusty things that looked like food were on my shirt. I picked one off. I knew I was looking at a piece of my own brain. My stomach clenched. I wanted to throw up. I wanted to pass out. Good thing I was alone in my aisle. I kept my head enough to gather the little pieces and put them in the sick bag I found in the back of the seat. I placed it safely in my carry on. Grabbing the book about Kurt Cobain, I did my best to try and read and forget about what I'd just been through. Somehow, I'd have the pieces analyzed to see what they were. Until then? The entire experience would just be one of those weird celebrity things everyone always reads about.

When the plane lifted off, Las Vegas looked like something out of Walt Disney World. It just didn't look real at all.

Not one bit.

✳✳✳

A few months later, life returned to normal. Ghost Soul were reinvigorated. Maddie seemed happy as a bee in honey. I was happy, too. Only thing was that whenever I had a good idea for a song or lyrics, that old crunchy feeling happened in my brain. Then the idea would seem to vanish as soon as it'd arrived. And then Lindsay would release a new song that felt strangely familiar to me, though I couldn't remember why. I hadn't heard from Lindsay since Las Vegas. Not a peep. Not a text. Nothing. I kept her note to me to myself, tucking it between my Jonathan Maberry zombie books.

Those little bits that were on my shirt? I gave them to Mr. Block, our science teacher. Told him I'd found them in my yard and was curious to know what they might be. We looked under the microscope, and he said, "The connective tissue and blood vessel patterns read it as some type of nervous tissue. Brain tissue. Poor animal." He gave me extra credit.

The more I thought about the night with Lindsay the more I came to believe she was something other than human. An energy vampire? An alien? Or something else?

One night I was hanging with the band in Maddie's basement where we practiced, and she had on the Global Music Awards show as inspiration. Lindsay Taylor was going to be on it, and the band teased me mercilessly that she was my girlfriend. "How come you never told us what really happened that night?" Maddie asked for the hundredth time.

"I can't really remember," I said, receiving much hooting and hollering. I shook it off.

Then Lindsay was on, her famous acoustic guitar strapped on. She started a new song.

Driving out of the city
Where the only light's the moon

Strange flashes in the sky so high
Still not sure what I meant to you

This crazy life makes you all alone
Until a special soul opens up
Sharing a world you've never known
Drink from that amazing cup

Deliver me from this evil world
Before it eats me up
I need a Holiday In The Midnight Sun
So I can find myself again
So I can find us again

There was something about how she said the first part of 'deliver' like it was my name, and when she hit the chorus, she looked right at the camera, and I thought, for sure, she was singing right to me, and singing about our night, and I know that because, deep down inside, something knocked on the door of my imagination, trying to get inside again, trying, needing, hungry.

Deliver me from this evil world
Before it eats me up

I pulled my hat down tight.

Her long, blood red fingernails fretted the guitar. "Sounds kind of like the stuff you were playing with her," Maddie said. "Wow."

She was right. I was speechless.

I need a Holiday In The Midnight Sun
So I can find myself again
So I can find us again

find...
us...
again...

Lindsay was finished. They moved to the next act. "Turn it off," I said. "I've got an idea for a song." And I did.

"Great," Maddie said. "What's it called?"

***

I'm not going to tell y'all what the name of the song is. That'd be too easy. You'd know it. If you listen closely, now that you know the story, I bet you'd probably be able to figure it out. If you can't, and you ever run into Lindsay Taylor? Maybe she'll whisper it in your ear.

Image by Davinia

Sport Pig

By Andrew Robertson

Every evening when I wake up, I wonder why I'm killing myself like this.

This evening it's particularly bad. I can hardly move. I'm weaker than ever, in pain, and I feel sicker than I've been in hundreds of years. I move to roll over in the bed and feel my nerves jump. I think there may be an open sore on my side. Is it wet? I stop moving. My mind tries to bury my anxiety about what that sore could mean. The news on the radio has been an endless litany about the new disease raging in New York and around the world, the scourge of the eighties, one that really liked to bring down men like me. Or at least the human ones. The religious nuts call it a punishment for the excesses of the era but being what I am, until now, I've never had a problem in any era with "excess".

I sigh and press my head into the damp pillowcase. It smells of metal, which soothes me a bit, but not enough. I close my eyes, trying to meditate, ignore, excuse…it's all too much.

Every night, I promise myself that I will change, but I don't. The hunger is overwhelming. I bargain with myself that I'll just have a little, but a little leads to a lot. The need to feed takes over, and I bend like a little bitch in heat, bashing my head into the same should've and could've internal dialogue after the fact. It's not that I want to stop feeding- that is my nature and prey is just prey. No creature like me would care about human livestock or the morality of my actions or any other bullshit sentiment like that. Does a leopard cry over the last antelope it ate? No. It's just that there's a certain type of food I've come to covet, and it makes me ill, but I want it in a way that makes me tremble.

In the near darkness, I look over at the other side of my bed and wonder if this kid propped at an odd angle against the ornate wooden headboard is alive or dead. His blood was delicious, but I had to bring him home to continue to feed. He did so much coke and ketamine that I thought I would end up in a k-hole in the club and not make it home before light. I reach over to touch his shoulder, thinking I may be able to drink a bit more off him and get some sustenance in me. Too cold. His body is stiffening and collapses toward me; his mouth hangs open. I guess I couldn't resist one last draught before I slipped into a blackout.

No good.

I curse myself for getting into this but find that I'm already thinking about how I'll get enough strength back to get out there for more. Every night now is the same. I wonder if I can make it down to the street and discreetly use what's left of my energies to draw someone behind the building, drain them, and dump the body in the river without being seen. My abilities may not work. It could get violent if they can fight back. I could get caught.

I'm surprised how little I care about being caught. I try to convince myself that I don't believe I will be, and the payoff is worth it. That's the bargain I make and the lie I tell myself in order to plan something so clumsy and stupid in my current state. Never trust a junkie.

I can hear Sharice in the living room, getting ready for a night on the Piers. She expects me to make a few appearances, so no one fucks her up. When I had more girls, they used to look after each other so I could do what I wanted, but that was before I got so deep into this addiction. They all took off and now I just have the one money maker. And now Sharice is getting mean, doing more drugs than she used to, talking back, and falling apart herself. She used to fear me enough that she was never a problem. She never used to ask so many questions.

It's all become a disaster.

I've become a disaster.

This is all Talulah's fucking fault.

***

"We've been doing the same shit for hundreds of years," Talulah said to me in my bedroom early one morning about a year or so ago when we were both suffering from a particular ennui all creatures like us suffer from time to time. "We've all sampled different delicacies, but what I'd like to propose is something new and dangerous. Maybe we'd call it a gross-out contest like the kids have in the clubs downtown. Maybe it's a triple-dog dare. I want to have some fun with you before I head down to New Orleans in a few days. I may just miss your cold and hard visage, my pale demon. You wanna know what I've got in mind, Lucien?"

Talulah sat at my antique vanity, teasing her red hair in the style of her most recent obses-sion, author Tama Janowitz. She'd been stalking her and Warhol and other underground stars around downtown Manhattan for years. I preferred to go to Paradise Garage and see Grace Jones hold court. If Grace was one of us, the world would surely be in trouble. I'd always been surprised when Talulah didn't feed on her obsessions instead of just watching them, it was her one peculiari-ty. I'd seen her decimate entire families, dynasties even, and laughed with her while carting off their gold and silver after the carnage.

"I'm suggesting that we taste what we've always been taught to avoid, play a little bit of Russian Roulette, a variation on the classic, and let's see how far we can take it. Have you ever heard of a Sport Pig?"

I shrugged in response as I stood beside the bed and adjusted my periwinkle frock coat. New York in the eighties truly was the perfect time for an ancient monster to hide in plain sight, with so many freaks and weirdos masquerading as artists. She popped open a vibrant red Chanel lipstick she took off a snack she had last night and layered it onto her full lips.

Her ideas were usually pretty wild, but this one already sounded like it was on the self-destructive side. We both usually stayed on the side of being the destroyers, but I was also so fucking bored. I'd just drank my fill of three young men, and I was feeling invincible and maybe a little drunk because they were pretty hammered.

"A Sport Pig is a gross young woman, or man I suppose. I know how you like your men. Have you ever eaten a woman? I don't recall." She laughs at her own joke. "A Sport Pig is just what it sounds like, used for sport. One you would never date or marry, but one you'll fuck for practice and just hope you don't end up with a tricky dicky. In our case, it's a pig we eat for sport. A dirty pig. I suggest we test our immortality a bit and see how far we can go tonight, find some fucked up prey and drink them dry, then compare results."

I shivered a bit at this prospect. I'd always been a bit of a prude. I preferred gorgeous young men and, occasionally, glamorous women to gutter trash, but I didn't like looking weak in front of her. She made me and never let me forget her superiority.

"Okay, but how far do we go?" Just one night, I figured, then she'd leave to manage her affairs down South, and I'd get back to my own business. "With all these kids downtown dropping dead from that new disease, couldn't we get so fucked up we can't come back from it?" Like any animal, our instincts kept us away from sick prey that could have unintended consequences.

She rolled her eyes dramatically.

"Don't be a fucking bitch, Lucien; just make it home before dawn and sleep it off. A little AIDS won't kill one of us at our age. It's just like the Black Death, just like cholera, just like the quote unquote French Disease. These are human problems, not our concern. We've survived the threat of all of it."

So we did it. We went out to a dive bar, then an after-hours, then some alleys, and found some of humanity's saddest participants. Junkie hookers, drug-addled runaways, then off to Times Square to finish off with some porn theatre clients who died with their tiny mushrooms nestled in their clammy hands.

"I think I'm getting a cold sore," Talulah laughed as we walked back to my place. "And my crotch itches. That really brings me back."

Talulah had an illustrious career in the House of Heaven back when prostitution was sacred, and it was there that she met her maker. They embarked on a long and successful career run-ning brothels in countries around the world, and after he vanished, she made me. She taught me the business because cash in hand is better for those of us who don't want to leave a trace, and now we each had our own business and army of ladies of the night to manage. With our abilities and strength, it was easy to keep them off balance and under control. Best of all, neither of us really cared about the girls who worked for us. They were a product, and we understood that every prod-uct has an expiration date. We could always find more product.

***

Things were great until that night with Talulah and her stupid dare. Because every night after that, I wanted what many like me would call bad blood, blood filled with drugs and angst, blood that screamed its way into my body to get me high, blood to make my senses reel in a way they hadn't before, and blood to help me forget so many things I wanted to forget, even for a little while. And the dirty blood excited me in a way that disgusted me, just not enough to stop.

My girls were getting pissed at me for blowing through all the cash they were making on the streets. I was using it to keep my prey high when they weren't already, or when they weren't high enough to satisfy my increasing desires. The girls got sick of me ignoring them when they asked for money for make up and food and clothes, for not being on the Pier when they were getting assaulted or ripped off by tricks and the other bitches out there. Sharice was so easy to control that I managed to keep her and at least some cash flow coming in.

Every night, I was out in the clubs and streets, docks and squats finding the poison inside men that gave me so much pleasure and every night I wanted to go a little bit further, but no one was there to keep track. No one would tell me when it was too much. I had no idea how bad it was becoming. Until she came back.

***

"You've gone too far, Lucien," Talulah said as she stood over my bed looking down at me with her eyes flashing in the dark. "You are degrading yourself and me, all of our kind, and that I will not tolerate you little pissant. Get your dignity off the damn floor."

When the fuck did she get here? I blinked myself into a horrible version of consciousness. Head full of broken glass, mouth full of a hairy tongue, no words found to be spoken into this con-fusion.

Her hair was bigger than ever, and the scent of Opium perfume hung in the air, surely a callback to the House of Heaven so many centuries ago. She was always a bit nostalgic when it suited her. "You don't look right, man. And is that a dead guy in your bed? So sloppy. He's sexy, though, for a corpse."

I pushed him around a bit, and he groaned. I'd glamour him and ditch him on the street later.

"I'm fine; I've just been having a bit of fun, that's all." My voice sounded alien to me. I wasn't expecting her back from New Orleans so soon. Or had it already been months? Could it have been months since we said goodbye? I was desperate to head out and score and get away from the interrogation to come. "Anyway, this was your idea. Shouldn't you be out looking for Tama? Go change her or do each other's hair, I don't care. Get off my back!"

Talulah looked shocked. Not angry. Just shocked, maybe hurt. I'd never seen her react like she did that night, and it gave me pause, but I quickly squashed the feeling.

"My idea, yes, but for one night! I haven't even been gone that long and you look insane! You have to stop whatever this is you've been doing. Where are all your girls? I've only seen the sad-looking one since I got here. She left hours ago. She smells of cheese and I hate it. Are you even planning on checking on her tonight? Or hunting? That sad piece of shit beside you smells so rank there's no way that bag of meat will keep your power up."

I looked at the clock. It was 3 am. I'd slept through half the night. I was suddenly in a rage. My thoughts were sticky and burned with a humiliation that was seeping out my pores in the dank bedroom. The walls felt close. Talulah was unwelcome, uninvited.

"Get out. Don't come back. Just get the fuck out!" As soon as I said it, my heart turned rot-ten, my throat was acid, and I regretted it but didn't say another word.

She ran her hands down her black PVC trench coat, smoothing the shining fabric while looking right into my eyes. Turning on a spike heel, she walked through the door into the living room, and in seconds, the front door slammed.

The clicking of her pace disappeared down the hallway.

That was the last time I saw her.

***

I hate the way these memories come back, and how often they repeat and race in my messy mind. So many regrets, past and future, pour over my dirty skin. I need a shower. I need help that I don't want. I need to get out of bed.

It's a slow and painful process. The smell in the room is

unbearable. I think the dead kid soiled himself. I need air. Hobbling over to the door, I pull my housecoat off the knob and reach to the vanity for some cologne, 'Obsession for Men.' That's mostly true, I think to myself and almost laugh. There's an eight-ball in a baggie that I grab and drop it into the pocket of the housecoat. I spray the room and myself heavily before I open the door.

Sharice sits on the bay window ledge, watching early stars through shattered clouds above the New York skyline. The sky is violet. I can feel a charge in the air, a mood. It's not good. And there is another odor out here.

She has the radio on. The new Cher song, If I Could Turn Back Time, is playing quietly. How fucking ironic.

Sharice was so beautiful, a perfect product for the streets. Now, I can't stand to look at her, which is likely because I can hardly stand to look at myself, but she has always made money for me. That's what she's always been here for, and what I've used part of my waning abilities to en-sure.

I remember the night I saw her for the first time. She was at the end of a block in the Meat-packing District, standing under a streetlamp and smoking a cigarette. It was laughable. Could she have looked any more like a hooker? Head tilted back, cigarette slowly lifted to her lips, a drag taken, and then exhaled off to the side, one eye trained on me, the other slowly winking. What, were we in a bad film? If we were, it was a porno. But fuck was she hot. Her lips were red and full with blood and excitement, and a subtle crimson lit up her cheeks on an ivory face. The wind ripped through her long blonde hair, and it looked so soft as the curls bounced that I just knew it would smell like cheap shampoo. One leg wrapped around the pole as I got within a half block of her, and flexed. She appeared to raise her whole body off the ground in one movement, as the hand holding the cigarette slowly caressed the pole, and her free hand beckoned me forward.

What else could I do? I walked toward her like a ship helplessly tossed by the sea. She would be great for business; I just needed to convince her employer to let her go. That part was easy.

Her green eyes glinted as she blinked against the dirt and dust flying in the chilly air.

"Hi," she almost sighed as I came in close. "I'm Sharice."

I wasn't sure what to say.

Her lips smelled like cherry cola lip gloss, the kind from the flat tin. She swung slowly back and forth off the pole, one arm wrapped around, the other swinging toward and away from me with the cigarette almost threatening to make contact.

"Are you dumb?"

I'm sure I looked shocked at the question.

"Like, can you talk, I mean?" she asked, almost apologetically, batting her eyelashes as she stared up at me. Her torn t-shirt read Teenage Jesus and The Jerks. Hard nipples pressed against the thin black fabric.

I could sense someone near, hear their heartbeat getting closer.

"Yes, of course," I muttered, turning slowly. There was a shadow at the mouth of a nearby gateway.

She quickly dropped the smoke and grabbed my face to turn it back toward her.

"Hey, all you need to see is right here," she whispered, trying to pull focus from whoever was shuffling behind us. "You have twenty bucks for me?"

That night I took her home then went back and killed her pimp.

Now, she's disheveled; hair a big knot at the back, a lit cigarette in her left hand, only wear-ing underwear and even those are looking greasy. She's ashing the cigarette out a crack in the window with a manic twitch I've noticed is getting worse night after night. Too many drugs, too much trauma, but this is our life, and she has her role. Go out and fuck and bring back money or else. Whatever else she does isn't my concern.

"Shouldn't you be out working?" I ask her with a hoarse voice I didn't expect.

She reaches down with her right hand and scratches at the heel of her right foot. It sounds like someone trying to unsuccessfully strike a match. The sound makes me feel sicker. She's a husk of that cherry cola dream now.

"What the fuck is going on, man? Who are all these young guys you keep bringing home and hiding in your room?" She's shrill. I ignore her question and close and lock my bedroom door behind me, swaying more than I want to.
My room is pitch black from the window coverings, but I don't want her to glimpse the latest young corpse who's still in there. I take a few weak steps to the kitchen table and sit down, legs giving out, landing hard.

"They all look fucked up, man! And that screaming I heard last night, what am I'm supposed to think getting home at 6 a.m. to that? And that guy Daniel who's been here a few times? He looks like he's been freebasing for years man, he's not even twenty! He was fucking golden when he first came by. He looks like he's got that disease that's going around, they all do. You've been decent to me over the years, but I'm not going to have some sissy as a pimp! I'll get fucked up out there. No one respects you now Lucien, and I'm gonna pay the price. And what if someone comes by during the day to mess with us? You're like a fucking corpse, I can't even get into your room or call for help, you don't even wake up when I knock and yell when I need money. Neither do your fucked up boyfriends."

Her whole monologue is delivered with her eyes unfocused, staring out the window, watching the darkening night come to embrace us, good or bad. "Also, you have a cold sore and it's grody."

She would never say this type of thing to my face before.

I reach up to my face and feel a crusty bump on my lip, something that has never happened since my transition. Then I remember the sore on my side and I feel my heart skip. As much as I want to totally ignore her and wait for this to simmer down, she's right. My appetites have spiraled downhill ever since Talulah's stupid fucking dare. And when I wake up after a bender, I'm never the same. It keeps taking longer to come back to myself again. But I want it all so badly. I'm so weak. I just need a little bit right now to get me going.

"Come over here," I say. "I feel bad. I'm so sorry. I promise I'll change. I'll be good to you."

She hesitates as affection is not something I'm known for. I take out the eight ball and dump the bag on the table. She's right to be apprehensive but, for her, drugs are a strong motivator. Desperation is colouring my decision but there's nothing I haven't been able recover from over the centuries I've been this creature. I feel that lie slowly sink into a grave at the back of my mind as soon as I think it. That grave is getting crowded.

"Want a bump before you go? Come sit on my knee and I'll get you set up. No screaming tonight, I'll fix everything, Sharice." With a shaky hand, I grab the perennial razor and rolled up one dollar bill from a mirrored tray in the middle of the table and set to work making a few fat lines for fat, sloppy Sharice.

The Killing Jar by Siouxsie and the Banshees is now playing on the radio, such a perfect soundtrack for the moment that is to come.

Sharice shuffles over, the dry soles of feet sounding like pages of a book being turned. She sits on my lap like a good little girl, just like I'm telling her to with my mind, strength ebbing but addiction giving me the power to get what I need before I leave tonight. Being this saccharine is making me feel almost as bad as the previous night's adventure.

She leans over and snorts a line before coughing as it hits

the back of her throat.

"Have another."

"I'll be high as hell when I get out there though."

"It'll make the night go by faster, let's just have some fun. Fun is always a good idea."

She gives a brief laugh and huffs another large line before she tilts her head back and wipes at her nose. I push her once lovely blonde curls behind one ear to expose her neck and then I smile with anticipation. A purple vein pulses beneath the surface, and I know that in a few seconds, maybe one more line of blow, that vein will be my path to shaking off this maudlin feeling hanging over me.

"Sharice, do you know what a Sport Pig is? Would you like to find out?"

A Little Red Thread

By Jonathan Fortin

Seren's gone. That's what the letter she left me says, anyway: so long, goodbye, thanks for all the blood. It sits there on the dining room table, unmissable, a big fuck you, my love that I am so tempted to burn.

Three years. Three years of biting my tongue whenever I wanted to tell everyone my goth ass was somehow dating a real, actual vampire. Three years of feeling weary from pervasive long term lack of blood (totally worth it, admittedly). Three years of showing up late to everything so I could drive her there at night, because Seren is *ancient* and too terrified to learn to drive herself and even more terrified of the subway. I wouldn't blame her—I'm terrified of the subway, too—but for me it's because creepy men talk to me on it. For Seren, it's because the trains move too fast. She can zoom across the room in the blink of an eye, but put her on a subway train and she gets like a cat: wide-eyed, hunched over, perfect black hair standing on end. If she had her way we'd still be riding horses everywhere. Then I realize I'd love that too, and I miss her all over again.

I inhale my tears and reread the godforsaken letter:

My dearest Carol,

Song of my heart, the time has come. For months now, my maker has once again been prodding my thoughts. Despite my best attempts, it appears that I cannot be rid of him. The pain in my skull has become indescribably awful. I've had enough. I must go and kill him. I wish I could promise that I will return, but there is something I have not told you. It is said that when a vampire lord dies, those who he turned shall perish as well.

Indeed, my maker has warned me of this many times to stop me from killing him. But now he stirs from his centuries-long slumber, and like a fat baby he cries and cries in the hopes that I will help him settle in the new world. I cannot be sure whether this is truth or myth, but should I perish, I would rather perish with love in my heart.

I understand if you are heartbroken or upset. Know that, while for me our courtship was like the blink of an eye, I have cherished it enormously. And it is for that reason that I must go. You met me at the twilight of my unlife, and I lament these circumstances greatly. Memories of your beauty will haunt me for the remainder of my nights, such as they are…

The letter goes on for another twelve pages about how much she claims to love me, as if the length makes up for the fact that it's a glorified suicide note.

My hands tremble with rage, the pages crackling between my fingers. How can Seren seriously think this the only way? Maybe she could beat up her maker so badly that leaves her alone for another hundred years. Or try to find a way to block out his psychic probing. Or…

I shake my head. Seren must have considered her options carefully; she isn't impulsive like I am. She's been talking about it for months, this pilgrimage to kill her maker; it's become routine pillow talk whenever I wake up to find her staring up into the darkness, wincing from some indescribable pain. But I'd never imagined such a mission would lead to her death. Hell, I hadn't even been sure how serious she'd been. Seren loves telling me straight up bullshit about vampires with this barely perceptive smile on her face, all but daring me to call her on it. Thinking about it now, I snort out a miserable, desperate laugh, convincing myself this is just another joke.

"You can come out now!" I shout. I turn off the lights and walk to the center of the den, in perfect position to be crept up on. I close my eyes and tell myself that she'll tap my shoulder just to hear me scream, and then we'll laugh and have awesome vampire sex and everything will be okay again.

But then I open my eyes, and I'm still alone. Seren is gone. The only vampire I've ever known is gone. And if she gets herself killed, I will never, ever have a vampire girlfriend again.

Fuck that, I decide. I'm going after her. I don't care if she can fly in bat form. I can travel during the day, and that means I'll be twice her speed. Seren always said her maker was in Romania, so I'll start there. I call my boss, tell her I have Covid, and head straight to the airport.

***

It only really dawns on me that I have no idea what I'm doing after I'm already on the plane. I've never been to Romania, and I have no idea where in the country Seren might be headed. (Seren doesn't like phones. I tried to get her to use one, I really did.)

When we land in Bucharest, it's snowing and already fairly dark. I have a mini-panic attack as I get off the plane, uncertain where the hell I'll go from here. I walk out of the airport with my one little bag, in no way prepared for a long stay.

A line of cabs is waiting outside, but only one has a driver standing in front of his car: a fat man smoking a cigarette. He smiles and waves like he's been waiting for me all day.

I freeze, something urging me to run. Then I tell myself to calm down. The cabbie doesn't know me. There's no way he knows me. He's probably just being friendly so I'll hire him instead of the others. He flicks his cigarette butt away and walks over, hand outstretched.

"Let me take your bag, miss." His accent is as thick as his figure. I'm still frozen, the fear not fully gone, but before I know it the bag is already in his hands, and he's opening his trunk. "You know where you're going?"

I stand there, uncertain what to tell him. Then a flock of bats flutters overhead. Nine, maybe ten. Again I'm stunned. We're just outside an airport. There shouldn't be bats here, right? Unless those bats were hiding on board, so they wouldn't have to tire themselves out across the ocean…

It's inexplicable. It defies all logic. And those bats might as well be flying red flags. But I don't have any other leads to follow. I don't know where else to go. And I'm scared that if I don't take advantage of this moment, I'll have lost my only chance at saving Seren's life.

"Follow those bats!" I tell the cabbie.

He looks up at where I'm pointing, then shrugs like this is just a normal thing in Romania.

I don't know how we're able to keep up with the bats given the traffic. Maybe the the creatures are keeping slow to guide us. Or maybe the cabbie already knows where to go. I want to bite my nails but that would reveal how nervous I am.

"You came all the way from America?" he asks.

I nod, not telling him more, focused on the city outside, and the bats in the dark gray sky above. Is one of them Seren? If so, wouldn't she have seen me while flying above me at the airport? And why would she be flying with others?

The bats lead us out of the city and into a snowy countryside, where it becomes so dark I can barely see. It doesn't help that the wind has picked up, causing the snow to blow around us like a storm of white ash.

"Are you okay going out this far?" I ask, after over an hour. The cabbie chuckles. "Of course, of course."

I check the meter. I'm gonna be broke by the end of this trip. On the other hand, outside it's cold as shit. I can't be out there on foot. "Can you still even see those bats?" I ask.

"Oh, yes. See? They're juuuust over there." He points, but I see nothing in the storming darkness.

The cabbie begins whistling as he veers a little to the right, and finally turns altogether. The air is so rife with snow that I can't even see a road to turn onto, but he seems to know where he's going. Like he's all too familiar with this path. Like he's driven here plenty of times before. His whistles become words, more mumbled than sang, barely audible over the crunching tires:

"It's a little red thread that binds us together
A little red thread of blood
A little red web I've got you wrapped up in
And it can never be cut..."

Cold snakes up my spine so rapidly I half wonder if a window opened. A single thought fills my head, the first in this whole trip focused on my own preservation: *I have to get out of this cab.*

I expect there are some people who would have been scared of Seren for her gothic aesthetic: the long sleek black hair, the pre-20th century clothes, the "Eastern European Villain Lady" accent. But all that had always just drawn me to her. So had her fangs, when she'd finally shown them to me. Even when we'd had that argument and she'd shouted loud enough to make the room shake, it had been immediately followed with apologies and tears and tender kisses. Seren never makes me feel afraid. And given how many cheesy vampire movies I've laughed at over the years, I never really internalized the idea of them actually being dangerous.

But right now, I'm absolutely fucking petrified.

I'll probably freeze if I run out, even with my winter coat. It's a dark, endless countryside, and I'd have no idea which way to go. Worse, there's no way I'd be able to outrun the cabbie in his car—or vampires, if they're out there too. All the same, the impulse to open the door is overpowering.

Just as I'm about to, the cabbie pulls to a stop. He looks over his shoulder at me, an unlit cigarette between his lips. Like he read my mind and is offering me the chance to try it. A cat, toying with his prey?

Then I open the door, and—

Be still my dumb goth heart.

We've stopped in front of an enormous castle, its dimly lit windows glowing in the dark. It's the most beautiful building I've ever seen. A towering, ornate, majestic ode to Gothic architecture, rivaling even Neuschwanstein Castle for sheer opulence. Any other night, I'd have given practically anything to live here. But right now, all I can think about is how much this snow smells like blood.

"You want to go up, yes?" asks the cabbie, lighting his cigarette as he emerges beside me, his other hand dipping into his pocket.

I shiver, holding my arms. This was a mistake. I should have trusted Seren to handle herself rather than recklessly going after her like this. "Can we go back?" I ask the cabbie, turning, as the canister he's holding beside my head sprays its contents into my face.

✳✳✳

I met Seren at the goth club, after getting so shit-faced that I could barely stand up. It had been months after my last breakup, but I've never handled being single well. I remember leaning on a stranger on the dance floor, singing badly along to the song while I let him grope me, the entire world spinning. Seren must have seen me, must have known I would end up blacking out and waking up at another strange man's place wanting to claw off my skin. The memory is hazy, even now, but I recall her deftly twirling me away, while the man holding me abruptly fell to the floor, passing out. Then Seren took me to a booth, got me snacks and water from the bar, and, later, held up my hair while I vomited into the toilet. Imagine, her seeing me like that and somehow falling in love with me anyway.

I woke up at my place alone, no signs of harm on my body, no marks on my neck, nothing to indicate I'd had sex with anyone.

A month later I found her there again, waiting in the same booth as before, a coy smile on her face. "Are you feeling better?" she asked.

We talked all night, her eyes dancing oh-so-casually across my rubenesque figure, my latest hair color—violet, I think. She admitted to taking me home, and said that she'd asked me why I was acting this way, why I was in such pain. But I hadn't talked about it, even drunk as I was. This fact made her smile. "You are trustworthy," she said. "Even when intoxicated, you can keep a secret."

A few months later, she told me her own big secret, and I'd never been so delighted to be burdened with one.

The memory ebbs like a red tide as I open my eyes, vaguely aware of a wrist hovering over my mouth, salty liquid landing on my lips, a raw soreness in my neck. I'm cramped, hard walls on either side of me locking my arms and legs into place. The cabbie's melody echoes from above, but it's hummed by a different voice this time. An older, more ragged voice.

Something slides across the wrist above me: a long black finger, ending in a sharp claw-like tip. More liquid drips into my mouth, and it's like I'm drunk at that club again, the black room spinning, time spinning with it, the whole world a murky mess. The salty liquid makes my throat dryer with every mouthful, but the more I drink, the more I want. I find myself reaching up to the wrist, overcome by a single thought: *Hunger. Hunger. Hunger.*

A snort of laughter echoes from above me, and the wrist

pulls away. With a desperate wail I reach up, scrambling to grab it again, but whoever was there is gone. I'm alone. Just like before I met Seren. Just like when Seren left me. I writhe in the narrow box, my scream so shrill it pierces my ears.

Then comes the sense of pressure in my teeth. Whenever I get a bad canker sore on my tongue, my jaws feel like a tight cage around it. The slightest caress of tongue against teeth brings unbearable pain, and the stress of this makes my entire mouth ache: every tooth shrieking at every minute with almost as much agony as the sore itself. That's what I feel now, as my canines stretch larger than my mouth has room for: pressure in my teeth like never before. Fresh pain bursts on my tongue and lower lips, and suddenly that dry, salty liquid is filling my throat again like sand.

*** *

Sometimes, things hurt a lot more than they tell you.

*** *

I awaken to music: classical, but unfamiliar. I'm still in the box—no, *coffin*, I realize. The pain must have been so bad that I blacked out. But even now, I'm hungry. So ravenous I feel like I could rip off my own skin.

This time, at least, I don't take too long to realize what must have happened. I don't know why he turned me, but it isn't hard to come up with a few theories, and God, this sucks so much more than I imagined. My entire mouth hurts. My bones feel weak. My throat is strained with a pervasive salty taste. I've never felt this sick or frail in my life.

I slowly push myself up to examine my surroundings: faded wallpaper, a rusty chandelier, a cabinet filled with human skulls of all sizes. The room reeks like it hasn't been cleaned in decades, the dusty stench made all the more pungent by the hunger clawing inside of me.

Suddenly pain reverberates through my skull like the

253

clanging of a gong, ten times worse than any migraine I've ever had.

Get up.

I sit up in the coffin, body moving on its own like I'm a fucking marionette.

Get up.

The voice crashes through my mind with the force of a runaway train, obliterating any thoughts in its path, and suddenly I'm standing. I regain control just as one of my feet passes over the edge of the coffin, and I'm so overwhelmed that I trip and collapse on the floor. "Wait!" I scream, trying to stand, but the waves of pain are already reverberating through my skull again.

GET UP.

I howl as my body lurches up once more, so rapidly the sheer velocity makes me nauseous. The voice sounds angry this time. Is this what Seren felt every time I saw her wincing? I thrust out my hand to push against the wall, steadying myself. It isn't easy to keep standing, even with the support; my whole body feels empty and wobbly, like I'm nothing but a jumble of crudely-connected sticks. "Wait," I pant, even though I don't know if the fucker can hear me. "Wait...I just need a moment..."

COME.

I almost fall over again, the voice a gust of wind blasting against my sticks, forcing my feet to take another precarious step. Another. I fall onto the door, gripping the knob for support as I open the door.

Ahead of me is a long hallway.

COME.

By the time I'm done stumbling down the hallway, I feel like I understand why Seren wants to kill this bastard. I open the door at the other end to find a big round dining room. The once-black table is caked with dust, and covered in dishes with crusted red stains. I cough as I lurch inside, the room still spinning. A gramophone plays some fuzzy old record.

"Good. You made it."

I look up. A withered man is hanging upside-down from the ceiling, veiny bat wings wrapped around him like a cloak. He's bald, with patchy grey skin and a face that I can only describe as looking like a shaved pug who got addicted to heroin.

"I know, I know, I need a maid. I was actually hoping you might consider filling that position when this nonsense with Seren is over. That cabbie is *awful* at cleaning. Better for him to just drop off morsels."

"What the fuck?" I yell, my voice hoarse.

He frowns. *SIT*, commands the voice in my head, and my ass launches into a chair so hard I'm surprised it doesn't shatter beneath me.

"Stop that!" I shout, skull still quaking.

The vampire tuts. "If I hadn't commanded you, you would still be in your coffin, in dire need of blood, and I'd have to go all the way down that hallway to give you some. And I'd rather not, just now. This is my ceiling time. So drink up. No need to clean the bowl. You needn't fear diseases now."

The bowl in front of me is dirty, but empty. In the center of the table is a large pot filled with deep red liquid. Blood, no doubt. And unfortunately, it smells really damn good. I ladle it into my bowl and sip—then tilt it up to gulp down the rest like a kid finishing his cereal milk. It tastes incredible.

"That's better, isn't it?" purrs the vampire.

"Fuck you," I say, ladling more blood into my bowl.

The vampire tuts again, his lip twitching, and I glimpse a fang longer than my middle finger. "You have a mouth on you. We'll need to work on that."

"I'm not gonna be your maid," I say, even as I gulp down more blood. "I'm not going to work for you."

One *GET UP* later, and I'm jerking to my feet, spilling

blood onto both the table and my shirt. *ON THE TABLE*, the vampire orders, and I'm falling onto the messy dishes, sending them clattering. Then comes a new command: *PAIN*. It's worse than any other psychic violation yet: sheer, overwhelming pain ricocheting through my skull. It feels like my brain is being torn apart, piece by piece. I writhe in pure agony, totally unable to control my own body or do anything but scream.

"Please don't tell me you think you have *options* here," says the vampire, rolling his eyes. "Seren's older, she can resist. But you? So young. So painfully, beautifully young. And of course, trying to lay a finger on me would kill you both. It would be ever so sad for someone as young as you to die in vain…"

I'm starting to think dying wouldn't be so bad. At least the pain would stop.

"You're putting it together now, aren't you?" he asks. "I saw you while probing Seren's thoughts. And when you came sniffing around for her, I decided to claim you. Honestly, I don't understand why she didn't turn you herself, but she always was squeamish about making slaves. Something about feeling shame for being at the top of the pyramid or some such ridiculousness. I wonder how she will feel about that when she arrives? Ahhh, well. You're my little chess piece now."

The pain in my skull finally fades. With a groan I sit up, white hot rage coursing through me. I feel stronger now that I've had some blood. Part of me even feels like I could take the fucker on. I bare my teeth, grab a butter knife stand on the table and lunge.

The vampire slaps me with a huge wing, knocking off the table. *PAIN* jolts through my head before I even hit the floor, and I spasm in agony, new teeth chattering hard enough to tear into my tongue.

"How about this? I'll let Seren live, and in return you be a good little maid for me. You'll never be alone. I'll always be there in your head. You could think of me as your…what's the word you children use these days? Bae, that's it. I could be your bae." He grins. "Or…you could try to kill me, and both die as a result. Poor Seren's blood all over your hands. That doesn't sound good, now, does it?"

He's right. As much as I want to kill him to be free, I don't want to kill Seren in the process—even if Seren was coming here to do just that herself.

A loud bell clangs, worsening the aches rippling through my head. "That must be her now," says the vampire. "She would interrupt my ceiling time. Are you going to get up by yourself or do I have to command you?"

In response I only growl. I refuse to make this easy on him. Maybe commanding my brain is like wiggling a finger for him, but even wiggling a finger gets exhausting after a while. If nothing else, it will irritate him.

He opens his wings and drops down from the ceiling, shifting mid-air to land on his feet like a cat. He's only wearing pants, and his gray skin looks almost leathery, covered with moles, liver spots, and snarls of white hair. His excessively long toenails spiral into themselves like ram horns. He probably hasn't trimmed them in centuries. I wonder if he'll make me do it if I really do become his maid.

The vampire commands me to follow him through more luxuriously decayed hallways, forcing my body onwards until we reach a vast entrance hall. The great staircase leads down to doors taller than most houses. What if it really is Seren on the other side? An ache fills my heart, longing to hug her, to kiss her. But how will she respond when she finds out I've been turned?

As we proceed down the stairs, the vampire flicks a clawed finger, and the doors grind open, revealing a dark, snowy night—and Seren, in the doorway. Her long black hair blows in the wind, and her beautiful porcelain face is lowered in submission. "Master Lazăr. I have come to answer your summons."

The vampire lets out a dry cackle, and Seren looks up and sees me. Her already white face somehow becomes even paler. "Carol…"

"No need to lie, little Seren," says the vampire. "Did you forget I can see into your mind? I know you only came here to kill me."

Seren's fist trembles, and only then do I notice the wooden stake it's gripping, tip already stained red, not to mention the sword at her belt…or the motionless body lying on the porch behind her. The cabbie, I realize with a start. A big red wound in his chest.

As Seren steps into the castle, the doors abruptly slam shut behind her, so loud and sudden that she flinches. It was probably to make her check her rear, but Seren doesn't dare break eye contact with her maker. She might not survive killing him, but he can kill her without harming himself at all.

MOVE BETWEEN US, commands the voice, and I stumble down the stairs, grabbing the rail for support.

Sorrow floods Seren's eyes. "Oh, Carol… Why did you come here?"

Shame courses through me. "I'm sorry. I just…I thought I could stop you. I didn't want to live without you. Please… Please don't hate me."

"Don't worry, song of my heart. I don't blame you for this." Seren's gaze flashes back to her maker. "I blame you, Lazăr."

Lazăr giggles into my ear, standing right behind me. "You understand your predicament, yes? Before, killing me would only end your own life. But now, it will end hers as well. Surely poor Carol doesn't deserve such a fate. She is innocent…so far, anyway." His sharp fingertip sharp traces against my jugular. Seren launches up the stairs, her eyes wide with rage, but Lazăr stops her with a bark of, "I wouldn't do that if I were you. She's still very weak, you know, and a single slice would open her throat. Unless you don't really care about her after all?"

"Don't…listen to him," I choke out.

Seren's eyes flash back to me, softening in worry. She remains planted, too scared to make a move.

"Ahh, what a beautiful thing love is," purrs Lazăr. "Let's make a deal, little Seren. Why not stay here and serve me for the next century? And in return, I won't kill you or Carol. She can even remain in your tower like one of your fairy tale princesses. Safe, alive. Well, as much as any of us are. You live, she lives, and everyone is happy. What do you say?"

Seren stares at me with a worried expression. She wants me to live, I know. And I want her to live, too. And while I desperately want to think Lazăr is lying, given how much psychic control he has over us, I have to believe it's the truth: if he dies, so will we.

But this is no way to live.

I tell Seren my answer with my eyes alone, and in her own flash worry, disagreement, acceptance, and finally fury. If we die, at least we die together, and on our own terms.

In the blink of an eye, she shoots past me—and Lazăr's finger is suddenly no longer against my throat. Nor do I feel him pressed against my back. I whirl around to find them at the top of the stairs. Lazăr is on the ground, Seren on top of him, jamming the stake into his chest. "You've gotten slow, old man," she says. "Must have spent too long sleeping."
Then she draws her sword.

"Wait!" Lazăr sputters. "It will kill you!"

"That's a risk we're willing to take," says Seren, bringing the blade's edge down onto his throat like a guillotine. Lazăr writhes, blood gushing out as Seren slices his head clean off his body. I freeze in terror as the light leaves Lazăr's eyes, preparing myself for death. Any moment now, I'll be gone, and so will Seren.

Seren pants, covered in her maker's blood. I rush to her,

pull her into an embrace, and kiss her, because if I'm going out, I want to go out kissing the woman I love. She squeezes me, a single crimson tear leaking down her cheek. "I'm sorry, my love," she whispers. "I should have warned you better."

"No," I say, clinging to her. "I refuse to die being mad at you."

I wait for death's cold grip.

And wait.

And wait.

"Are you sure he's dead?" I ask.

Seren scowls down at Lazăr. His severed head and staked body appear totally lifeless. She picks up his head with one hand and his body with the other, then drags them down the stairs and throws them out into the snow outside. "Sun's coming up soon," she grunts, slamming the doors shut again.

An hour later, the sun does come, and we watch through the window, holding hands, as Lazăr's body bursts into flame. Neither of us do, though.

Seren clicks her tongue. "I can't believe how long I believed him."

"Right?" I ask. "That guy was an asshole."

We head upstairs to find the least repulsive bedroom. Cleaning this place up will take time, but I have a feeling it will be worth it. It's our castle now.

The End

About The Authors

Jonathan Maberry – JONATHAN MABERRY is a New York Times best-seller, five-time Bram Stoker Award-winner, anthology editor, comic book writer, executive producer, magazine feature writer, playwright, and writing teacher/lecturer. He is the editor of *Weird Tales Magazine* and president of the International Association of Media Tie-in Writers. He is the recipient of the Inkpot Award, three Scribe Awards, and was named one of the Today's Top Ten Horror Writers. His books have been sold to more than thirty countries. He writes in several genres including thriller, horror, science fiction, epic fantasy, and mystery; and he writes for adults, middle grade, and young adult. Jonathanmaberry.com

Dacre Stoker – Dacre Stoker is the great grandnephew of Bram Stoker and the international best-selling co-author of *Dracula the Un-Dead* (2009), the official Stoker family endorsed sequel to *Dracula*. Dacre is also the co-editor of *The Lost Journal of Bram Stoker: The Dublin Years* (2012). Released in October of 2018, *Dracul*, a prequel to *Dracula*, co-authored with JD Barker, was the UK's # 1 Bestselling Hardcover Novel in Horror and Supernatural in 2018. A native of Montreal, Canada, Dacre taught Physical Education and Sciences for twenty-two years, in

both Canada and the U.S. Dacre and his wife Jenne have lived in Aiken SC for the past 30 years, he is currently the Executive Director of Aiken Streetscapes, a foundation dedicated to the preservation and protection of Aiken's grand trees. Dacre has consulted and appeared in recent film documentaries about vampires in literature and popular culture. *The Real Vampire Files* (2010 History Channel), *The Tillinghast Nightmare*, (2014 Historical Haunts), *Secrets of the Dead* (2015 PBS), *Mysteries at the Museum*, (2017 Travel Channel) *Legend Hunter* (2019 Travel Channel) *American Vampires* (2022 Fox Nation).

Linda D. Addison – Linda D. Addison is an award-winning author of five collections, including *How To Recognize A Demon Has Become Your Friend*, and the first African-American recipient of the HWA Bram Stoker Award®. She has been honored with HWA Lifetime Achievement Award, HWA Mentor of the Year and  SFPA Grand Master of Fantastic Poetry. She has published over 400 poems, stories, articles and is a member of CITH, HWA, SFWA, SFPA and IAMTW. Find her in anthologies: *Black Panther: Tales of Wakanda; Predator: Eyes of the Demon; Qualia Nous Vol 2; Shakespeare Unleashed; The Book of Witches; A Unioverse Anthology; Deathrealm: Spirits.* lindaaddisonwriter.com

Gabrielle Faust – Author, editor, entertainment journalist and illustrator Gabrielle Faust is best known for her internationally renowned post-apocalyptic cyberpunk vampire series ETERNAL VIGILANCE. To date she has successfully released twelve novels and anthologies in the horror and poetry genres. Her work has appeared in magazines and websites such as *Weird Tales Magazine, SciFi Wire, Girls and Corpses Magazine,*

Austin Food and Wine Magazine, Fatally Yours, Examiner, Doorways Magazine, Fear Zone, and *Gothic Beauty Magazine,* as well as various anthologies. In addition, she has served as the lead editor on seven novels and two anthologies, including BLOOD GAMES: A VAMPIRE ANTHOLOGY. She is represented by the renowned New York literary agency the Knight Agency. In 2013 she was crowned "Vampire Royalty of New Orleans". Faust is currently at work on several new literary projects, as well as her first cookbook. More information about Gabrielle Faust can be found on her website gabriellefaust.com.

Sèphera Girón – Sèphera Girón is the award-winning author of over twenty published horror novels and dozens of short stories. Recent work includes *Weird Tales of Terror* and a collection with Andrew Robertson called *Dearly Departed.* Her interactive book, *Let Us Burn,* is on the TALES app. Sèphera has stories in *Phantasmagoria, Dark Rainbow, Group Hex 1, Group Hex 2, Abandon, Amazing Monster Tales No. 1, Creatures in Canada - A Darkling Around the World Anthology, The Pulp Horror Book of Phobias 1* and *2,* and more. Sèphera attended the Stowe Story Lab Fellowship Screenwriting Program 2022 in Birmingham, Alabama for her horror TV pilot, *The Calling* after being a finalist in the NYX Horror Collective. She has written several pilots and features. Sèphera has appeared in the horror movies *Pandora* (short, 2023), *Killer Rack,* and *Slime City Massacre.* In 2023, Sephera began the journey of writing a horror novel in tiny slices and publishing it online for free on a weekly basis.

Serial Vlogger is an experiment in publishing and will be completed in 2024 on both Substack and Patreon. sepheragiron.ca

Jeff Strand – Jeff Strand is the Bram Stoker Award-winning author of over 50 books, including PRESSURE, DWELLER, and TWENTIETH ANNIVERSARY SCREENING. Despite what "The Car" may lead you to believe, when he plays Monopoly he always wants to be the dog, although he's  not whiny if he doesn't get his way. You can visit his Gleefully Macabre website at www.JeffStrand.com

JG Faherty – Born and raised in New York's haunted Hudson Valley, JG Faherty is the author of 19 books, 3 collections, and more than 85 short stories, and he's been a finalist for both the Bram Stoker Award (twice) and ITW Thriller Award. He writes adult and YA horror, science fiction, dark fantasy, and paranormal romance,  and his works range from quiet, dark suspense to over-the-top comic gruesomeness. He is proud to be a relative of Mary Shelley. His hobbies include bourbon, wine, bad movies, and building guitars. You can follow him on X, Facebook, and Instagram as @jgfaherty.

Roh Morgon – Roh Morgon writes fantasy, supernatural suspense, and horror for adult, young adult, and middle grade readers. A past winner of the International Vampire Film & Arts Festival Silver Stake Award, she is best known for her supernatural suspense series, THE CHOSEN and WORLD OF

THE CHOSEN. Roh dreams up her dark tales while driving and hiking through California's Sierra Nevada foothills. But it's her time spent in more remote locales—the soaring peaks of Colorado, the windswept plains of Wyoming, the mysterious Carpathian Mountains of Romania—that provides the settings for her stories, and opens the door into

hidden worlds filled with seductive, lethal creatures and the secret lives they lead. Based in Central California, Roh shares her home with her very patient husband and an extremely demanding cat who helps her write by periodically walking on the keyboard. Roh and her stories can be found on her website (www.rohmorgon.com), Facebook, and Amazon.

Rain Graves – Rain Graves is a two-time Bram Stoker Award winner, TOI/ FOI Priestess, and retired Tangonista. Publisher's Weekly hailed her poetry in 2009 as "Bukowski meets Lovecraft." She lives and writes in Houston, with all the other things in the wilds of South Texas that are trying to kill you. raingraves.com

David C. Hayes – David C. Hayes is an award-winning writer of many novels (*Cannibal Fat Camp*), screenplays (*Rottentail*), graphic novels (*Kringle*), stageplays, poetry, and more. By day, he holds a PhD in forensic psychology consults on cold case homicides. Visit him online at www.daviechayes.com and www.hayescriminology.com.

Michael H. Hanson – Michael H. Hanson created the ongoing SHA'DAA shared-world anthology series currently consisting of "SHA'DAA: TALES OF THE APOCALYPSE", "SHA'DAA: LAST CALL", "SHA'DAA: PAWNS," "SHA'DAA: FACETS", "SHA'DAA: INKED", "SHA'DAA: TOYS," and "SHA'DAA: ZOMBIE PARK", all published by Moondream Press. Michael's short story "C.H.A.D." appears in the Crystal Lake Publishing anthology "C.H.U.D. LIVES!", his short story "Rock and Road" appears in the Roger Zelazny tribute anthology "SHADOWS AND REFLECTIONS," his short story "Born Of Dark Waters" appears in the Independent Legions Publishing anthology "THE BEAUTY OF DEATH 2: DEATH BY WATER," and his short story "Night Shopper" appears in William Morrow Paperbacks' OTHER TERRORS: An Inclusive Anthology. Michael also has stories in Janet Morris's Heroes in Hell (HIH) anthology volumes, "LAWYERS IN HELL," "ROGUES IN HELL," "DREAMERS IN HELL," "POETS IN HELL," "DOCTORS IN HELL," "PIRATES IN HELL," "LOVERS IN HELL," "MYSTICS IN HELL," "LIARS IN HELL," and the soon to be published "MONSTERS IN HELL." Michael has had over 110 short stories published in the fields of science fiction, fantasy, and horror.

Jonathan Fortin – Jonathan Fortin is a neurodivergent author and voice actor from Oakland, California. His debut novel LILITU: THE MEMOIRS OF A SUCCUBUS was published in 2020 by Crystal Lake Publishing, and his short fiction has been published by such markets as Dark Recesses Press, Mocha

Memoirs Press, and *Siren's Call Magazine*. In 2017 he won the Next Great Horror Writer competition from HorrorAddicts.net. He is an affiliate member of the Horror Writers Association, a graduate of the Clarion Writing Workshop, and a *summa cum laude* graduate of San Francisco State University's Creative Writing program. When not writing, Jonathan enjoys wearing elegant gothic attire, growling along to black metal, and exploring all things odd and macabre in the San Francisco Bay Area.

Andrew Robertson – Andrew Robertson is an award-winning queer horror writer and editor. His most recent release is *Dearly Departed*, a dual-author short story collection he shares with Sèphera Girón. This thirteen tale volume features their favourite frights and gravest hits over the past decade. Andrew has three  short stories heading to the moon as part of *Lunar Codex: #WritersOnTheMoon*. These stories will be part of the largest single collection of contemporary art ever put on the Moon, and will fly there on the first commercial lunar flight in history. A lifelong fan of horror, Andrew's work has appeared in multiple anthologies and literary magazines. He is the founder of The Great Lakes Horror Company small press and a member of the Horror Writer's Association. Find GLHC on Instagram at @glhorrorcompany.

Gustavo Bondoni – Gustavo Bondoni is a novelist and short story writer with over four hundred stories published in fifteen countries, in seven languages. He is a member of Codex and a Full Member of SFWA. He has published six science fiction novels including one trilogy, four monster books, a dark military fantasy and a thriller. His short fiction is collected in

Pale Reflection (2020), *Off the Beaten Path* (2019), *Tenth Orbit and Other Faraway Places* (2010) and *Virtuoso and Other Stories* (2011). In 2019, Gustavo was awarded second place in the Jim Baen Memorial Contest and in 2018 he received a Judges Commendation (and second place) in The James White Award. He was also a 2019 finalist in the Writers of the Future Contest. His website is at www. gustavobondoni.com

John Palisano – John Palisano's novels include *Dust of the Dead*, *Ghost Heart*, *Nerves*, and *Night of 1,000 Beasts*. His novellas include *Placerita*, *Glass House* and *Starlight Drive: Four Halloween Tales*. His first short fiction collection All that Withers celebrates over a decade of short story highlights. He's won the Bram Stoker Award® in short fiction for "Happy Joe's Rest Stop" and Colorado's Yog Soggoth award. His short stories have appeared in *Weird Tales, Cemetery Dance, PS Publishing, Independent Legions, Space & Time, Dim Shores, Kelp Journal, Monstrous Books, DarkFuse, Crystal Lake, Terror Tales, Lovecraft eZine, Horror Library, Bizarro Pulp, Written Backwards, Dark Continents, Big Time Books, McFarland Press, Darkscribe, Dark House, Vincere Press* and many more. Non-fiction pieces have appeared in *Blumhouse Online, Fangoria,* and *Dark Discoveries* magazines and he's been quoted in *Vanity Fair, The Writer* and the *Los Angeles Times*. He's a recent past President of the Horror Writers Association. You can find out more at: www.johnpalisano.com

Sumiko Saulson – Sumiko Saulson is a Bram Stoker Finalist and Elgin Nominated poet for their 2022 collection *The Rat King: A Book of Dark Poetry* (Dooky Zines), and an award-winning author of *Afrosurrealist* and multicultural sci-fi and horror whose upcoming novel *Somnalia* (sequel to *Happiness and Other Diseases*) will  be available on Mocha Memoirs Press. Sumiko has an AA in English from Berkeley City College, writes a column called "Writing While Black" for a national Black Newspaper, the *San Francisco BayView* and is the host of the SOMA Leather and LGBT Cultural District's "Erotic Storytelling Hour."

OTHER TITLES FROM NIGHTSHADE PUBLICATIONS

If It Bleeds by Darryl Dawson Brown

Revenge by Gabrielle Faust & Solomon Schneider

Eternal Vigilance: From Deep Within the Earth by Gabrielle Faust

Eternal Vigilance: The Death of Illusions by Gabrielle Faust

Eternal Vigilance: Bound in Blood by Gabrielle Faust

101 Ways to Fall Apart by Gabrielle Faust

Lineage by Gabrielle Faust